Cover Design and Interior Format
© KILLION
GROUP INC.

LAKOTA DREAMING

CONSTANCE GILLAM

OTHER BOOKS BY
CONSTANCE GILLAM

LAKOTA MOON RISING:
A historical prequel to the Lakota Series

LAKOTA BLOOD MOON:
Second in the contemporary Lakota Series

DEDICATION

In loving memory of my mother, Elnora Burks, a magnolia with roots planted deeply in the soil of her faith. Her indelible spirit will always be with me.

CHAPTER ONE

THE SUN'S LAST RAYS BLAZED over the mountains of the Badlands, across prairie grass oscillating just beyond the deserted South Dakota highway and into the SUV as it ate up the distance between Pierre and the reservation.

Zora Hughes adjusted the visor against the glare. She glanced over at her Nikon in the passenger seat, longing to take just one shot of this magnificent scenery. But she didn't dare. One shot would turn into a hundred, and night encroached. She touched the vehicle's cue screen instead, activating the phone. A dial tone resonated.

She still had a signal, so why hadn't Claudia called? "Come on," she muttered. Her hands tightened on the steering wheel of the rental, willing the phone to ring.

"Claudia, I need this job." The words tasted like a bitter pill, a pill too big to swallow. But if begging would get back her editorial position at *Haute*, she'd beg. She'd also turn this car around and forget about this trip to the reservation. A decision that would cause her therapist to question Zora's sanity. How could she ditch this trip when it was the culmination of two years of counseling? Not when Zora was so close to putting an end—

The phone rang. Claudia's number flashed on the display.

For a moment Zora couldn't move, tears of gratitude pricked her eyelids. She plastered a smile on her face and hoped the smile and not the tears could be heard in her voice. "Hey, Claudia—"

Static filled the car. In her periphery—a blur of fur and hooves.

———◆———

"Sheriff? You out there?" The dispatcher's voice crackled over the radio's airwaves.

Without taking his eyes off the road, John Iron Hawk grabbed the radio mouthpiece. "What's up, Maggie?"

"Got a couple of calls about shots fired up old man Tyler's way. I called him. Says he's got coyotes up at his place killing his chickens. Says he's going to—and this is straight out of his mouth—'make them a new asshole.'"

John cursed. Chet Tyler was ninety if a day. He'd probably shoot his foot off. "Tell him to stay inside. I'll drive by his place in about an hour."

"Where are you?"

"Twenty-eight miles out. Should be back in the office in about twenty minutes." John replaced the radio.

Streaks of purple and pink tinted the blackening sky. The coyotes bayed in the distance, a lonely sound. This was the best time of the day, a lull before the casino crowd poured into the area en masse. His jaw clenched until his back teeth ached. The casino: a blessing and a curse. Yes, the casino made money, but his people hadn't seen much of it.

Up ahead, a late model SUV sat on the shoulder, facing the wrong direction, its grill and hood busted to hell. Almost at the same time, he spotted the animal carcass sprawled on the side of the road. Making a U-turn, he angled his service vehicle behind the mangled car, and picked up his radio.

"Maggie, run this tag for me."

"Okay, Sheriff."

Technically, he was Captain of the Little River Reservation Tribal Police Force, but after trying unsuccessfully for two years to get Maggie to call him by his correct title, he'd given up.

She was back in less than two minutes. "Rental out of Pierre."

"Thanks." Pulling a flashlight from the console, he stepped out of the Jeep. As he scanned the vehicle's interior for movement, he unsnapped the flap over his gun.

———◆———

Overhead, the early morning call of the hawks captured Julia's attention as they sailed above the dry landscape, so different from her native Louisiana. The air held the promise of another fine September day. The sage-scented wind calmed her like her husband's hands on her face after their early morning loving. At the river's edge, she lifted her deerskin dress over her head and placed it with her fresh garments on a nearby rock. Walking slowly into the river, she allowed her body time to adjust to the shock of the cool water. She enjoyed these moments alone, away from the hate-filled eyes of the village, especially the women. But her babies would awaken soon and need to be fed, so she washed quickly, removing the smoke from the cooking fires from her hair.

She submerged herself, allowing the water to close over her head. When she surfaced and cleared the hair from her eyes, a strange heavy mist surrounded the river. A figure stepped out of the vapor, and Julia's heart pounded. She chastised herself. The stranger had to be someone visiting the village. Women did not wander the land alone.

Julia smiled in shy welcome. The woman moved slowly into the water, never taking her eyes off Julia. Shunned by her husband's people, Julia was happy someone now sought her out.

Only when the woman neared did Julia see death—her death—reflected in the empty eyes.

———

Zora surfaced from the dream, a scream frozen in her throat, her pulse swishing in her ears. A deflated airbag sagged across her lap. When she touched the thin and surprisingly soft fabric, images exploded in her mind: the deserted highway, the call, the deer. She jerked to a sitting position and blinked against the glare of lights that filled the SUV's interior.

A man stood outside her car.

"Police, ma'am. You okay?"

She swallowed her fear. "May I… may I see some identification, please?" She sounded a little like Elmer Fudd as the words passed over her swollen lips. She was lucky. Swerving at the last second, she'd missed hitting the deer head on. Somehow she didn't think the animal had been that lucky.

She glanced up at the officer before checking out his badge plastered to the car window. Black hair peeked out from a Stetson he'd pushed off his forehead. Dark eyes stared back intently at her, steadiness and concern in his gaze. She opened the car door and stepped out into a night of sage and wildness. Her knees buckled, and he reached out a hand to steady her.

"I hit a deer." She peered through the darkness at the road behind them.

"An antelope. I saw it." His eyes locked on her lips. "Are you sure you're okay?"

She touched her mouth and winced, grateful the airbag had saved her from more serious injury. "Yes." But was she really? The dream had left her a little woozy.

"May I see your driver's license and rental car agreement?"

She hauled out her overnight bag then extracted the items.

Head bent, he quickly scanned them. His hair was long

and pulled back from a rugged face. His street clothes gave her a moment's qualm. "Are you off duty?" She'd read about people being stopped by phony police officers.

He glanced up. Two vertical lines appeared between dark thick brows. Male musk and the smell of worn leather filled her nostrils.

Pointing to his leather jacket and jeans, she said, "That's not the usual policeman's uniform."

"For me it is."

His voice held a hint of a smile. A smile she waited for and was disappointed when it didn't materialize.

Dark eyes held hers for a heartbeat, making the muscles in her stomach tighten. She glanced away.

"A long way from home, Ms. Hughes." He handed back her papers. "Where you headed?"

"Little River Reservation."

His gaze stabbed her with its intensity. "The casino?"

"Umm… no."

"Do you have family on Little River?"

She shook her head.

Taking in her wrecked vehicle, he said, "There's no lodging on the reservation. May I ask why you're here and where you'll be staying?"

She couldn't tell him why she was here. Her quest would sound crazy. It sure sounded crazy to her. After all, it had been more than one hundred and fifty years.

Hoping to stop his questioning, she rummaged in her bag for the two computer sheets she'd printed before leaving her great-aunt's home in Nebraska. "I'm staying at the Starlight Motel." Finding the sheets, she squinted at the print. "The motel is located—"

"I know where it is."

Something in his tone made her glance up. The deep grooves between his brows had reappeared.

"That picture you have there is old." He pointed at her computer printout. "The motel changed ownership about

two years ago. Hank hasn't done much to fix the place up."
John Iron Hawk glanced at her wrecked SUV. "It might
not be what you'd consider comfortable."

She studied him. How did he know what would be comfortable for her? "Do you have any other suggestions?"

He pushed the brim of his hat up. The band had made a
crease on his forehead. "No, ma'am."

"Then it's Hank's, isn't it?"

He gave a resigned shrug and motioned her toward the
Jeep.

Once she was seated, he moved around to the driver's
side. Reaching through the open window, he picked up
a handheld radio. "Maggie, I need someone out here to
remove an antelope carcass." He gave her the mileage
marker. "Call Ted over in Rosemount and have him tow
this rental."

"Sure 'nough, Sheriff."

He replaced the radio and turned his attention to Zora.
"You got luggage?"

She shook her head. "Just this." She patted the overnight
bag nestled in her lap. "Everything else is in my hotel room
in Pierre."

"Give me a minute."

He walked around her wrecked vehicle, taking notes,
stopping once to rub the back of his neck. When he
climbed back into the Jeep, the scent of man and earth
filled the interior.

"Okay, let's get going. I'll have a completed report for
you to give to the rental agency in the morning." He
started the engine then pulled out onto the highway.

Zora pulled her cell from her overnight bag and held it
up to the meager light. Had Claudia attempted to call her
again? The screen was blank. No missed call.

"Reception's poor out here," Officer Iron Hawk said,
taking his gaze off the road to glance at Zora. "Not much
better on the reservation."

"Great." How was she supposed to exist without her phone?

"There's a landline at the motel."

"Okay." She fidgeted with her cell, before reluctantly tossing it into the black hole of her handbag. "Thanks."

Who would she call once she reached the motel? Claudia? Not after hours. No one intruded on Claudia's time after six p.m.—not if they valued their jobs. And since Zora was trying to get hers back, the last thing she wanted to do was piss off her boss—ex-boss.

Her mother? "By the way, Mother, I've lost my job."

No way in hell. Janine Simpson—she'd reverted to her maiden name after the divorce from Zora's father—would send this long silence that would transmit across the line like a glacial freeze. The silence that said she hadn't expected any better from William Hughes's daughter. It didn't matter that Zora had held the position of editorial director of the most exalted fashion magazine for six years—five of those years brilliantly.

No, she wouldn't call her mother. And she definitely wouldn't tell her about this visit to South Dakota.

"You sure you're okay?"

She felt his gaze on her.

"We don't have a doctor on the reservation, but I could drive you to the clinic in Rosemount."

"I'm fine." Except for her swollen mouth and some sore muscles, everything seemed in one piece. Mentally, she was far from fine, but he wasn't asking about her psyche.

To discourage further conversation, she stared out the passenger window. But she couldn't escape him. The muted glow of the dash superimposed his broad-shouldered image on the stark, barren landscape that sped by. His big hands confidently gripped the steering wheel. She tried to focus her thoughts, not on this man, but what she would say to Claudia once she got her boss...ex-boss on the phone.

The police car came to a stop in front of a seedy one-story structure. The 'L' in Starlight on the motel's electronic sign flickered. Even the semi-darkness couldn't mask the shabbiness of the area. "Is this *it*?"

"Don't say I didn't warn you." Officer Iron Hawk hopped out of the vehicle.

She didn't move just stared at the structure. "But it looks nothing like its picture."

His mouth tightened. "No, it doesn't." He turned and then strode across the broken asphalt. She followed more slowly.

The motel's office held a couple of sagging armchairs, an old Mr. Coffee perched on a white plastic stand, and a counter with a bell the officer now pounded. A few moments later, a wrinkled old man lumbered out from a door behind the counter.

"Got a customer for you, Hank."

Hank worked a toothless lower jaw. "Room twelve's available. Just need to see a credit card."

She handed him her Visa.

"Good luck, Ms. Hughes." The officer's dark eyes held hers for a long moment, and then he nodded at Hank and was out the door in three strides.

Zora stared at the empty space where he'd been a minute before.

"Sign this."

She studied the dusty book Hank had pushed in her direction. Did any hotel still require their guests to sign in? She added her name and glanced at the signatures above hers. Not an entry in three weeks.

The two wings of the motel fanned out from the office with all rooms facing the parking lot. When she opened the door to number twelve and flipped on the light, bugs scurried across the linoleum floor. She squealed, jumped back into the parking lot, and slammed the door.

Could her life get any worse? No job, stranded in South

Dakota, and now spending the night in a bug-infested motel.

CHAPTER TWO

——◆——

JOHN PUT HIS JEEP IN gear but braked when Zora Hughes' tall willowy frame came into view through the motel office's dirty window. He couldn't resist studying her. Slender but with curves, she was a beautiful woman with honey-colored skin and big brown eyes, but behind those expressive eyes lurked shadows. Those shadows coupled with the outward picture of sophistication peaked John's curiosity. He noted the expensive camera and hoped she wasn't a journalist planning to do some insulting story about the "Plight of the Indian." John could feel his ire beginning to rise at the thought. He clamped a lid on it. These days it didn't take much to make him angry. His unproductive trip to Pierre hadn't helped.

The wind sent trash tumbling around the potholed parking lot. He didn't like leaving her in a crappy place like Hank's. But what were the alternatives? He couldn't invite her to his house, not that he thought she'd accept.

He drove out of the lot only to spot Danny Matisse's tricked-out blue Dodge parked in front of the Iron Horse Café. John's mood darkened. Like father, like son. Where Danny hung out, trouble soon followed.

The wind had picked up and now buffeted the Jeep. Fat raindrops splattered on the windshield. Instead of heading out to Chet Tyler's place, John drove across the road and into the Iron Horse's parking lot.

He made it inside just before the heavens opened up.

Nodding to Foster behind the bar, John took off his hat and slid into a booth at the rear of the café.

Danny Matisse, Billy Joe Strickland, and Mac—John couldn't remember this kid's last name—racked up balls at the billiard table. Billy Joe was a white kid who'd been hanging around the reservation for the last few months. John had pegged him as the ringleader of this trio of troublemakers.

"What'll ya have, John?"

Sylvia, the café's only waitress, stood at his booth, pad in hand. Her bleached hair was pulled back into a ponytail, giving her sallow face a pinched appearance.

"Coffee."

She returned carrying three bottles of beer and his coffee.

"Who's the beer for?"

A flush crept over her washed out features. "Ah…for Billy Joe."

John sipped his coffee, staring at the pool players. "He's drinking all three bottles?" To his knowledge Danny Matisse and Mac were not yet twenty-one.

"John…"

He glanced up at her.

She shifted from one foot to another. "Don't cause trouble. Not tonight. Let 'em drink. It'll make my night easier."

He nodded. Technically, he had no jurisdiction here. The café was outside reservation land, but he just couldn't turn off the policeman in him.

She scurried off toward the billiard table.

The pressure in the room changed as the café's door swung open. Zora Hughes stood poised in the opening, causing a current of fresh air to swirl through the stale odor of the bar.

"Well, shut the damn door. You trying to drown us?" Foster shouted.

She closed the door then hung a dripping gray poncho

on the coat rack. With long trouser-clad legs, she moved confidently toward the bar. Her entrance wasn't lost on the crew at the pool table. Billy Joe, mouth ajar, watched her progress. His partners nudged each other, laughing at him.

"Chardonnay, please," Zora said to Foster. Her thick dark hair was twisted into some kind of knot at the nape of her long neck.

John chuckled when Zora grimaced at the first sip of the Iron Horse's finest. She obviously thought she was still in New York.

What exactly was she doing here? No one intentionally traveled to the reservation unless they had family here or came to gamble.

"—Joseph Bearkiller."

John's head snapped up. He strained to hear the conversation between Foster and Ms. Hughes over the laughter of the pool players.

On a wave of catcalls and hoots, Billy Joe sauntered over to the bar.

He tapped Zora on the shoulder. "Hey, sweet thang. We don't get many of your kind in here."

John flinched. The kid was a class act.

Zora's reply was lost, but it caused Billy Joe to turn scarlet. She stood and started to move around him. He grabbed her arm. She shook him off.

Danny and Mac bent over with laughter.

John rose and moved toward the bar. He clamped a hand on Billy Joe's shoulder. "Go back to your game."

"This ain't no concern of yours, Tonto."

The racial slur rolled off John like water off greased rawhide.

Billy Joe tried to move, but John only tightened his grip. He nodded toward Danny and Mac. "Get him out of here before I throw him in jail."

"On what charge?" The whites of Billy Joe's eyes were bloodshot, his malty breath filled John's nostrils.

"Disturbing the peace."

"I—"

Danny Matisse and Mac each grabbed an arm and dragged Billy Joe toward the exit. When the door opened, sheets of air-driven rain splattered the bar's already wet floor.

"I'll be back, Iron Hawk," Billy Joe shouted over his shoulder.

John ignored him. He turned to Zora. "Are you okay?"

She nodded. "I'm fine. Thank you for—" She waved a long-fingered hand in the direction of the door.

"My job," he said.

Though she said she was okay, the bleakness in her eyes contradicted her words. Turning away, she pulled a ten-dollar bill from her trouser pocket, laid it on the counter, and walked away.

"She asked me the strangest thing," Foster said, watching Zora as she grabbed her poncho.

"Which was?"

"Who was the oldest person on the reservation?"

The café's door closed behind her. "And what did you say?"

"I told her it was old Bearkiller," Foster said.

Now why was she asking about the oldest tribal member?

Curious, John followed her. When he stepped outside, a flash of lightening made the buildings appear stark against a sky as bright as day.

She stood under the overhang as sheets of water cascaded off the roof. "Can you give me a ride over to the motel?"

She'd added some glossy pale lipstick to her swollen mouth, and he almost missed her question. "Ah...yeah."

Stepping from underneath the protection of the overhang, he turned his face skyward. Rain pelted his skin, cooling the anger generated while dealing with Billy Joe and the lust that had sprung up just watching Zora Hughes's lips move.

Pulling the Jeep up to the café, John leaned across the passenger seat and opened the door, motioning for her to hop in. She dashed from the café, her long legs making short work of the distance. Her fragrance—something that smelled like flowers—filled the small space.

Driving to the end of the parking lot, he stopped and studied the road through the rain.

She shifted restlessly beside him. He frowned and cut her a sideways glance. "Why are you interested in old Bear-killer?"

She stiffened. An array of emotions played across her face, caution, anxiety and what looked like fear. Her face and body language relaxed as though she'd come to some decision. "I need his help with a story I'm writing. Can you tell me how to find him?"

Not all of his blood had drained south. "What kind of story?"

Her face, so full of expression a minute earlier, became guarded. "Let's just say I'm working out the details."

John studied her closed face a moment longer and then accelerated out onto the road. He stopped in front of number twelve.

"So will you tell me where to find Mr. Bearkiller?" She leaned toward him. Her damp blouse clung to her small breasts.

He focused his gaze on her face. "No journalist travels to a place without knowing what they're writing about. So I'm asking again, what's the story?"

Her eyes were now almost black with anger.

Used to getting her way, he thought.

Ignoring the rain, she opened the door and hopped out of the Jeep. "I can locate Mr. Bearkiller without your help. I just hoped—"

"That I'd make it easy for you? Not gonna happen."

She took a deep breath then shot him a look that should've seared the hairs off his body. Slamming the Jeep's door, and without looking back, she darted toward her room.

Now what had gotten into him? He'd always tried to make visitors to the reservation feel welcome. But he knew the reason. He didn't like secrecy. And Ms. Hughes was hiding something.

CHAPTER THREE

MIKE MATISSE GLANCED AT HIS watch as he headed up the stairs of his two-story home. Nothing stirred. "Damn lazy boy," he muttered. He'd heard his son come in last night around two a.m., stumbling up the stairs just like his grandfather used to do, both trying to outrun their demons. Not bothering to knock, Mike threw open his son's bedroom door. The smell of dirty socks, stale food, and an unwashed body hit him in the face like a two-by-four. Clothes littered the carpet and empty beer bottles decorated almost every available surface. At least Dottie, when she was here, had picked up behind the boy.

If Mike had had a bucket of cold water, he would have tossed it on the boy. Instead he yanked the sheet off his son's body. "Danny, get the fuck up."

Danny opened one red-rimmed eye, said something unintelligible, and plopped a pillow over his head.

"You've got ten minutes to get dressed and come downstairs or I'm selling that car."

Nine minutes and thirty-five seconds later, Danny stomped into the kitchen. "What's got you so all-fired mad?"

Mike didn't answer, just continued to read the newspaper.

Bottles clacked as Danny opened the refrigerator.

Mike folded the newspaper, laying it on the table. The clock over the stove read 8:10. He studied his son.

"Thought you had an eight o'clock class."

Danny gave all his attention to the refrigerator's contents. "Dropped it."

The boy took one class during the summer session and couldn't even get that right. "Why?"

"'Cause I was failing and I didn't want an 'F' on my transcript."

"And why were you failing?" Mike asked through clenched teeth.

"'Cause the professor wouldn't let me in class to take the exam. Said I was too late. I was only ten minutes late."

Probably more like twenty or twenty-five. Mike didn't bother asking any more questions. It was the same old song with the boy. Always someone else's fault. "I want you to get a job."

The refrigerator door slammed, and Danny faced him. "Doin' what? Working at the casino?"

"And what's wrong with working with me at the casino? It's better than riding around and drinking beer all day with those hoodlum friends of yours."

"They're not hoodlums."

"Billy Joe's got a rap sheet a mile long."

Danny didn't respond. There was nothing he could say. They both knew his buddies were thugs.

"There's no food in the house. When's Dottie coming back?"

"She isn't."

Danny's eyes narrowed. "You sent her away, didn't you?"

Mike stood, straightened his tie. "She decided to go back to her people."

"I told you nothing happened." Taller than Mike, Danny leaned over his father.

Mike gave Danny a cold smile. The kid might be taller, but Mike was meaner. He'd had to be impervious to intimidation to work around some of the thugs on the reservation. "It doesn't matter, does it? She's gone, and she's not coming back." He walked to the door leading to the garage. "Get a job, or you'll be out of here too."

Julia fought the swamp, running as quickly as her soaked dress would allow. The heavy fabric wound its way between her legs, slowing her progress. A sharp pain in her side forced her to stop and catch her breath.

The marsh became eerily still as she panted, her hands on her knees. Then an unsettling sound raised the hair on her neck. Dogs. Their baying broke the silence, causing her heart to slam against her chest and prodding her feet into motion.

Daylight hadn't improved the motel office's appearance. It looked shabbier than the night before. Sunlight danced off dust motes and a worn linoleum floor. Zora's mouth twisted with disappointment when she noted the sludge at the bottom of the coffee pot. She needed caffeine to chase away a night of tossing and turning in the only chair in the room, a ratty blue number. She also needed the stimulant to lift her out of the depression she fell into after dreaming about Julia.

Zora's gaze slid over a receptionist, whose head was buried in a book, to hone in on a spiral phone at the end of the counter. "May I?"

The girl never looked up from her novel, just nodded her approval. Zora dialed the offices of *Haute Magazine*.

Claudia's secretary answered.

"Kathy, this is Zora Hughes."

Silence, then a bright, "Good morning, Zora."

Not the usual, "Good morning, Ms. Hughes," she expected to hear. The line seemed to hum with a challenge. A challenge Zora decided to ignore. She was *persona non grata* at the moment, but that would all change when she was back in New York—back in her old position as *Haute's* fashion editor.

"Is Claudia in?"

"She's in a meeting." The customary response when Claudia didn't want to be disturbed.

"She called me last evening, but the call dropped. Would you let her know I'm on the phone?" Desperate, Zora softened her tone. "Please."

Silence. Zora could almost hear Kathy struggling with that request.

"Just a moment. I'll see if she can break away."

Right. Claudia was probably sipping her mocha skinny latte, deciding who would be her next workhorse. She'd almost certainly have fired Zora's replacement.

"Zora, how are you?" Claudia said in her preppy New England accent. "More importantly, *where* are you?"

Zora took a deep breath. "I'm fine. I'm in South Dakota."

"Oh."

One word that held a wealth of censure.

"I thought you'd gotten past all that nonsense."

"I'm working on it. I should be back in New York in a couple of days." She took a deep breath. "I want to come back to work, Claudia."

"Are you sure you're up to it?"

Claudia had a right to question Zora's mental status and a right to question her ability to do the job. She'd made mistakes that had cost the magazine money. But she'd also at one time been the hottest, brightest star in the fashion industry. She hoped Claudia remembered that. "I'm more than up to it."

"Well, call me when you're back in the city. Must run."

A click. Zora stared stupidly at a dead phone. She'd expect more from the call. A definite time for the two of them to get together, a lunch date to talk over her return to the magazine, something more than what she'd gotten, which was nothing.

"Hank won't like you making long-distance calls."

Poreless skin, sullen mouth and a rainfall of dark hair, the receptionist's black-eyed gaze connected with Zora's over the top of a romance novel.

"He can bill it to my room." Zora glanced at the coffee machine and sighed. "Where can I get a decent cup of coffee?" Maybe with caffeine and a lot of luck, she could find Mr. Bearkiller, learn what he knew about Julia's death and be on the evening flight to New York.

"Iron Horse doesn't open until two p.m."

Zora rubbed her forehead. The muscles in her scalp tightened into a mother of a headache. "What about a car? Is there one I can borrow?"

"Hank's got the only car."

"Where is he?"

"In his room."

She hadn't expected Hank to live on the premises. "Will you tell him I need to speak with him?"

"He's asleep."

Gritting her teeth, Zora responded slowly and with patience she didn't have, "Would you wake him, please?"

With an exaggerated sigh the girl placed the book face down and walked to the end of the counter to pick up the phone Zora had just used.

"You're wanted up front." A pause as she listened. "Number twelve." Another pause. "I don't know." She hung up the phone and went back to her novel.

Forever came and went before the door behind the counter opened. Hank stepped out, disheveled and unshaven, dressed in a ratty blue bathrobe. His white hair stood on end.

"This better be good," he growled. He cast a look from beneath bushy brows.

"I need to borrow your car."

Startled, he drew himself up and squinted at her. "My

car? Why?"

"I need transportation to the reservation."

He grunted. "I don't loan anyone my Bessie." He started shuffling back to the door.

"I'll pay you."

That stopped him, and he pivoted. "How much?"

"Twenty bucks."

He snorted and turned to leave again.

"Fifty dollars." As hard as she tried, she couldn't keep the hint of desperation out of her voice. She knew he heard it.

"For one hour," he said over his shoulder.

Parked behind the motel, the car, a twenty-year-old death trap, sputtered to life when Zora started the engine. The rusted tin can jerked and coughed its way out of the lot never accelerating above forty miles an hour. She could see the road through the holes in the floorboard as the car limped along the highway. She cursed Hank all the way to the sign marking the beginning of Little River Reservation.

Driving down one dusty road after another, Zora faced the truth. She was afraid, afraid she'd never get her job back. Afraid once she found this Joseph Bearkiller and told him her story, he'd think she was crazy. Afraid this trip to the place of Julia's death would not rid her of the dreams.

She passed a yard full of children playing on a home-made jungle gym. On impulse she parked the car on the side of the road, picked up her camera and stepped out. Whenever she needed to ground herself, she'd pick up her camera and just shoot. She did that now.

Although she'd never had the desire to reproduce, she did find children fascinating. Maybe as an only child, it was the fascination with a species she knew nothing about. But their laughter was infectious.

"You shouldn't take pictures of them without their parent's permission."

A teenage girl stood on the other side of Hank's car,

arms folded across her small chest. About average height, her short black hair was moussed so it stuck up all over her head.

"And why is that?" Even though she would never publish pictures without the written consent of the individuals, or in this case their guardian, she felt the urge to engage this girl in conversation. Maybe it was the eyes; they seemed to look bleakly out on the world. A world Zora knew all too well could be a harsh place for a teenager.

"'Cause you could use the pictures on the Internet." The girl's sloe-shaped eyes were heavily kohled, which, instead of making her look older, made her look vulnerable.

She hid a smile at the earnestness of the girl's expression. "You're absolutely right." With a snap, she placed the cap back on the lens. "What's your name?"

The girl appraised Zora.

"I'm not going to take your picture. Not unless you want me to." She wanted to take a couple of shots of the girl, but only if she could catch her unawares. She wanted to see the wariness in the girl's expression disappear.

"Laura."

"What a beautiful name."

The girl shrugged. The word "whatever" hung in the air.

"Have you ever read *Their Eyes Were Watching God*?"

When Laura shook her head, a frown marring the smooth brown skin between her eyebrows, Zora continued, "The author is Zora Neale Hurston. My father named me after her." She stared down at her camera caressing the lens. "He gave me my first camera when I was twelve."

No response.

"He and my mother had just divorced, and I guess he was trying to make himself feel better about leaving me." She had never mentioned that to anyone, not even her great-aunt. What would it hurt to share this with Laura? Zora was leaving today and would never see the girl again.

"Dads can be assholes," Laura said.

The word hung in the air between them. Obviously the girl was having her own problems with her father. When Zora said nothing, Laura turned to leave.

"Wait. Can you tell me how to get to Joseph Bearkiller's home?"

If the girl was wary before, she was absolutely hostile now. "Why do you want to know?"

"I'm a reporter. I'd like to do a story about him." She felt bad about lying to Laura. The girl deserved honesty.

"I don't know him," she said and turned to walk across the dying lawn of a small ranch.

She was lying, but Zora couldn't blame her. She wouldn't volunteer information to a stranger. "Can you at least tell me where I can get a cup of coffee?"

"The consignment shop."

Before she could ask the directions, the girl had disappeared inside the house.

Back in Hank's car, she decided to stick to the main road. She got lucky. A short distance from where she'd encountered Laura, a short, thick police officer leaned into the open window of a car loaded with teens.

Zora pulled over and parked on the opposite shoulder. The officer stepped back from the car, a black two-toned job. The vehicle shot away in a squeal of tires and burnt rubber.

"Don't make me haul you guys in," he shouted after them.

Catching sight of her, the officer strutted across the road. "Darn kids. What can I do for you, ma'am?"

"I need directions to the consignment shop."

"Next door to the casino. About two miles further down this road." He studied the car. "Isn't this Hank's old heap?"

She nodded, plastering a smile on her face. She wanted to curse Hank's name but thought this might not be the time. If he thought she and Hank were friends, it might make what she wanted to ask next easier. "Do you also know the way to Joseph Bearkiller's house—" She glanced at his nametag. "—Officer Levant?"

"About ten miles along this road, you'll come to a cottonwood tree. Turn left. Can't miss it. Tree's been hit by lightning. Old Joseph lives down that road."

"Thanks."

Little River Casino, a perfectly landscaped oasis in a sea of poverty, rose out of the mountain face as she traveled further into the reservation. Zora pulled the car off the road, reached for her Nikon and took the shot.

Quickly realizing the camera presented a chance to win back her father's love, she'd taken picture after picture, saving each one for his next visit, basking in his praise, feeling dejected when he didn't give it.

That was a long time ago. She'd moved on. Her father had stayed with this wife, maybe because she subjected her desires to his, unlike Zora's mother.

Janine had let no man or child stand in the way of what she wanted. The path to full professorship was littered with the corpses of her colleagues. Zora had spent many nights alone as her mother wined and dined someone critical to her advancement in the Black Studies department. Many lonely nights.

Zora drove on. Nestled at the base of the mountain were three small businesses, all painted maraschino to match the casino's bright hue. A sign painted in bold blue letters proclaimed: The Consignment Shop.

When she parked the car and shut off the engine, it sputtered for a full minute before falling silent. She wanted to kick the tires but was afraid they might fall off their rims. She settled for glaring at the bucket of metal, visualizing Hank in its place.

Ignoring the other two businesses, she was pulled like a magnet toward the nutty aroma of coffee, wafting out of the shop's open door. She made it as far as the shop's window display.

Although the sun was warm on her back, a shiver started in her gut and spread to her extremities until she felt encased in ice. Spread on a bed of black velvet like a woman awaiting her lover, a bracelet of multicolored stones shimmered in the store's display window.

"Beautiful, isn't it?"

Zora jumped. She'd been so enthralled by the bracelet she hadn't heard the tall, gaunt woman approach. Dressed in jeans, with flawless bronze skin that stretched across prominent cheekbones, the woman appeared to be around forty. Hair as shiny and black as a crow's wing hung in one braid down her back.

"It's quite old. The stones are turquoise."

Frowning, Zora stared intently at the bracelet. "I thought turquoise only came in one color—blue green?"

The woman smiled. "Most people do." She swept an arm toward the shop. "Come in. I'm Lydia by the way."

"Zora."

"Welcome, Zora."

The interior of the shop surprised her. Although small and sparsely stocked, the space was attractively arranged. Against a backdrop of warm yellow walls, handmade snake-skin boots and belts were artfully displayed on velveteen cloth. Stetson hats sat atop brown-faced mannequins. But Zora moved as though pulled by an invisible string back to the open display case and the bracelet nestled there. She glanced at Lydia. "May I?"

The woman nodded.

With reverence, Zora lifted the piece and placed it on her wrist. The silver felt warm to the touch. She shivered.

"Before you become too attached, it's not for sale."

Zora raised a brow. "Why display it?"

"It brings in tourists," Lydia smiled, "like you."

"I'm no—"

The wind chimes above the door clattered.

John Iron Hawk stepped into the shop, clearing the

doorframe with only inches to spare. He removed his Stetson. Sunlight glittered off black hair peppered with gray. Stripping off his sunglasses, at first he obviously didn't see Zora, as she stood in the alcove to the left of the front door.

"Where's Hank?" His deep voice sounded gravel rough.

Lydia shrugged. "How should I know?"

Zora must have made some sound, because he turned in her direction.

"I'm driving his car."

He nodded in greeting. "Ms. Hughes." He had a jagged scar on his chin she hadn't noticed the night before.

"Officer Iron Hawk." In amusement, she bobbed her head in imitation of his greeting. A very formal man or maybe he was just formal with her.

"If you want to stop by headquarters before you leave this morning, I'll have your accident report ready."

"I'm not leaving, at least not right away. I have to see Mr. Bearkiller before I do." She smiled sweetly, taking perverse pleasure in spoiling his day.

He held her gaze in a long unblinking stare. His eyes were as black as onyx and just as cold. What was it about this man that made her so riled? They'd met less than twenty-four hours ago, yet she felt as though they'd fought for so much longer.

"Did you want something, John?"

He shifted his attention back to Lydia. "No. Nothing. I'll talk to you later." He pulled a card from his shirt pocket and handed it to Zora. "Come by the office when you're ready to leave." Without another word, he turned on his heel and stalked out of the store.

Placing her hands on her hips, Lydia cocked her head and stared after the departing police officer. The Jeep's wheels spewed gravel as the vehicle shot from its parking space.

She turned an inquisitive gaze on Zora. "What was that all about?"

Zora tried not to squirm. "I must've rubbed him the

wrong way last night."

"You *rubbed* my brother the wrong way last night?" Lydia's eyes lit with humor. "I'm all ears."

"He's your brother?" Other than height and hair color, they didn't resemble each other.

Lydia nodded. "Baby brother. So what've you done to ruffle his feathers?"

"I don't know. I just wanted to meet Joseph Bearkiller. Your brother wouldn't tell me where he lived. Do you know him?"

Lydia nodded. "I do. He has a homestead a few more miles outside of town. What's your interest in him?"

Not wanting Lydia to think she was certifiably crazy, Zora gave an edited version of the truth. "My great-aunt always spoke of a female relative who lived among the Lakota Sioux, and since there weren't many black Indians, I wanted to find out some information about her. I hoped Mr. Bearkiller would be able to help me."

"How long ago did this relative live in these parts?"

Zora cleared her throat. "About one hundred and fifty or so years ago."

Lydia's mouth fell slightly ajar. "You're joking, right?"

Zora shook her head.

"That's a long time. Our history is oral. And I wouldn't rely on the memories of some of these old timers."

"But there must be someone that remembers something. Maybe a story an older relative passed down to them? Anything."

"I doubt it." Lydia held out her hand, and Zora remembered she was still wearing the bracelet. She ran her fingers over the stones before pulling it off. She felt as though she were removing a part of herself.

"What was your ancestor's name?"

"Julia."

"Beautiful name. Did she have an Indian name?"

Zora hadn't thought of that. Her dreams of Julia had

been without sound, just flashes of images against an emotional backdrop of pain, joy, and the horror of death. The little factual information had come from a journal her Aunt Callie had in her possession. It had belonged to Julia's son, and he never spoke of his mother by anything other than her Christian name. "I don't know."

"Her Lakota name might have jogged someone's memory. Oh, well." Lydia shrugged. She busied herself replacing the bracelet and straightening the black cloth. When the chimes tinkled again, a willowy blonde and a male companion entered the store.

"Look around," Lydia said to Zora and moved off to greet her new customers.

Zora roamed the store until she came to an isolated corner. Two paintings depicting the Great Plains stood on easels. One painting was of a regal elderly male Indian in full headdress, standing in a field of waving yellow wheat. His unsmiling face resembled old leather, brown and wrinkled. In the other painting, a herd of buffalo stampeded across a wide expanse of prairie with armed white horsemen at their heels. In the foreground of the picture, two lone braves stood watching the slaughter of the animals.

The stoic faces of the Indians as they watched their world being destroyed evoked an unexpected emotional response in her. She'd let the dreams of Julia take a toll on her professional and social life. The Indians at least had fought back as their world was destroyed. She had unwittingly trained her own replacement at the magazine, only to be forced out of a position that had meant everything to her.

Zora took a few more minutes to admire the rest of the shop's wares but was drawn back to the bracelet's display case. How had it come into Lydia's possession? She touched the glass lightly with her fingers. Her blood hummed with the life force radiating off the stones.

Knowing she probably looked crazed to the customers,

Zora grabbed a Styrofoam cup of coffee and retreated to a bench across the street from the shop to formalize a persuasive argument to get Lydia to sell the bracelet to her.

———◆———

John strode into his office and threw his hat on his desk. He hadn't wanted to talk to his sister with Zora Hughes around. He'd go back later this evening.

He picked up a pile of mail. "Maggie, any calls?"

The dispatcher filled the doorway of his office with her ample build. "More complaints about shooting out at old man Tyler's."

John let out a loud sigh of frustration. He'd gone out to Chet Tyler's place last night after leaving the Iron Horse, but the rain had obliterated any paw prints. The house had been dark, so he hadn't knocked on the door. "Anything else?"

"Let me the hell out of here?" The voice came from the vicinity of the holding cell.

John glanced at Maggie.

"Billy Joe Strickland. Oscar picked him up here on the reservation for drunk and disorderly late last night, decided to let him sleep it off in a cell."

"I kicked him out of the Iron Horse. Should've brought him here instead." John didn't want to deal with Strickland right now. Unable to concentrate, he threw the mail down on his desk. Turning, he unlocked the gun cabinet and removed a Remington 30.60 rifle. "I'm going out to Tyler's place again. Radio if you need me."

"What about Billy Joe?"

"Let him stew a little longer. It won't kill him."

As the Jeep traveled east on State Route 154, the stray dogs wandering on the side of the road looking for food and the barrenness of the landscape barely registered on John's consciousness.

He'd left the reservation twice in the past, once to join the Marines and again to take a job on the St. Paul, Minnesota, police department. After ten years on the force, he'd returned home two years ago.

Poverty still ran rampant here. The young people who didn't move away from the reservation worked in the casinos, but there weren't enough jobs for everyone. The ones who didn't want to work eventually came under his radar.

He passed a dead cottonwood tree, stopped, put the Jeep in reverse, and made a left onto the road. He dodged potholes until he'd traveled about a mile before turning onto a graveled drive. Shrubs surrounded the base of the trailer. Emma Bearkiller had attempted to make the place as homey as possible with a scattering of flowers.

He sat in the car, pondering over what he was going to say. He didn't want his visit to be construed as anything other than business.

The screen door opened and Emma stepped out onto the stoop. "You coming in, John?"

Any thoughts he had about turning around and going back were now over. He stepped out of the car. "Good morning, Emma."

She smiled. "Kinda formal, aren't you?"

He groaned inwardly. This was what he hadn't wanted. One night after returning to the reservation, he'd had a few drinks with Emma, and one thing led to another. Before he knew it, they were fucking each other's brains out. She was a nice woman, but he didn't want to repeat the experience. Emma was looking for something he couldn't give her. "Just stopped by to see your grandfather. Is he having a good day?"

Her smile faded. "Depends. Why?"

John ran his fingers along the rim of his Stetson. "I wanted to ask him a question."

"What is it?" Her big black eyes were her best feature. They now held a pleading he didn't want to see.

"This is a question for your grandfather."

She held his gaze a moment longer then entered the house. John followed.

The interior of the small home smelled of fried food.

"It's good to see you, John Iron Hawk."

The curtains were drawn against the bright morning sun, and John had failed to make out the wheelchair that sat in the shadows of the hall. He walked toward the elder Bearkiller. "It's good to see you too, old wise one."

The old man grunted. "How wise can I be? I'm sitting in this chair. Let's go to the den."

John grabbed the handles of the wheelchair. Emma followed closely behind them. Her eyes bore into his back as he pushed her grandfather toward the rear of the house.

A small television sat on a wooden cart, and an unlit pot-bellied stove filled the corner of a room used as a family gathering place.

John took off his hat and spun it round. "There's a woman in town who might come out to see you."

Bearkiller's eyebrows rose with interest. "Who is she?"

John cleared his throat. "Name's Zora Hughes."

The old man frowned in concentration. "Is she from one of the nations outside the Dakotas?"

"Aw... no." John avoided making eye contact with Emma. "She's a black woman from New York City. Young. Dresses expensively." With Emma listening to every word, he couldn't say Zora Hughes was one of the most attractive women he'd seen in a long time.

"I do not know of such a woman." Joseph cocked his head, his dark eyes probing John's face. "What does she want?"

John shrugged. "Don't know. She works for some magazine."

"Tell Ms. Hughes I will meet with her."

"I wouldn't advise it. Couldn't be anything good."

Joseph smiled, his gaze turned inward. "We'll never know

unless I talk to her."

John clamped his mouth closed. Sometimes talking to the old man was like talking to a brick wall. He turned to Emma, hoping she might discourage her grandfather from meeting with the reporter. The hungry look she directed at him had him turning back to the old man, words forgotten. But his granddaughter's interest in John hadn't gotten past the old man.

"John, why have you not married again?"

Emma straightened from her position against the doorjamb. "Grandfather."

John blinked, blindsided by the old man's words. "I'm not interested in repeating mistakes." He reached out and shook Joseph's hand. "Sorry to have taken up your time with this matter. I'll see myself out."

Emma caught up with him before he'd even gotten the door open.

"John, I'm sorry about…" She pointed in the direction of the den.

"It's okay." He opened the door. Why in the hell couldn't he just have kept his dick in his pants?

"Can we go out again?" Her voice was low, husky.

The plea in her tone stopped him in his tracks. He needed to end this right now. He opened his mouth to tell her their being together had been a mistake, but he could hear the grind of the chair's wheels coming up behind him. Not wanting to embarrass her in front of her grandfather, he said, "I'll call you."

She rewarded him with a big smile. He ducked his head to clear the doorframe and beat a hasty retreat to his Jeep.

———◆———

Outside, John's car engine roared to life.

With her hand lingering on the front doorknob, Emma struggled to keep the smile off her face. It had been two years since that night. Two years she'd waited and hoped, and now maybe there'd be another chance.

"John is a good man and would make you a fine husband."

She stiffened. Keeping her face neutral, she turned to face her grandfather. "And what makes you think I'm interested in him or any man as a husband?"

He didn't speak, but only stared at her in the dim light of the entry. "I'm eighty-six years old. I don't have much time left and none at all for denials."

He rarely meddled in her affairs, but when he did, he always saw to the heart of the matter. "I could just be interested in having a good time." She'd wanted to say maybe she only wanted John for sex, but she respected her grandfather too much to say such things to him. And it would be a lie. She wanted John for much more. She wanted to make a life with him. She just had to convince him he wanted a life with her.

CHAPTER FOUR

———

LIGHTENING MUST HAVE HIT THE tree dead center because the trunk was split evenly down the middle. Zora made the left turn and traveled slowly down the road. The federal government hadn't done the Indians any favors when they'd created the reservation. The land resembled a wasteland, arid and barren, but somehow eerily beautiful. A majestic mountain range filled the horizon, and hawks with broad wingspans flew above the land. Zora could almost see the teepees dotting the land, and buffalo stampeding across the terrain. She imagined she could feel the earth tremble.

There were no names on the mailboxes. A little further down the road, she spotted a young woman hanging laundry on a clothesline with a child playing in the dirt at her feet. Pulling into the driveway, Zora leaned across the passenger seat. "Can you tell me where the Bearkiller family lives?"

The rattle and sputtering of Hank's car probably frightened the toddler because he began to wail. His mother picked him up and settled him on her hip.

Zora smiled. "Sorry." She patted the steering wheel. "It's a little noisy."

The woman gave the car the once over. Zora fully expected her to ask if the car belonged to Hank, but instead she pointed down the road. "It's the place with tires in the front yard."

"Thanks." She knew the house the moment she saw it. The tires were spaced randomly over the front lawn and from their centers grew a variety of wildflowers in bright vivid hues of blue, pink, red, and orange. A screened-in porch had been added to the trailer at some point, and because the structure faced away from the sun, Zora didn't see the old man until she'd stepped onto the porch.

In sleep, he looked older than death, his face a mass of wrinkles and his skin the color of brown leather. She hesitated, not wanting to wake him.

"Sit beside me."

Zora jumped and almost stumbled off the wooden porch.

Without opening his eyes, the old man patted the plastic chair next to his wheelchair. "I knew you'd come."

She cleared her throat. "How—how did you know?"

"It was written on the wind." When he opened his eyes, there was a twinkle in the depths. He smiled. "John told me."

John Iron Hawk talked to him about her? Why should that be a surprise? Last night, he'd given her the impression he was very protective of his constituents. It would make sense he'd warn Mr. Bearkiller that someone sought him.

She relaxed and returned his smile. "I guess it wasn't a stretch to know I was the one he spoke of."

"No."

She took the seat. Now that she was here, she didn't know where to begin.

"Start at the beginning," he prompted.

It was if he could read her mind? She stared out over the landscape. Wild grass grew in profusion across the road from the trailer. The mountains, the grass, the cry of the birds seemed to put her into a different place, a different time.

The truth she'd withheld from John Iron Hawk spilled easily from her lips as she sat companionably with this old man. "A female ancestor of mine lived among the Sioux many years ago. She was a slave from Louisiana. She found her way to this land and married an Indian. She bore him a son. I want to find out what happened to her... and if she has any family left in the area."

The man was silent for such a long time Zora thought he'd fallen asleep.

"Why do you hunt for her family? And why now?"

To anchor myself to something. To stop the dreams. Zora shrugged. "I've always wanted to know about my family. I'm...I'm on vacation and thought this was a good time to come."

"John says you are from New York City."

"Yes."

"A long way to come on such a mission."

His voice was hypnotic and her muscles started to relax. The peace she felt in the old man's presence was mystifying. She wanted to tell him about the dreams. She opened her mouth but closed it when a beat-up old truck rumbled up the road. Dirt churned and flew around the Ford like a Tasmanian devil. The truck skidded into the drive. A slender woman, attired in a frumpy dress and cowboy boots, jumped out of the cab. As she pulled a bag of groceries from the truck, she frowned at Hank's car. Bounding up the porch steps, she stopped short when she saw Zora.

"Who are you?" The ugly twist of her mouth made her pretty face appear harsh and bitter.

"Zora Hughes."

"From New York City," the old man finished for her.

The woman stiffened then shifted the bag from one hip to another. "What do you want?"

Hoping to ease the woman's suspicions, Zora smiled. "I was hoping that..." she turned to the old man realizing she didn't know his relationship to the young woman. "That your..."

"Grandfather," he supplied.

"That your grandfather might be able to help me with

some research I'm doing."

The granddaughter dropped the bag of groceries inside the front door and moved to his side. "I don't know how."

"I thought—"

"You thought wrong." She pushed her grandfather's wheelchair toward the door, barely missing Zora's shoes. "He's an old man and needs his rest."

Joseph Bearkiller placed a gentle hand on his grand-daughter's arm. "Emma, you are being rude to our guest." He turned to Zora. "Come back later, Zora Hughes. We will talk."

Emma pushed her grandfather's chair into the house and let the door slam in Zora's face.

Stunned, Zora stood on the porch trying to figure out what had just happened. Emma hadn't the slightest idea why Zora needed to speak with her grandfather. Why was she so hostile? What had Zora done to offend her?

A dog of undetermined breed snapped at John's heels as he made his way to Chet Tyler's front door.

The Tyler place was five miles further down the main reservation road from Joseph Bearkiller's. A barn in need of paint sat behind the main farmhouse. With Chet Tyler's advancing age, and no family, the place had fallen into dis-repair.

The door opened at John's knock and old man Tyler stepped out, wearing what had once been a white T-shirt. He wore pants with suspenders that flapped around his hips, no shoes and carried a double-barreled shotgun aimed at John's chest.

"Whoa!" John grabbed the shotgun barrel and shoved it up before the old man could accidentally fire it. Raising his voice, John shouted, "It's me, John Iron Hawk."

The old man studied him with rheumy eyes. Bushy

white hair surrounded a long narrow face. "'Bout time you got here. Them coyotes been at my chickens and I aim to get rid of 'em."

John studied the foothills. There were thousands of coyotes living up there, and it would be impossible to find the one terrorizing Tyler's place. "I'm going to take a look around. Stay in the house and put that gun away."

John walked the boundary of the small farm. The ground was still moist in spots from the rain, but in the daylight, he could make out a paw print or two he'd missed the night before. Tyler's eyesight might be failing, but he was right about this being the work of coyotes. John doubted shooting one or two of them would help. If the pack were hungry, another would take the place of the deceased one and continue killing Tyler's chickens. John walked back to the farmhouse. The old man hadn't taken his advice but sat rocking on the porch, his gun across his lap.

John stopped on the bottom step. "Mr. Tyler, I can set traps, but I'm not sure that will solve the problem."

"I got what will solve the problem." The old man patted his shotgun. "If you can't take care of them scavengers, I will."

John had no doubt the old man would shoot something, maybe himself. Coyotes had been known to attack people. If the animal turned on Tyler, John doubted the man could move fast enough to get himself to safety. "Okay, Mr. Tyler, I'll send someone out tonight to set the traps and keep watch."

John started toward his vehicle then turned back. "By the way, I was down at Joseph Bearkiller's place."

Tyler squinted. "He ain't dead, is he?"

"No, sir."

"Too bad."

John smiled to himself. The old men played checkers together. If Joseph Bearkiller died, Tyler would be mourning an old friend.

"Bearkiller got coyotes?"

"Not that I know of."

"So why'd ya bring him up?"

Since Tyler and Joseph were about the same age, John thought about warning the old coot about Zora Hughes. She might come around asking questions, but she seemed fixated on Joseph. "No reason."

He climbed into the Jeep. He had more important issues to deal with than trying to figure out why Zora was in these parts. He needed to get his mind back on police business and figure out a way to bring Mike Matisse down.

———◆———

When Zora returned with Hank's car, Wilma—Zora now knew the receptionist's name—was in the same position, reading her book. Zora handed over the keys and wandered over to the Mr. Coffee stand and picked up a year-old edition of *People* magazine. No way was she returning to her room. God would have to come down from the heavens first.

Flipping through the magazine, she found an article about Dr. Phil. She tossed the rag back on the shelf underneath the coffee pot and strode to the phone at the end of the counter.

She dialed a familiar number. "Are you busy?" She turned her back to Wilma and whispered into the phone.

"I'm between patients," Dr. AnaMarie Eidson said. "Did you make it to the reservation without a problem?"

"Ah…not exactly. I hit a deer."

"You what?" AnaMarie's voice rose in alarm. "Are you okay?"

"Yes, but my rental is totaled, and I can't get another car until the wrecked one is evaluated for repair."

"I'm so sorry." Zora's therapist voice was soothing and a balm for her overwrought nerves.

"Where are you staying?"

Zora glanced over her shoulder at Wilma. The girl appeared to be engrossed in her novel, but Zora couldn't be sure, so she lowered her voice even more. "In a motel that has bugs."

AnaMarie coughed.

In addition to being Zora's therapist, she was also a friend. One of the only true friends she had. A conflict of interest, but Zora didn't care. She didn't make friends easily; when she did, she held on to them. "It's not funny."

"Something was caught in my throat."

"Right."

"Still having dreams?"

Zora's mouth tightened in frustration. "More than when I was in New York."

"Well, I advised you that might happen. It was worth a try. Can someone drive you to the airport?"

Zora stared out at the road. "Maybe. The police captain is more than willing to drive me out of town."

"Sorry?"

Zora gave her the rundown on her encounter with John Iron Hawk.

"Interesting. Is he cute?"

"What a question for a therapist to ask."

"I'm asking as a friend."

Zora thought about the police captain. "Tall, long hair—"

"Hmm, sexy," AnaMarie said.

Wilma cleared her throat.

"Look, I'm using the motel office. I'll ring you as soon as I get back in town."

She replaced the phone in its cradle. Maybe she could throw herself on John Iron Hawk's mercy and ask him to drive her back to Pierre. He would be all too happy to see the last of her. Once in Pierre she would get the first plane back to New York.

Pulling John Iron Hawk's business card from her purse,

she picked up the phone again.

"Do you want your message?" Wilma asked. She held up a white sheet of paper that looked to be torn from a spiral binder.

Zora returned the receiver in its cradle. The message was from Joseph Bearkiller.

Thirty minutes later and another fifty dollars poorer, Zora sat on the Bearkiller's front porch. "Where's your granddaughter?"

"She is taking food to an elder who does not drive."

Somehow, Zora couldn't picture his granddaughter doing anything for anyone. Maybe it was just Zora she had a problem with.

"I am sorry for the way she acted this morning."

"No apology needed."

"I have been thinking about what you told me." His gnarled hands tightened on the wheels of his chair. "And there might be a way we can help each other."

Zora's heartbeat quickened with interest. She scooted to the edge of the plastic lawn chair. "How?"

"I will call on a vision to find out what you want to know about your ancestor."

She frowned. Had she heard him correctly? "A vision?" This had moved into the macabre.

He stared intently at the long brown grass billowing in the field across the road. "Why are you afraid?"

She swallowed against the dryness in her throat. "Afraid? I'm not afraid."

"But you doubt."

She rose. "Look, maybe this was a mistake."

He turned his dark gaze on her. "Only if what is in your heart is not true."

This was getting out of control. It sounded too much like Eastern mysticism.

A hawk cried out somewhere over the foothills. Zora stared down into the fathomless depths of Mr. Bearkiller's dark eyes. "You don't know me. Why are you willing to do this?"

"For Emma. I want her to be happy."

Zora studied him for a long time, waiting for him to say more. When he didn't, she did. "How is seeking a vision about my ancestor going to make her happy?"

In contrast to his body, his eyes were those of a far younger man. "When you are happy, you can help Emma find happiness."

Zora remembered the look of hostility on Emma's face this morning. "What can I possibly do for her?"

"Get John Iron Hawk to marry her."

CHAPTER FIVE

"I AM NOT A MATCHMAKER," ZORA mumbled as she drove back to the motel. The same words she'd said to Joseph Bearkiller twenty minutes earlier. What could she possibly do for his ill-tempered granddaughter? It would take a miracle and a major attitude adjustment to make Emma attractive to any man.

And what was so special about John Iron Hawk? He was a man just like any other. Okay, so he was tall and muscular, but his craggy features couldn't compare to the model-like face of Terrance. A little ache in the vicinity of her heart caused a moment of regret. She and her ex had had something beautiful once. Maybe when she got back to New York, she'd call him. Maybe they could start again.

Heat shimmered off the black asphalt. The hot wind blew dust and probably all types of pollen in through the open windows of Hank's car. When she sneezed, a bead of sweat rolled down her neck and into the valley between her breasts. What she wouldn't give for a long soak in her garden tub in her nice cool, clean townhouse.

At first, she thought the shouts and screams that floated on the afternoon breeze were a product of her heat-induced daydream, until she saw the car in the distance. As it drew closer, she could see hands and arms waving from its open windows. The vehicle weaved across the yellow line before jerking back into its lane. The distance between the two cars diminished quickly. The other car veered once again across the yellow line and, this time, stayed in Zora's lane. She clutched the steering wheel. Were they crazy? Should she pull over onto the shoulder and let these fools have the road?

Like hell, she would.

But as the bright blue beast bore down on her, she realized she might be the loser. At the last minute, she swerved off the road and a hail of gravel and dirt flew in through the window. As the blue demon machine sped past, teens, their black hair billowing in the wind, shouted obscenities at her. Someone hurled a bottle. It hit Hank's car with a thud and a spray of liquid flew into the window. A yeasty sour smell filled the interior. She wrinkled her nose in disgust. Splotches of liquid spotted her favorite Dolce blouse. Muttering some obscenities of her own, Zora turned the Chevy around, stomped down on the accelerator, and trying to keep the blue NASCAR in sight, sped back to the reservation.

***

She lost the blue beast twice as she tailed it back to Little River. Each time she was about to give up the chase, she'd spot it again. With each mile, her temper cooled. What would she do once she found them? Give them a lecture on reckless driving? Somehow she didn't think anything she had to say would make much of an impression on this gang.

Just when she'd decided to turn around and head back to the motel, she spotted the car. Parked in front of a trailer on a grassless lot, the bright blue Dodge stuck out like a Dior in Walmart.

Beer cans littered the ground around the vehicle. She needed to call John. What if the teens got back on the road and this time injured or killed someone?

She rummaged through her bag until she found her cell.

Please, please, she begged as she held the phone up, looking for one little bar. She found it, lost it, found it again. Quickly with her body twisted like a pretzel to keep the reception, she dialed 911.

The dispatcher answered in a bored, disinterested voice. Identifying herself, Zora relayed her location and was describing the problem when the call dropped. Short of standing on her head, she couldn't get reception back.

Would John come? What if he didn't? She got out and walked cautiously toward the vehicle.

A mangy liver spotted dog watched her approach from his resting position beside the car. Bones littered the ground around him.

"Nice doggy."

His tail thumped, stirring up dirt as she moved close enough to the Dodge to peer inside. Living in New York, she didn't own a vehicle and didn't consider herself a car aficionado, but this one was over the top. There were more gauges on the dash than in a Boeing 727.

"Well, if it ain't the lady from the bar."

A shirtless young man stood in the open door of the trailer. He stepped out and strolled toward her. His thin hairless chest made him seem young, but the eyes were empty and cold. Caught off guard, Zora blinked several times then straightened as she tried to place the face. The only young people in the bar had been the pool players. Other than the one called Billy Joe, she wouldn't recognize the others if her life depended on it.

"Who is it, Danny?" The trailer door opened and a young girl with a pixie cut stepped out. She spotted Zora at the same time Zora recognized her. "Laura?" She'd removed the mousse from her hair and now the straight black strands fell just below her ears.

"What are you doing here?" The disapproval must have come through in Zora's voice, because Laura walked over to the punk and wrapped her body around his skinny frame.

He pushed her back, looking down into her face. "You know her?"

Laura shrugged. "Not really." She closed the distance between them and linked her arms around him, lifting her head to give him access to her neck. He ran a long lizard-like tongue up and down the slender column, studying Zora as he did so.

She repressed a shudder of repulsion.

The smugness left Danny's face at the same time Zora registered the sound of an approaching vehicle. Frowning, he pushed Laura away.

John Iron Hawk's white Jeep pulled up behind Hank's car. He stepped slowly out of the vehicle. His face was a stony mask as he moved past Zora without acknowledging her. When he unsnapped the flap covering his gun, Zora's stomach dropped. Her gaze flew to his face. She wanted him to talk to the teens, not shoot them.

"Get in the car," John said to the girl.

Some emotion flickered across the teen's face and just as quickly was replaced by defiance.

"I said get in the car, Laura."

Without looking at John, Laura marched past him, her head up and her thin body ramrod straight.

Danny, having recovered from John's unexpected appearance, now displayed a swagger in contrast to the fear in his eyes.

The officer moved closer. He smiled, but there was no humor in it. "I could run you in. She's a minor."

"But you won't." The boy's voice cracked.

John towered over the young man by at least six inches and outweighed him by fifty pounds. He shoved Danny toward the blue vehicle. "Place your hands on the hood and spread your feet." Not waiting for the young man to comply, John spun him around and used his boot to shove the boy's feet apart.

A crash from the interior of the trailer made John's head snap up. Quickly, he patted the boy down, removed keys from Danny's pocket then shoved him toward the driver's side of the Dodge where he handcuffed the teen to the steering wheel.

With gun drawn, John moved toward the trailer. "Come out with your hands up."

Laura had left the patrol car and now stood next to Zora.

"Don't hurt them, Daddy," she whispered.

Zora's head jerked around to stare at the girl. Daddy? John Iron Hawk was her father? No wonder the policeman's handling of this scene seemed over the top.

The trailer door eased open, and John took a step back, keeping both the trailer and Danny within his sight. Another male stepped out, his hands raised above his head. Long black hair fell past his shoulders. At least he was fully clothed.

"Anyone else in there?" John asked.

"Gilly."

"Tell her to come out."

"She can't, man."

"What do you mean, she can't?"

"She's wasted."

John's mouth tightened. Zora could see the wheels of his mind turning.

"Bring her out."

Somehow, this whole scene had moved beyond Zora being terrorized by a car full of drunks. Something dark churned beneath the surface. She'd come to the reservation to find out about her ancestor, go back to New York, and put the dreams behind her. Now she was mired in another nightmare of sorts, poverty, teen despair, and family squabbles. It wasn't too late. She'd pay Hank for the use of his car and drive to Pierre, hop a plane, and be back in New York by tomorrow morning.

With a girl's head lolling over his arm, the second boy

exited the trailer. The girl's black hair almost trailed in the dirt. She moaned.

John opened the rear passenger door of the Jeep. "Put her in the back seat."

Once the teen had done as John commanded, he handcuffed the boy to the roll bar. John's long legs ate up the distance between the Jeep and the Dodge. He released Danny and dragged him toward the police vehicle and into the back seat where he cuffed him. The unconscious girl lay between the males, her head in one boy's lap and feet in the other. John motioned for Laura to get into the front.

He marched back to Zora. "You had no business being here. Didn't the dispatcher tell you I'd handle it?"

"No." Her chest rose and fell as she tried to hold her anger in check. "I had no idea whether you'd come at all."

He looked away. The muscles in his jaw rippled. "What would one lone woman do against these boys?" He jerked his chin toward the two in the Jeep. "You could've been hurt. You don't belong here. Get off the reservation and go back to New York."

"You can't tell me what to do." Her words sounded childish and whiny. And to her horror, she was about to cry. She was heartsick at the way this had turned out. She wished now she'd not reported the incident. But as she imagined the blue car mangled and in pieces and Laura hurt, she knew she'd done the right thing.

John didn't spare her a glance, just jumped into the Jeep and pulled the vehicle with its teen prisoners onto the rutted road and sped away.

She stared after the vehicle until it was lost in the dust kicked up by its passing. Nothing about this trip had turned out the way she'd expected. She moved slowly toward Hank's heap. Hand on the car's roof, she studied the area one last time. Rocky terrain, scrawny trees, and earth devoid of greenery. The desolation of the area matched her mood. Time to go home.

The mangy mutt barked just as she opened the car door.

Glancing over her shoulder, she gave him a grim smile. "Sorry, pal. No room on the plane."

But he hadn't been barking at her, but at a young girl dressed in white and wearing moccasins who leaned against the end of the trailer.

Zora straightened. Why hadn't the others mentioned there'd been another person in the trailer? Had they been trying to protect this girl? Laura might have, but Danny didn't strike Zora as willing to protect anyone but himself.

"Hello."

The girl didn't respond.

"Are you okay?" Zora shut the car door. As though approaching a skittish deer, she moved cautiously toward the teen.

The girl watched Zora with narrowed eyes. She swayed and braced her hand against the trailer's dirty side.

Was she stoned too?

When Zora came within ten feet of the girl, the dimension of time seemed to slow to a stop. She couldn't comprehend what her eyes told her. Mouth dry, heart thudding loudly in her ears, she stared into Julia's face.

CHAPTER SIX

———

ZORA GAVE HERSELF A MENTAL shake. Of course it wasn't Julia. Julia had been dead for over one hundred and fifty years. From the look of her, this girl must be a Native American descendent of Julia's. A relation Zora hadn't expected to find.

Happiness bubbled through her for the first time since— since forever. She'd found a living descendent, someone who could tell her what had happened to Julia. It was more than she'd dared hope for. "Who are—?"

The girl's knees buckled. Zora caught her before she could tumble to the ground. "What's wrong?" The teen's arms felt like sticks.

The girl stared up at Zora with mute appeal but didn't utter a word. Zora glanced around frantically for help. There wasn't any. John was long gone.

"Let's get you inside, out of the sun." She could almost count the girl's ribs as she lifted her. She was so thin. Probably pills. She'd seen enough models who lived on speed to keep from gaining weight to recognize another victim.

Once inside the trailer, Zora wished she taken the longer trek to her car instead. The stench of weed—pungent and herbal—permeated the small space. Light from the open door only penetrated a few feet, but it was enough for her to see a banquette-style sofa lining one wall and opposite it a small kitchenette. She lowered the teen to the sofa. Closed plastic blinds covered the one window in the kitchen but couldn't hide a pile of food-encrusted dishes in the sink. Two doors opened onto a short corridor, which led to the end of the trailer. She had no desire to investigate. If the kitchen were any indication, the rooms in the back would make Hank's motel look like the Waldorf.

"Let's get you some water. Maybe a cool cloth for your forehead." Zora moved toward the small kitchenette but stopped cold when a dirty dishtowel moved on the counter. She took an involuntary step back. She glanced at the teen. The girl needed water, but Zora couldn't bring herself to touch anything in the kitchen.

She remembered a bottle of water in her bag. "I'll be right back." It would be warm, but it beat drinking out of the glasses in the trailer. She ran out, gulping untainted air as soon as her feet hit the steps. Maybe her reluctance to return made the search for the bottle of water take longer. Whatever the reason, by the time she'd returned, the girl was gone.

———————◆———————

Zora had driven up and down the dusty roads around Danny's place looking for the teen. No luck. The girl obviously didn't want to be found. She probably thought Zora would turn her over to John and she'd suffer the same fate as her friends. She had no way of knowing how important she was to Zora.

Finally giving up on locating the girl, Zora had paid Hank to let her borrow the car one last time and driven to Pierre. There she'd packed her clothes and checked out of the hotel, but not before she'd had a long hot shower. She'd also stopped at the rental car agency. The sales rep explained again in bored tones that Zora had to wait for the estimate of repairs on the Cadillac before they'd rent her another car.

Now, Hank's deathtrap, with the old geezer driving, rattled out of the Bearkiller driveway, belching gas and carbon monoxide fumes. So here she was with her luggage at her feet and no car. But she had a mission, a definite lead to Julia. She just needed to find this friend of Laura's.

The screen door creaked open and Joseph appeared in the opening. His eyes lit in warm welcome. "Let me have one of your bags."

She handed him her overnight case, and he placed it on his lap. With arthritic fingers, he maneuvered his wheelchair down the dark narrow hall. Zora followed.

"Where's Emma?"

"She had an errand to run," he tossed over his shoulder.

Translated that probably meant she hadn't wanted to be here when Zora arrived. "Did you tell her why you invited me?"

"No."

Zora stopped in her tracks. "Why not?" But Joseph was no longer in the hall. She followed him into a small, but clean room where the smell of pipe smoke lingered in the air. The room held a twin bed and a chest of cherry wood. "This is your room?"

He gazed up at her apologetically. "We have only two bedrooms."

"Where will you sleep?"

"We have a small den."

She should decline his hospitality, but Julia's face sprang to mind. "Let me sleep there." She grabbed the bag from his lap. "Lead the way."

"You'll have no privacy," the old man said. His crooked fingers lay motionless in his lap.

"Privacy is an overrated commodity. Lead me to the den."

She followed him further down the corridor to an even smaller room.

A plaid sofa took up half the den's space. A television sat

on a cart across from the sofa and a black potbellied stove sat in one corner. "This is cozy."

Joseph grunted.

She placed one of her suitcases on the sofa. She opened the bag then looked around for somewhere to hang her clothes.

"I'll bring you some hangers. You can put your clothes on the hook behind the door."

"Thank you." She held his gaze. "Why didn't you tell Emma the reason you invited me?"

His eyes grew sad. "She's a gentle soul. A young bird easily crushed."

Zora did a mental eye roll. Emma was a barracuda.

"It would hurt her to know that I knew of her love for John and had shared that with you."

Zora could only stare at him. She'd never known anyone as selfless as this old man. Definitely not her parents, nor—if she were completely honest—herself. There'd been many times her staff worked longer hours because she hadn't been satisfied with a layout. It shamed her; at times she'd glimpsed her mother's manic drive in herself but didn't know how to do it differently.

"Tell me about John Iron Hawk," she said casually, not looking at Joseph, not wanting him to read her thoughts.

When the old man didn't respond, she glanced at him. "You're not being disloyal by telling me. I can't help her unless I know something about the man."

Joseph nodded. "John is a very private man. A good man."

This was going to be like pulling teeth. "Why do you think Emma would make him a good wife?"

Joseph leaned forward and lowered his voice. "John has a daughter, Laura, a wounded bird. She needs a mother."

Yes, Zora would definitely agree. Laura was a troubled young woman. She'd been surprised to learn John had a child, but there'd been no reason for her to know. She and John weren't friends. He'd made that perfectly clear.

Zora nodded sagely. "And you think Emma would make a good mother?"

He hesitated. "She could only be better than John's ex-wife."

Zora hated to admit to herself she wanted to know more about John's ex-wife. What type of woman did he find attractive? She closed her eyes and put a brake on the direction of her thoughts. She didn't need to know about John's love life, just about his daughter and her friends. "Tell me more about the daughter."

A sad look stole over the old man's face. "The child..." he paused. "John has raised her for the past three years."

"Where's her mother?"

"She's dead."

Zora stopped her mindless task of unfolding her clothes. "What happened?"

"Mina and her husband were killed in a car accident. The husband had been drinking."

Joseph must have seen the confusion on her face. "John and Mina married young. He was still in the Marines. I think she couldn't handle him being away so much. There was another man..."

"So they divorced..." Zora prompted.

Joseph nodded. "The day of the crash, Laura was with her grandmother."

"Thank goodness," Zora muttered.

As though coming back from a far distance, Joseph gave a little shake of his head. "John brought the child back to the reservation."

"Poor baby," Zora whispered. She cleared her throat. "I saw her today."

Joseph threw her a sharp glance. "Laura?"

As she recounted the day's events, his eyes grew misty with sadness.

"There was another girl with the group, short, petite."

Joseph shook his head. "I don't know that one. Maybe

Emma does. She helps out at the Boys and Girls Club."

Emma appeared to be the woman of the hour. If Zora was going to find this friend of Laura's, she might first have to go through Emma. *Great.*

———◆———

John leaned against the doorjamb of his studio and sipped whiskey. Pale sunlight streamed into the room, illuminating a dozen unfinished canvases—their faces turned to the wall. He studied the back of the paintings so long the sunlight turned from pale yellow to golden to blood red and the liquor in his stomach went from mellow to acidic.

Draining his glass, he sank to his haunches and picked up the nearest canvas. Sketched in charcoal, the outline of the Black Hills at sunset filled the page. The shadow of an American eagle as it flew across the face of the dying sun captured the sense of freedom he'd tried to portray. The rest of the canvas was as empty as his creative spirit.

Sighing, he propped the canvas back against the wall before closing the door on a room that had more dust and shadows than a crypt.

As he walked down the hall to the kitchen for another drink, the thumping bass couldn't drown the strident vocals from music Laura played to annoy him.

The thought of his daughter being with Matisse's son made bile creep into his throat. As much as she drove him crazy, she deserved to be treated with respect and love. And one thing John knew, Danny didn't respect her and didn't know the meaning of love.

The whiskey had lost its appeal. He poured the liquor down the sink then made a pot of coffee.

Seated at his kitchen table, he stared down into the black, oily depths of his cup and thought of ways he could get rid of Danny Matisse.

"Well, at least it isn't a glass of whiskey."

His hand shot out almost knocking over the cup. Coffee sloshed over the sides, burning his fingers. Lydia stood just inside the screen door of his kitchen, not two feet away. Some police officer he was. He hadn't heard her enter. She took a seat opposite him at the kitchen table.

"You heard?" he asked, mopping up the spilled coffee with a dishrag.

"News travels fast. Word is the woman from New York was there."

He sat back down at the table, took a sip of the remaining coffee and grimaced. "Yep. They ran her off the road. Drinking, she says."

"You believe her?"

He stared down into the cup for a long moment then looked in the direction of Laura's room. "Yep. One of the teens, Gilly, was out cold. Dropped her off at the clinic."

"What're you gonna do?"

"There's nothing much I can do. I didn't catch them behind the wheel. I let them reflect on the error of their ways in the holding cell. If Zora Hughes wants to press charges…" John shrugged. "What I really wanted to do was beat the shit out of them."

Lydia gave him a knowing look. "But you didn't."

"Naw. Matisse showed up before I could lay a hand on them."

Lydia rolled her eyes. "You and I both know you wouldn't have harmed those boys. That's the trouble with you, John. You're too good. Now I know a couple of men who'd be happy to get the job done."

He gave his sister a hard stare. Sometimes he didn't know if she was serious or kidding. "As much as I think those boys deserve it, I can't let that happen."

She snorted. "If you'd play dirty on occasion, you could beat Matisse at his own game. You and I both know he's stealing money right out of the mouths of the people."

John stood. Walking to the kitchen window, he stared at

the sun sinking behind the foothills. "Yeah, he needs to be brought down."

A sound made him turn. Laura stood framed in the kitchen door. Her big usually expressive eyes, so like her mother's, were devoid of expression. John wanted to go to her, but he couldn't. He was still too angry.

Lydia motioned Laura into the kitchen. Tall like her aunt, Laura carried herself with grace. She took a seat at the table and stared down at her clasped hands. The act of humility didn't fool him. He'd seen the fire in her eyes before she'd lowered her gaze. She wasn't remorseful and that made him angrier.

His sister cleared her throat. "Is Gilly okay?"

Laura shrugged. "I don't know. I haven't been allowed to leave the house." She threw John a withering glance from beneath long lashes.

As far as he was concerned, she'd be old and gray before she left the house. He knew he was being irrational, but at the moment, he didn't know what else to do. He was at his wit's end with the girl. He'd send her back to her mother, if she were alive.

"Everything would have been okay if that bi—"

"Don't let that word come out of your mouth," John warned. "If Zora Hughes hadn't alerted me, Gilly could have died."

Laura jumped up from the table, her chair scraping against the faded linoleum floor. "You don't care about Gilly or me. It's your precious job you care about. Well, Danny's dad says you're just a flunky. Says you couldn't make it with the real police force so you came back to the reservation."

John took a step toward her, stopped and forced himself to breathe. Blood pounded like a ceremonial drum behind his eyes. "Stay away from Danny Matisse."

"You can't make me." She turned and ran.

John started after her, but Lydia's restraining hand on his

arm stopped him.

"Let her go. She needs time alone."

John wanted to give her all the time she needed—in the spirit world.

———✦———

Zora stood haloed in the light of the refrigerator, studying its meager contents. She made a mental note to do some shopping tomorrow, if she could convince Emma to let her borrow the truck.

Dinner, cooked by Emma, had consisted of over-baked chicken floating in greasy gravy and side dishes of starch, starch, and more starch. Even if Zora had found the food appealing, the hostility radiating off Joseph's granddaughter would have been enough to kill her appetite. Plus, thoughts of the afternoon encounter with the teens, John's anger, and seeing Julia's look-alike had taken away any desire to eat.

A knock sounded at the front door. Startled, Zora jumped, bumping her head on the freezer compartment. Rubbing the sore spot, she strode to the door and peered out the curtain- covered window. Laura Iron Hawk stood on the porch.

When Zora opened the door, Laura took a half step back in surprise. "What are you doing here? Where is Emma?"

Pulse kicking up a notch, Zora peered beyond the teen, looking for John's Jeep. It wasn't there. In fact, there wasn't any vehicle in the drive. How had the girl gotten here?

Not wanting to wake Joseph, Zora stepped out onto the porch. The light from a full moon illuminated the teen's pale face. From the haunted red-rimmed eyes, she was obviously hurting and had come looking for comfort. Joseph had not overestimated the bond between Laura and Emma. "Emma is working tonight."

"Oh." Laura stepped backwards off the porch.

"Wait."

She froze.

"How is your friend?"

In the dim light, Zora saw caution etched on the girl's face. "Gilly?"

"The unconscious one?"

Laura nodded. "I don't know. I'm on lockdown."

Yet, you're here. She recognized the anguish on the girl's face, and that anguish pulled at Zora's heartstrings. It reminded her of her own angst at that age. "And your other girlfriend?"

Laura frowned. "What other girlfriend?"

"The one in the white shift. The one you left at the trailer."

Shaking her head, Laura backed further down the drive. "There wasn't anyone else at the trailer."

"Of course there was," Zora insisted. "She was about this tall." Zora raised her hand to the level of her shoulder.

"If you say so." Laura turned and strode toward the road, her jean-covered legs making short work of the distance.

Feeling like an idiot, Zora dropped her hand. Maybe the other girl hadn't been with them but just hanging around. Zora hadn't actually seen her come out of the trailer. "Sorry, I thought she was with you guys."

Feeling it was too dangerous for the teen to walk alone at night, Zora grasped at the first thing that came to mind. "Hey," she shouted. "Do you want some dinner?"

Laura stopped.

Zora took that as a yes. "I'll heat it up." She retreated into the house and held her breath as she listened for the girl's footsteps to cross the threshold.

In the kitchen, Zora pulled the remains of dinner from the refrigerator. Maybe someone would like the meal Emma cooked. If Joseph's granddaughter wanted to win John Iron Hawk's heart, she'd better find another way than through his stomach.

As Zora heated the chicken, she was acutely aware of Laura standing in the door. "Joseph was kind enough to offer me a place to stay. He thought I'd be more comfortable here than in the motel."

When Laura didn't speak, Zora rambled on. "I'm tracing my family tree. I have a Lakota ancestor." She glanced at Laura. The girl's face was expressionless. Definitely not impressed.

Zora set the plate of food on the table. When Laura didn't move from the door, Zora wiped her hands on a towel. "Well, I'll just go to my room. If you want to talk about anything, I'm in the den."

The girl stepped back to allow Zora to pass. She walked silently down the hall but stopped when she noticed the light spilling out from underneath Joseph's door. She knocked softly.

"Come in."

Zora stepped into the small bedroom and quietly closed the door. Joseph was propped up in his twin bed, reading. When she'd entered his room initially, she'd noted the hoops of netting that adorned his bedroom wall.

"Dream catchers," he said now in response to her interest.

She wanted to ask about them, but now was not the time. "Laura Iron Hawk is in the kitchen. She came looking for Emma."

Joseph glanced at the clock on his nightstand. "She's alone?"

Zora nodded.

"We should call John."

Remembering the girl's tear-stained face and John's hard, unrelenting demeanor earlier today, Zora didn't think that was a good idea. "Can't we wait until Emma gets home and let her take the girl home?"

Joseph shook his head. "John will be worried." He reached for the phone.

Not waiting to hear the conversation between the two men, she walked back to the kitchen. Laura was gone, and the plate of food, untouched.

Zora took a seat on the porch to wait for John. The plaintive cry of a coyote howled in the distance. She shivered. Laura obviously didn't have a good relationship with her father. But at least she had one. Zora worried about the girl, worried about her safety and her state of mind.

Ten minutes later a vehicle's headlights bobbed along the rutted road. John's Jeep barreled into the drive, skidded to a stop, and without turning off the lights, he hopped out. She rose from her vigil and walked to meet him.

"Where is she?"

"She's gone."

He cursed under his breath, turned and started in the direction of the open field that lay in darkness across the road. "Where could she be? I didn't pass her."

His hair was pulled back and tied with a leather string, leaving exposed his neck tanned a deeper copper by the South Dakota sun.

"Is there anything I can do?"

He turned back to face her, his face a hard mask. "No. You've done enough."

Her back stiffened in anger. Images of his hand opening the flap over his gun as he approached the trailer that morning flashed through her mind. He didn't know how to handle teens. Neither did she, but somehow, she thought she could do a better job of it. She clamped down on her anger and softened her voice. "May I make a suggestion?"

His generous mouth was set in a hard straight line. "Stay out of this. It doesn't concern you. I know what I'm doing."

"You're not doing so great a job of it."

Fire flashed in his eyes. "I thought I told you to leave. You're putting your nose into things you don't understand."

She flushed. For a moment, all she heard was the swish

of blood pounding in her ears. She closed the distance between them and poked her finger against the hard wall of his chest. "How do you get off telling me what to do? I'll have you know—"

"Move your finger."

Anger had her by the throat. "Or you'll do what?"

He grabbed her shoulders and pulled her toward him until his mouth was mere inches from hers. His breath— smelling of coffee—fanned across her face, causing the hairs on her arms to quiver and the muscles low in her belly to tighten.

Mouth suddenly dry, she licked her lips. Like radar, his gaze zeroed in on her mouth. Through one long thudding heartbeat, she stood frozen, waiting, wanting. The harsh beams of a vehicle released her from the spell.

John dropped his hands and stepped back. She wrapped her arms around her body suddenly chilled.

Emma bounded out of her truck. Without a word of greeting, she rushed past them and into the house.

"Shit." He glanced uneasily at the closed door then turned to Zora. "I've got to find my daughter." He stalked off to his Jeep.

As the taillights of the police vehicle faded down the narrow road, she pressed her hands to her lips. He'd almost kissed her. And Emma had seen it. That little scene was not going to make getting information out of her any easier. Zora sighed as she walked back into the house. She had to convince Emma what had passed between her and John meant nothing. She pressed her hands to her lips again. Hadn't it?

———◆———

Driving slowly, John divided his attention between the road and the ditch. He wouldn't put it past his daughter to jump down into a gully when she heard his Jeep. Why did parenting have to be so hard? He'd rather spend his days tracking serial killers through the foothills than deal with one headstrong teenager girl. A jackrabbit darted onto the road. Caught in the Jeep's headlights, it froze, its pink eyes large and glowing in the bright beams of the vehicle. John cursed, slammed on the brakes, and the Jeep skidded to a stop. The animal seemed to give him a woeful stare, then hopped over the ditch, and disappeared into the grasses.

He stomped on the accelerator and his vehicle leapt forward. Would it have been better to let Mina's mother raise Laura? He instantly dismissed the idea. Sometime after they were married, he realized Mina had married him to escape her critical and domineering mother. No, Grace, Mina's mother, was not the person he wanted raising his daughter.

At least Laura had found a friend in Emma. Thinking about Emma brought Zora back into his thoughts. His hands tightened on the steering wheel. What the hell had happened back there? One minute he'd wanted to throttle her, and the next he'd wanted to kiss her senseless. He didn't go for the caviar and champagne type. And Zora Hughes was definitely a woman with expensive taste, way out of his beer budget.

John slowed the Jeep as Mike Matisse's two-story home came into view. Had Danny driven Laura to and from Joseph's house? That would explain why John hadn't seen her on the road.

But the blue beast wasn't in the driveway. Now what? Was Laura even with Danny? One more place to try. Turning the Jeep around, John headed back to the main road.

He found Danny's car in the parking lot of the Iron Horse Café. He sat in the Jeep getting his temper in check before barging into the establishment. All conversation and laughter stopped when he stalked through the door. As usual, Danny, Mac, and Billy Joe were playing a game of pool. Laura was nowhere in sight.

"Coffee, John?" Foster asked from behind the bar.

John shook his head, then turned around, and headed back to his patrol vehicle. By the time he reached his house, he'd worked himself into a real frenzy. "Please let her be home," he chanted.

No light shone from underneath her bedroom door. He eased open her door, and holding his breath, tiptoed to the head of her bed. His daughter lay on her side, her back to him. He didn't know whether she was truly asleep or faking it. He didn't care. He was just glad she was home.

CHAPTER SEVEN

South Dakota, 1855

JULIA FELT THE GROUND SHAKE underneath her feet as a hunting party of warriors thundered through the camp. Tied by the ankle to a stake in the ground, she attempted to move out of the path of the horses, but her ankle, raw and bloody from the rope, chose that moment to collapse beneath her. In the next instant, her breath was knocked out of her when something landed on her. Whoever lay on her weighed more than three hogs in a bag, and she couldn't breathe.

"Get off," she gasped.

The weight shifted. She glared up into the face of a male savage. Sharp angles and burning dark eyes stared down at her. He said something to her in his harsh guttural language.

"I do not speak Indian." And never will.

The stranger touched a finger to her face, his expression thoughtful. Obviously he had never seen a woman of her color before. He rose and pulled her to her feet. She grimaced when pain shot up her leg and would have collapsed if he had not grabbed her by the shoulders.

Her captor's mother stared at the corn it had taken Julia all morning to grind. The grain had been pounded into the dirt. The old woman picked up a green twig and proceeded to whip Julia about the head and shoulders. The newcomer grabbed the old woman's arm and said something low but sharp to her. She dropped the twig and bowed her head, moving backwards quickly.

Julia knew this Indian was important. She did not know how important until he returned to her captor's teepee the next morning with four horses and bargained for her.

———————

The remnants of the dream clung like cobwebs to Zora's psyche when she woke. This was the first time John Iron Hawk's face had taken the place of Julia's Indian lover, and it shook Zora to the core. What did it mean? Did it have something to do with the almost kiss? She really needed to get on with her business and back to New York and away from this reservation. But first, a promise was a promise. She had to do something to make John sit up and take notice of Emma.

When Zora entered the kitchen twenty minutes later, Emma stood at the stove cooking breakfast. Her shoulders tensed, but she didn't turn around. Zora glanced at the old-fashioned percolator that sat on top of the gas burner. How badly could someone mess up coffee? She got her answer a moment later when she took a sip.

"Did John find Laura?" Zora asked. She placed her cup on the table and vowed to take over the coffee-making duties as long as she stayed.

"Yes," Emma said, turning bacon over in a skillet.

That was a relief. "Where was she?"

"At home."

Zora waited for Emma to say more, but the other woman ignored her. Zora's lips tightened in irritation. "Look, about last night—"

Emma swung around, meat fork in hand and took a menacing step toward Zora. "What about last night?"

Whoa. Zora took a step back. As she did so, she couldn't miss the look of smug satisfaction on Emma's face. She righted herself quickly. Score one for Ms. Bearkiller.

"I know you don't want me here, but I'm here at the

invitation of your grandfather. When I finish my business, which hopefully will be in a few days, I'll go back to New York. How fast I leave will depend on you."

The meat fork lowered just a fraction. "What do you mean?"

Zora had the other woman's full attention. "You've got a thing for John, don't you?"

Emma's shoulders stiffened. "We're friends."

"But you'd like to be more."

Emotions flitted across Emma's face. She might play tough, but the vulnerability and yearning were there for anyone to see. John must be blind or, at this thought Zora paused, didn't want to see Emma's desire for him.

She rubbed an imaginary speck of dust off her black boots, giving Emma time to get her emotions under control. "I can help you win John." Images of the dream invaded Zora's mind. She quickly blocked them.

"How do you know I want him?"

Zora couldn't reveal Joseph's part in this. "I saw how you looked at him last night—like you could eat him whole."

"And you weren't looking at him the same way?"

Zora opened her mouth in denial but shut it instead. This was about Emma and John, not Zora and John. And anyway, that almost kiss meant nothing to her or to him.

"John is not my type. I like them a little more…cultured."

Fire blazed in Emma's eyes at the put-down.

Zora jumped right on it. "So you see, you have nothing to worry about from me."

She studied Emma. Wearing old jeans, a hideous plaid shirt, and hiking boots, she looked like a Salvation Army reject. "First we need to find some sexier clothes for you. What else do you have in your closet?"

Emma looked down at her attire. "My clothes are just fine." She turned back to the stove, and with jerky movements, removed four pieces of burnt bacon from the smoking skillet.

"You're not going to get him to notice you unless you do something different. Men are into the physical. They notice your body long before they notice your mind."

Emma didn't turn around or acknowledge Zora's words. She held her breath. Had she struck out? Would her attempts to find out about her ancestor end before they'd even begun?

"What's in it for you?" Emma asked, pivoting to face Zora.

She thought about Julia's murder. *A chance to right a wrong*. But of course, she didn't say that to Emma. It would invite too many questions. Questions she didn't want to answer even if she had the answers. So she settled for part of the truth. "Your grandfather is going to help me trace an ancestor."

A doubtful expression filled Emma's dark eyes. She turned back to the stove, poured some of the grease from the bacon down the sink, and then cracked two eggs into the hot oil. "It's two hours to Pierre where all the good shops are."

Zora let out a breath she didn't know she'd been holding.

———◆———

Zora handed a gray silk blouse over the dressing room door to Emma. "He hasn't dated anyone since coming back from Minneapolis?"

"Nope." Emma's voice sounded muffled.

Zora found that hard to believe. A man with as much animal magnetism as John—and yes, she'd give him that—had to have a woman or women on the side. Maybe Emma just didn't want to think there were other women. "What social gatherings do you have in Little River?"

"None."

"Hold on. There's got to be something—a dance, cookouts?"

Emma stepped out of the dressing room. Her slim figure was showcased in form fitting jeans and the gray Kenzie top.

"There're the monthly council meetings. John goes to those."

"No, I mean somewhere that you can sit down and have a drink—"

Emma flushed crimson, ducked her head and hurried back into the dressing room.

Her embarrassment confirmed what Zora suspected last night, that there was history between John and Emma. "You've already had those drinks, haven't you?"

"Yes."

Then there was silence for so long, she thought Emma had clammed up. "Have you and John ever…" She couldn't get the words out, maybe because she didn't want to know.

"That's none of your business."

Something twisted in Zora's gut. Emma's evasion of the question told her more than the woman's spoken words would ever do. They'd had sex.

Without realizing it, Zora had twisted a Valentino blouse into a ball. She smoothed out the wrinkles and placed it back on the hanger. Knowing Emma and John had been intimate put a new reflection on the situation. Somehow it was easier helping Emma when Zora thought the other woman hadn't a snowball's chance in hell, but now…

She gave herself a mental shake. She needed to focus. Find out about Julia's life and get back to New York. Next week, the reservation and its police chief would be a distant memory. "Laura seems like a troubled girl."

Emma stepped out of the changing room. Her eyes were guarded, their earlier camaraderie gone. "Why do you care? And for your information, she's had a rough time."

Zora couldn't ruffle Emma's feathers, not if she wanted information. She shrugged. "When she came to the house last night, she'd been crying. I was concerned."

Emma placed the unwanted clothes back on their hangers. "Like I said, she's had a hard time of it."

"How did you two become friends?"

"I volunteer at the Boys and Girls Club. Laura hangs out there sometimes."

Zora had heard of the club before coming to Little River. She was just surprised to see it on an Indian reservation. "Do most of the teenagers belong to the club?"

"Some of us adults have tried to get the older kids involved, but they think it's a white man's trap."

Zora frowned. "A white man's trap?"

"Some of the teens are very anti-establishment."

Zora found that interesting. She'd have thought the adults would want to keep the old ways and it would be the teens wanting to move away from Native traditions. "Are all of Laura's friends in the club?"

"Laura doesn't have any friends," Emma said. "That's the problem."

"What about Gilly?"

"That's about the only one."

"What about the short-haired girl?"

Deep lines furrowed Emma's forehead. "What short haired girl? Laura's the only one I know of with short hair."

How could Zora describe Laura's friend? Oh, she looks like my great-great-great-grandmother. "Yesterday, Laura was with two boys and two girls. One girl was Gilly. I didn't hear the second girl's name."

Emma shrugged. "I don't know of another girlfriend other than Gilly. The boys I know." She grunted in disgust, sounding very much like her grandfather. "Billy Joe's flunkies, Danny Matisse and his pal, Mac."

Slinging the clothes she wanted over her shoulder, Emma strode toward the checkout counter.

With her longer legs, it didn't take Zora two strides to

catch up with Joseph's granddaughter. "So you've never seen Laura in the company of another girl other than Gilly?"

"No, not unless it's someone she met recently. I know all the teenage girls on the reservation. There're not many of them."

"Could she live off the reservation?"

Emma whipped around. "Why are you so curious about Laura's friends?"

Buying herself time to come up with a suitable answer, Zora dug in her purse for her credit card. "She seems lonely."

Zora could feel Emma studying her.

"She is, but she doesn't need your pity. She doesn't need you pretending to be interested in her."

Oblivious to the sales woman listening to their conversation, Emma held up the clothes she wanted. "It's okay to use me 'cause I'm using you but leave Laura and my grandfather alone." She marched to the checkout counter, plunked the clothes down on the counter and said to the sales clerk, "She's paying," and stomped away.

Five hours after they'd left the reservation, Emma had in her possession a simple black sheath, some sexy lingerie, a few flattering tops, and three pairs of jeans. Zora had in her possession a Chrysler 200 convertible. She and the rental car agency had finally come to terms.

A grizzly old man with white hair and whiskers, and dirty clothes sat on the couch Zora now called her bed when she and Emma arrived back at the Bearkiller residence.

"This is Chet Tyler," Joseph said. "Homesteads a couple of miles from here."

"Come here, girl." Tyler, teeth stained brown, pulled

Zora down on the couch next to him and inspected her face. "Don't look like blood to me. What's your tribe, girl?"

"Lakota," Zora said.

Emma laughed.

Confused, Zora glanced at Joseph.

"The Lakota nation is made up of seven tribes," he said. "I am of the tribe called Oglala. If your ancestor lived here among us then you are also Oglala."

Zora tried the foreign sounding syllables out on her tongue. "I'm Oglala."

Joseph nodded his approval.

"You vouch for her?" Tyler said, squinting at Joseph.

"I do."

Tyler nodded his bushy head. "So be it."

"What?" Zora asked.

"We," Joseph pointed between himself and Tyler, "are the oldest on the reservation. Chet has also agreed to help you."

Zora glanced uneasily between the old men. "What are you two planning?"

"We will speak to the spirits on your behalf."

Emma advanced into the room. "You two are going to do *what*?"

Joseph met her question with silence.

Emma marched over to her grandfather's chair. "Don't do something stupid." She included Chet in her hot glare. "You don't even know this woman. She could be lying, having a joke at the expense of two old Indians. What do you really know about her?"

Joseph only stared at his granddaughter.

"You're two old fools. She doesn't want your help. She's slumming."

Emma stalked over to Zora and stopped within a foot of her. "I want you out of this house, and you can take those fancy clothes with you."

"Emma." Joseph's voice was soft but commanding. He

waited until his granddaughter faced him. "She is family. We will help her."

A flush the color of an overripe pomegranate flooded Emma's face. She opened and closed her mouth like a hooked salmon then shot Zora a look of pure hatred before stomping out of the room.

CHAPTER EIGHT

R EMOVING HER SUNGLASSES, ZORA ALLOWED her eyes to adjust to the interior of tribal headquarters. The one and only time she'd been in the building was to report the incident on the highway involving Laura Iron Hawk and her friends.

Immediately to the left of the entrance was the police department. She had no interest in seeing John, so she turned her attention to the other occupants of the one-story structure. The tribal council office was at the end of the hall, and the Boys and Girls Club ran the length of the building directly opposite the police department. *Bet that kept the kids in line.*

The dribbling of a basketball echoing off concrete walls greeted her when she opened the club's door. One lone boy of about twelve, with long legs and big feet, ran down the length of the court with another boy in baggy gym shorts pursuing him. A few bored kids, a mixture of boys and girls, lounged on the floor or leaned against the walls, watching the pair.

Zora glanced at her watch. It was one o'clock and summertime. She expected to see more kids, and where were the teens?

"Can I help you?"

A short woman with blunt-cut hair stood in the door of one of the rooms that encircled the gym. From a distance, she looked about twenty, but as Zora approached, she realized the woman was probably closer to forty. Her plump face was free of wrinkles but the eyes were those of a person who'd seen change and not all of it good.

"I'm visiting and wanted to check out the club." Zora didn't want to put the woman on the defensive by asking immediately about the girl at Mac's trailer.

"I'm Viola Black Elk. I run the facility."

Facility? The word sounded as though she referred to a prison. "Zora Hughes."

"Are you familiar with the Boys and Girls Clubs?" Viola asked.

"Not really."

"The organization has been around for over one hundred years, helping underprivileged children find their way in society. It keeps them off the streets." Her spiel sounded rehearsed.

Zora glanced around. "Not many kids?"

"We've had to cut back on services. We lost our basketball coach last month."

Zora nodded toward the kids leaning against the walls. "What are they waiting for?"

Viola followed her gaze. "For the art instructor. He's running a little late."

"Where are the teens?"

"They usually show up later in the day. They tend to sleep late when school is recessed for summer."

Or sleeping off hangovers, Zora thought.

Time to get down to business, but she wondered about the best approach. As her great aunt said, "Honesty is always the best policy." Or as close to the truth as possible, Zora thought. "I met three teenage girls yesterday." No need to describe the circumstances surrounding the meeting. "One was Laura and the other was Gilly, but I failed to get the name of the third teen. About five-foot-four, short dark hair."

Viola's dark eyes bore into Zora's. She fought the urge

to look away.

"That description fits about sixty percent of the teenage girls on the reservation. Why are you looking for her?"

"I wanted to ask them if they'd be interested in modeling." Zora hid her face as she dug into her purse and pulled out a business card. She was not a good liar.

Viola took the card. "Zora D. Hughes, Fashion editor, *Haute Magazine*, New York, New York." She handed the card back to Zora. "I know Laura. She has a friend named Gilly, but I don't know the other girl. Best to talk with Emma Bearkiller. She volunteers here a couple of days a week and knows the teenage girls a lot better than I do."

A young girl of eight or nine walked up to Viola, holding a swatch of cloth to her chest. The color—a shade of yellow with orange undertones—clashed horribly with the child's skin.

"You teach sewing?" Zora asked.

Viola shrugged. "Yes, but I'm not good at it."

"Neither am I." Zora loved the touch and smell of fabric, but she didn't have the patience for sewing. "What are you making?" she asked the child.

"A blouse." The girl hugged the material, smiling shyly.

"Is it for you?"

The girl nodded.

Zora groaned. Awful choice. "A caramel-colored blouse would look beautiful on you."

The child's face scrunched into a frown as she studied the fabric. Her lower lip trembled.

"Go back to your sewing. I'll be there in a minute," Viola said.

Downcast, the girl walked slowly back to her machine. Viola turned to Zora a look of censure in her eyes. "We don't have a lot of fabric. She'll be dissatisfied with her choice, now that you've pointed out its flaws."

Zora winced. "I'm sorry. I didn't think."

Without saying goodbye, Viola turned and headed back

to the sewing room. Zora had just been dismissed.

Just before she stepped out into the sunshine, Zora heard the swish of a door opening behind her. She turned in time to see John rush into the Boys and Girls Club. If he'd turned his head just a little, he'd have seen her standing at the entrance. She shrugged off the hollow feeling of disappointment that lodged in the pit of her stomach.

Once back on the street, she realized she was no closer to finding the teen than she'd been twenty minutes earlier. No one knew the girl. Granted, Zora hadn't given them much of a description, but…

She glanced up and down the empty road. White wispy clouds floated in a blue sky. If she were a teen on summer vacation where would she hang out? There wasn't a mall within a reasonable distance. Where could they go and goof off? Taking a gamble, Zora headed for her car.

Hard rock blared from the jukebox when Zora entered the cool dark interior of the Iron Horse Café. She paused in the door, letting her eyes adjust to the radical change from the bright sunlight. Danny, Laura, Mac, and another boy occupied a back booth. Their conversation stopped abruptly when they spotted her. The song ended and you could hear the ping of the next compact disc as it slid into place. The Eagles wailed "Desperado."

She walked to the bar and ordered a Coke. As she sipped the cold amber liquid, she tried to decide on how to approach the group and get them talking about this mysterious girl.

Her opportunity came when Danny pulled Laura toward the small dance floor. After he gathered her close, his hands slid down her back to her butt. He gripped a cheek and squeezed. Laura squealed and removed his hands.

Zora picked up her drink and strolled toward the back

booth. The smile froze on Mac's face when he saw her.

"What do you want?" His eyes were black mercurial pools of hate. "'Cause of you, we spent time in the holding cell."

Her natural inclination was to fire back a scathing response, but she held her tongue. She needed information from this punk. "Think of it this way. I might have saved your life."

"Fuck you, lady," Mac muttered.

Gritting her teeth, Zora ignored him. "You guys left another friend at the trailer. Nice of you not to tell John she was there."

Mac's eyes shifted back and forth like he was reading a cue card and not understanding the script. "Huh?"

"This tall," Zora lifted her hand shoulder height, "short hair, thin."

"Who the hell you talking about, lady?"

The other boy, his face pock-marked with acne, smirked.

"She may be in trouble." She didn't know where this knowledge came from, but some instinctive place in her gut practically screamed with certainty.

"Trouble from who?"

"I don't know." She felt inane admitting it and well deserved the incredulous glance he gave her.

"Lady, you're nuts."

That brought a giggle from the other kid.

Zora leaned over the table and put her face close to Mac's. She wished she hadn't. His breath stank of onions and poor dental hygiene. "Do you know her?"

"I know lots of girls, but there wasn't any girl around the trailer but Laura and Gilly."

"Maybe she lives near you."

Mac must have heard the desperation in her voice because his face closed down, and he folded his arms across his chest. "Lady, get the—"

"I said stop, Danny."

Zora turned to stare at the couple on the dance floor. Laura removed Danny's offending hands from her ass and stepped out of reach.

He held out his arms. "Okay, baby. Come on, let's finish the dance." He gave her a grin that someone had obviously told him was cute.

Laura pivoted and headed for the door.

"Whoa!" Danny ran after her and grabbed her arm. "Where you going?"

"Home." Laura glared down at his offending grasp. "Let go."

He dropped her arm. "It's a long walk back to the reservation," he said to her retreating back. Laughing, he strolled back toward the booth. Drawing level with Zora, he gave her the once-over before sliding into the seat opposite his friends. "What'd she want?" He inclined his head toward Zora.

"Nothing, man," Mac said. "She's cracked."

The males laughed.

Feeling she'd gotten all she was going to get out of Mac, Zora dug money out of her purse, slapped it on the bar, and rushed out.

Laura hadn't gotten very far down the road when Zora pulled up next to her in the convertible. "I'm on the way back to the reservation if you want a ride."

Laura stopped, glanced back at the cafe then at the long dusty road that stretched out in front of her. She climbed in. They traveled in silence for the first few miles.

"How is your friend Gilly?"

From beneath thick black eyebrows so like her dad's, Laura shot her a hostile glare. "Why do you want to know?"

"Just concerned."

She snorted. "Right."

"Does she live on the reservation?"

Laura turned in her seat so she faced Zora. "Just who are you anyway? You just show up and start asking questions.

Are you with the Bureau?"

Confused, Zora frowned. "The FBI?"

Laura laughed. The sound put a smile on Zora's face. It was good to hear the teen's laughter, even though she knew it was at her expense.

"No. I was just kidding. There's no way you're a Fed. Your clothes are too expensive, too flashy."

Zora looked at her attire. Flashy? She wore jeans, a shirt and boots. What was flashy about that?

"The fabrics shout money," the teen said.

"You have an eye for fabric?"

"I study the pictures in *Vogue*."

Zora heard the wistfulness in the girl's voice. "Clothes aren't everything," Zora lied. She didn't add that next to clothes and money everything else was a distant third, including love.

"Spoken by someone who has it all."

Zora didn't want to dishearten the girl even more, so she changed the subject. "You deserve better than Danny." She studied the teen from out of the corner of her eye. Just like her father when he was angry, Laura's jaw rippled. Never one to know when to quit, Zora plunged on. "In fact, I'd say he's an opportunistic snake." She thought Laura would tear into her for that remark, but the teen surprised her with another burst of laughter.

"Where do you get these expressions? You mean he's a S'unka."

Zora frowned and took her eyes off the road to stare at the teen. "A what?"

"A S'unka, a dog."

Zora smiled. "There are a whole lot of S'unkas in this world."

The rest of the ride back to the reservation passed in silence. With directions from Laura, Zora pulled the car up to the small utilitarian one-story she'd taken pictures in front of several days ago. At the time, she hadn't known the place belonged to John or this was his daughter.

A study in brownness, the house resembled a tired old eagle. Someone had attempted to enlarge the home by adding a wing on either side of the main body. Wings that now sagged under the weight of a roof repaired many times.

Trying to put a positive spin on the bleakness of the place, Zora said, "You must get a lot of natural light." She nodded toward the large picture window at the front of the house.

"John uses it for his hobby."

Zora cocked her head with interest. "What's his hobby?"

"He thinks he's an artist."

Zora smiled. Within the derision in the girl's words, she thought she detected a hint of pride. "Being an artist is a good outlet for tension."

"Yeah, right." The girl stepped out of the car.

Before Laura could dash off, Zora said, "The girl I asked you about might be in trouble. I want to help her."

John's daughter studied her, probably judging her sincerity. She gave an abrupt nod, slammed the car door and jogged across the grassless yard to her front door.

It wasn't lost on Zora that in an unguarded moment, Laura, at Mac's trailer had called John: Daddy. Here with Zora, she'd showed disrespect by calling him by his first name. Zora's smile was bittersweet. There was a small, insecure child lurking in that mature body. A child who probably wanted her father's love, but didn't know how to go about asking for it, or, and this thought brought a sting of tears to Zora's eyes, didn't think she deserved it.

Before pulling away, she waited for Laura to unlock her door and step into the house. Because she saw a definite parallel in her own life with her father and Laura's with John, Zora wasn't sure whom her tears were for.

CHAPTER NINE

———

"I STAYED OUT AT OLD MAN Tyler's place for five hours," Oscar Levant said in disgust. "Nothing happened. What a waste of time."

John sorted through the morning's mail, listening to his deputy's whine with half an ear.

"—chased a kid off the property—"

John's head shot up. "What?"

"A girl. 'Bout fifteen. Caught her in the hen house, trying to steal eggs."

John frowned. "What did she look like?"

"Like a girl. Thought she was a boy at first with that short hair." He grinned. "But then I got a look at those boobs."

John had tried to teach his only deputy to use his eyes and ears to improve his policing skills, but Oscar was a lost cause. "Indian or Caucasian?"

"Indian."

"Slim or heavy?"

"Slim."

This was going to take all day. "So what did you do with this girl?"

"I ran her off, of course," Oscar said.

John closed his eyes in exasperation. "Did you get a name, maybe followed her?"

Oscar's eyes widened. "You told me to check out Tyler's place. I stayed."

"Okay. Okay," John said. He wondered if this was the cause of the disturbance on Chet Tyler's property. "Put some feelers out. See if anyone else has seen the girl or had chickens stolen."

Oscar stared out the window of John's office. John could practically see the wheels turning in his deputy's mind. "Do you think this girl is the problem not the coyotes?"

It took a while for Oscar to get from flash to bang but eventually he got there. "Could be both. I want you back out there tonight."

Oscar groaned.

"And if she shows up again," John said, "follow her."

———◆———

"Dinner was good," Joseph said, pushing his wheelchair back from the kitchen table.

Zora had stopped at a grocery in Pierre and picked up frozen lasagna along with other food items. The lasagna hadn't been as good as that of Marciano's, but it was still better than anything Emma could have cooked up.

"So where are you ladies off to tonight?" he asked.

"We're attending the monthly council meeting," Zora said, stifling a yawn that threatened to crack her jaw. This wasn't exactly how she wanted to spend her evening, but a night of jazz and a martini were three thousand miles away.

Joseph placed a worn, paper-thin hand on top of Zora's. "Thank you."

"For what?"

"Taking her to Pierre—" He glanced toward the kitchen door and his face brightened. Emma stood in the doorway, wearing jeans and her Kenzie blouse. The scooped neckline showed off her slender neck and shoulders.

Zora gave herself a mental pat on the back. She'd done a damn fine job of selecting clothes that showed off the young woman's figure. They'd picked up makeup while in the mall, and a makeup artist had shown Emma how to select eye shadow to complement her clothes. John would be knocked off his feet.

"You look very nice," Zora said later, as they bounced along the highway toward the tribal center.

"Thanks. I just hope John thinks so."

Zora turned and stared out the window of the truck. The idea that John's dark eyes would look at Emma with admiration left a sour taste in her mouth.

When they arrived the small council meeting room was filled to capacity. Even so, Zora spotted John right away. He stood a head taller than anyone in the room, with the exception of her. Emma moved restlessly beside her. Not wanting to witness the meeting between the two, Zora moved off toward the refreshment table.

———

When Zora and Emma entered the council meeting room, John, who'd been speaking to one of the council-men, lost his train of thought.

Zora wore a multicolored skirt that swished around her long slender legs as she strolled toward the refreshment table. When she leaned forward to pick up a paper cup, her breasts molded to her short-sleeved blouse.

"Hello, John."

He blinked twice and reluctantly shifted his eyes down to Emma. There was something different about her. He couldn't put his finger on it. Maybe she'd cut her hair. He opened his mouth to say, "Nice haircut," but shut it. What if it wasn't her hair that had changed? "Hey, Emma. Didn't know you were coming tonight."

She smiled up at him, her black eyes glowing. "Zora wanted to see a tribal council meeting so…" She shrugged.

Matisse strolled up to Zora. Grasping her hand in one of his meaty paws, he gave her the once-over.

"—house tonight?" Emma asked.

"Huh?"

Her lips compressed into a tight line. "I asked if you're coming by the house tonight."

What the hell for? He was saved from replying when Zora marched toward them, body taut with emotion.

"That guy is full of it," Zora said.

Laughing loudly, Matisse pounded Fred Red Elk on the shoulder.

"Yes, our council president does have a high opinion of himself," John said.

Zora's eyes narrowed as she studied him. "I'd think you'd make a better tribal president."

He shook his head. "I'm not a bought man." He needed to get away from Emma's hopeful eyes and Zora's alluring presence. He needed air. "If you ladies will excuse me." He kept the exit in his sights as he maneuvered through the crowd.

———

Was Matisse taking bribes? Zora studied the short, stout tribal leader. There appeared to be no love lost between him and John, but that was no concern of hers. She needed to find the teen. Once she found the girl, she could get answers to what happened to Julia. Zora had read up on visions in Indian lore and found peyote mushrooms were used, producing an effect much like LSD. She shuddered. She hoped Joseph hadn't planned to seek his vision by using mushrooms. She didn't want him putting his life in danger for her.

She turned to Emma. "How did it go?"

"Fine until you came back."

"Yeah," Zora said dryly. "It looked like you had him all but wrestled and hog-tied."

Emma narrowed her eyes. "You don't fool me, you

know."

Zora raised a brow.

"You want him as much as I do."

At a loss for words, Zora tried to laugh it off. "You mean Mike Matisse—"

"Cut the bullshit," Emma said. "John may find you different, but the two of you have nothing in common. Men like him seek their own kind." She turned on her heel and stomped away.

Mouth open, Zora stared after the woman. She didn't find John Iron Hawk the least bit attractive. Okay, yes, there was something different about him. The men in her life, and especially Terrance, had been smooth, well dressed and cultured, something John Iron Hawk definitely was not. Her eyes widened at the mental picture of that tall muscular body in a tuxedo and his blue-black hair flowing on his shoulders. Her throat went dry. She scanned the crowd until she found him. Wide-shouldered, he stood near the entrance to the room, listening patiently to two old men.

"Find your seats," Mike Matisse bellowed. He stood at a table at the front of the room, gavel in hand.

Emma had taken a seat between two grandmother types. Zora knew it was an intentional slight. Scanning the hall, she found an empty place next to a mother with two small children.

The mother gave Zora a shy smile. Two sets of black eyes peered at Zora curiously from the safety of their mother's arms. Watching the girls watch her kept Zora awake through the dry recitation of committee reports. When the girls fell asleep, Zora found herself zoning out. The rap of the gavel jerked her back to consciousness. Whatever she'd missed must have been a doozy. The air in the small room fairly crackled with tension.

"I said, I wanna know what's happening with the money coming from the casino," a young man shouted.

Voices rose in agreement. Mike Matisse, growing redder

with each pounding of the gavel, shouted, "One at a time."

"That's been on my mind too, Matisse." This from a round woman with braids looped around her head. "What about the money that's supposed to fund the library?"

"And the Boys and Girls Club," someone else shouted from the back of the room.

Mike raised a sheet of paper over his head. "It's all here in the budget."

"That budget's bullshit, and you know it," someone else said, voice raised above the growing melee. "The casino's making more money than that."

"The casino's got operating expenses," Mike said. "Extra money goes to our police department for the security of the casino. Maybe you should ask John Iron Hawk about those funds."

Zora glanced around the room, looking for John. She wondered what he'd say to these allegations, but he'd disappeared.

"I left the disbursement of those funds in John's hands. Maybe I was wrong in putting so much trust in one person." Matisse raised his hands in a calming gesture. "You have my word I'll look into what's happened to the money, and if Iron Hawk has misused the funds in any way, I'll have his job."

She hadn't known John very long, but she knew he was no thief. She glanced around to see how the crowd reacted to Matisse's statement. They'd grown silent. Did this mean they believed Matisse?

———◆———

In the darkness of the starless night, John's car headlights merged together about two hundred yards down the main road. Oscar had paged, probably after failing to raise John by radio. He hadn't left a message.

John depressed the talk button on the patrol car's radio.

"Maggie, have you heard anything from Oscar?"

"No, sir. Not for at least two hours. He was heading out to Chet Tyler's. Is everything okay?"

"Everything's fine." He didn't want to alarm Maggie or have her inform half the reservation that something was going on out at the Tyler place. John punched the accelerator.

The Jeep barreled down the highway. He reduced his speed then pulled into Chet's drive. Removing his Remington .22 from the rack, he hopped out of the Jeep, walking quietly toward Oscar's abandoned vehicle. The driver's door stood open, the vehicle's dome light extinguished. Oscar's shotgun was missing.

A muted television played a rerun of *The Andy Griffith Show* as John walked through the small house, looking into all four rooms. No Chet. No Oscar.

Back in the living room, he studied the images on the TV. Andy berated Barney. John scanned the darkened living room. Smoke spiraled from a still burning cigarette.

With a sickening premonition, John glanced in the corner by the front door. Chet Tyler's shotgun was missing.

Sliding out the front door, John kept to the shadows as he moved toward the barn. The structure had no doors. Normally, you could stand at the front entrance and see all the way to Chet's back pastures, but clouds hid the moon. He slipped quietly inside and listened. Nothing. No restless rustling of animals or high-pitched sounds of distress. Confident no one was in the barn, John moved through it and out through the rear. Fifty feet outside the barn, he stumbled over a prone form.

Kneeling, he turned the body over.

Chet Tyler.

John found a weak pulse in the old man's neck. "Chet? Can you hear me?"

No answer.

John ran his hands over the body. Not a mark on him.

Probably a heart attack. John slung his rifle over his shoulder and easily lifted the old man. He stopped. Something had moved in his peripheral vision. He eased Chet back to the ground, and swung his rifle in the direction of the chicken coop. "Who's there?"

Silence.

"Come out with your hands up." The shadow had definitely been human.

From the shifting shadows, a small form rose from behind the coop. The half moon moved out of the shadow of the clouds to reveal a girl with short-cropped hair and a pale formless dress.

"Who are you?" John asked.

She stared mutely at him. Was this the girl Oscar had chased off Tyler's property the night before? "Have you seen my deputy?"

When she didn't respond, he repeated the question in the language of the people.

"He has been shot." She spoke, her voice halting and slow.

"Where is he?"

"The old man shot him."

"Where is he?" John repeated.

"Here." She pointed to an area a foot from where she stood.

He moved toward her. She backed away. He stopped. "I won't hurt you."

The grass surrounding Oscar's body glistened with a dark substance. John fingered it. Blood.

He knelt and ran his hands over his deputy's body and found a hole in Oscar's left shoulder. A few more inches down and Oscar's soul would have departed this earth. "There's a first aid kit in the Jeep, get it for me."

John tore his shirt and pressed it to Oscar's wound to staunch the bleeding.

She didn't speak but continued to stare at him. There was

something familiar about her. Time enough later to question her. He needed to get these two men some medical help. "Hurry." He glanced down at Oscar. "Hang in there, buddy."

What the hell happened here? Did the old guy need glasses in addition to a hearing aid?

The clouds shifted and moonlight flooded the pasture. Oscar's face, partially hidden by scraggly grass, was gray. Blood continued to seep into the dirt.

What was taking her so long? Blast it all.

He dashed for the Jeep.

Grateful for his four-wheel drive, he pulled behind the barn. Using the first aid kit, he made a bandage for Oscar's wound, then lifted his deputy, and deposited him in the back seat. John went back for Chet. Scooping the old man up in his arms, John laid him gently on the front seat. The old coot was nothing but skin and bones.

John jumped into the vehicle and turned the Jeep around in the Chet's pasture. Once on the road, he floored it.

Chet Tyler rested with his head propped against the car's doorframe. Except for the slightly blue tint of his skin, he looked as though he slept. Trying to keep one eye on the road, John grabbed the old man's wrist and felt for a pulse. Weak, but still beating.

John picked up the radio. "Maggie?"

"Yes, Sheriff?"

"Patch me through to one of the docs from the clinic." This was why Little River needed a full-time doctor on the reservation. They had a clinic, but the doctor came in from Pierre only twice a week. Any emergencies had to be driven to Stonewater, halfway between Pierre and the reservation. John planned to do something about the situation.

Chapter Ten

EARLY MORNING SUN POURED THROUGH the thin sheers in the Bearkiller den, leaving pools of yellow light on the worn carpet. Zora lay huddled on the sofa, listening to the pounding of her heart.

Since she'd arrived in South Dakota five days ago, the dreams had increased, become stronger, and more vivid. On waking, it took her longer to remember this was 2014, not the 19th century. If being on the reservation was the cause of the change, maybe she needed to rethink what she hoped to accomplish here. Maybe the dreams would never disappear. Maybe she needed to return to New York.

She pushed to a sitting position. Her suitcases sat in the corner of the room. All she had to do was pack. She'd could return the rental car to Pierre and take a flight to New York. She could be back in her apartment by nine p.m. There were other magazines. She had a reputation for quality work. It wouldn't take her long to land another position, and she'd call Terrance as soon as she returned. They'd iron out their problems, and it would be smooth sailing from that point on. Maybe she'd start planning a wedding. Yes, a wedding. Lots of bridesmaids, a flower girl—

She jerked when Joseph's wheelchair moved into her line of sight, cutting off her view of the suitcases.

"You're thinking of leaving?"

Blocking out the disappointed expression on his face, she

stood, donned her robe, and began removing her clothes from the back of the door. "Emma has clothes and makeup. She'll be fine."

"She has a long way to go to capture John's heart. Clothes alone will not do it."

Zora moved around the wheelchair and picked up a suitcase. "I'm not a matchmaker. I can't make him love her. I couldn't straighten out my own love life."

His sunken brown eyes seemed to bore a hole into her soul. Hopefully, he couldn't see all the fear and uncertainty hiding there.

"Running will not make your problems go away. It will only make them worse."

"I'm sorry. I don't mean to renege on our agreement. I just…" She stared down at the worn carpet then glanced up into his wrinkled face. "I just can't do this. I thought I could, but I can't."

He didn't reply, but his sorrowful gaze shamed her more than any words he could have spoken.

She closed her eyes. All her life she'd done what was necessary not to disappoint her mother, her teachers, or her bosses. Obviously, she'd failed in Claudia's eyes. Why else would her boss have put a twentysomething in Zora's position? A twentysomething Zora had trained. She closed her mind to the fact her erratic behavior of late could have contributed to her being fired.

She turned to face him. "Look, John and Emma need to work this thing out on their own. Maybe it's not meant to be." Or you don't want it to be, a little voice in her head said. She reached for more clothes, all the time feeling Joseph's dark eyes on her.

"John is a good man. Emma, a good woman. Don't you agree?"

Was John a good man? According to Mike Matisse, maybe not, and the jury was still out on Emma.

"Give me a week to find the answers you seek," the old

man said.

Zora whirled on him. "A week!"

His talon-like fingers gripped the arms of his chair. She shook herself out of her self-absorbed state to really study him. He looked tired and dispirited. The humor that normally shone in his eyes was gone.

"What's wrong?"

The old man sighed and turned his wheelchair to stare out at the field across the road. "Chet had a heart attack last night. John found him and took him to the hospital."

So that was where John had disappeared to. Zora placed a hand on his shoulder. "I'm so sorry. Is he going to be okay?"

Joseph's smile was grim. "He will be fine. At least long enough for us to commune with the spirits."

Zora was too disheartened to even smile at the mention of the visions. She sank onto the sofa that until a few moments ago had been her bed. "I've decided it doesn't matter any longer. I will live with the dreams. I'll go back to New York and work out my problems."

His body stiffened. "What dreams?"

She blinked several times, feeling like an animal caught in the beams of an oncoming train. Had she spoken of the dreams aloud?

"You have visions?"

"Ah, not visions, just dreams, occ...occasionally." She jumped up, closed her luggage and moved to place the piece at the door. Joseph maneuvered his chair to block her path.

"Tell me about the dreams."

Zora rubbed her forehead. "They're not important."

He studied her with his dark eyes. "Tell me."

With a sigh, she sank onto the sofa. "I've had them all my life. They've gotten worse in the last two or three months." She went on to tell him about the dreams and about the teenage girl who resembled Julia. She didn't tell him about Julia being murdered, and she didn't mention that sometimes Julia's husband's face became that of John Iron Hawk. What was this power Joseph Bearkiller had over her? He made her reveal thoughts she hadn't shared with anyone else.

"Has anyone else in your family had these dreams?"

She shook her head. "I asked my great-aunt Callie. I'm the only one. Do you think I'm crazy? Losing my mind?"

He smiled and moved his chair closer to her. He took her hands in his rough ones. "No, little one. You have a gift. For some reason this Julia has found a receptive spirit in you. She speaks through you."

Zora shuddered. "Like possession?"

His face was solemn. "Do not be afraid. She is telling you her story for a reason. Possibly there is some uncompleted task. Maybe something she wants you to do because she cannot. The young girl's family may hold more answers."

"I haven't been able to find the girl or anyone who knows her."

"We will search for her together. I will help you and Julia find the answers you seek here among the People."

When John stepped into his sister's store, the clang and clatter of the brass chimes made his teeth grind. Because he'd gotten only three hours sleep his head throbbed to each tinny rattle. Normal people had the chimes outside the store, but not Lydia.

He wandered around, checking out the new merchandise as he waited for his sister to finish with a customer. He fingered the leather belts Chet had tooled.

Chet's heart attack had been mild, but his age had complicated his condition. The doctor at the clinic in Stonewater had arranged for an ambulance to take him to Pierre, but only after they sedated him. John chuckled.

When Chet had regained consciousness and found himself in the hospital, he'd tried to dress and leave. It was hard to keep down someone as crusty and opinionated as Chet Tyler. A battleship of a nurse had gleefully injected Valium in his IV line.

"What do you have to smile about?" Two vertical worry lines were etched between Lydia's brows.

For the first time, John realized how tired his sister looked. Caring for an invalid husband and working all day was wearing her down. "Glad to be alive, I guess." He'd barely slept the night before and now operated a one-man department, but two members of his community were alive, which meant a lot.

"You haven't been to your office?"

He shook his head. "Why?" Something told him he wasn't going to like what she had to say.

"Several concerned citizens are calling for an audit of the police department finances."

"*What?* "

"After you left the council meeting last night, someone questioned Mike about the funds generated by the casino and how they were being used. He implied the funds had been misused by the police department."

"Meaning me."

"Meaning you," she said.

"Son of a bitch."

"Wonder if he's got a burr up his ass because Dottie left him."

John couldn't stop a grin from spreading over his face. Somehow, Matisse's misfortune made him feel good. "She's gone, huh?"

"Heard she took the Greyhound to St. Louis a couple of weeks ago."

John scratched his head and tried unsuccessfully to wipe the smile off his face. "Good for her."

"The rumor is he put her out 'cause she and Danny

were getting it on when Mike was away in Pierre, meeting with the bigwigs."

John stopped smiling. "That punk was screwing his stepmother?"

"Seems so."

Images of Danny touching Laura out at the Mac's trailer flashed through John's mind. His hands tightened into fists. Fists he'd like to shove down the little cretin's throat. If Danny was screwing Laura, that would be statutory rape, grounds for him to throw Danny's punk ass in the jail, but only after he'd rearranged the little shit's face.

John relaxed his hands and shoved his Stetson further back on his head. He'd deal with Danny Matisse later. "Chet Tyler shot Oscar last night. Think he mistook him for a coyote."

Lydia's eyes widened. "Is there a full moon? What's going on?"

John shrugged. "Beats me.

The wind chimes clattered. A heavyset white couple stepped into the shop.

Lydia smiled at them. "Look around. I'll be with you in a moment." She turned her attention back to John and lowered her voice. "How do you mistake a man for a coyote?"

"I don't know, but there was a girl out on the property who might be able to shed more light on what happened. *If* I can find her."

"Who was she?"

He shook his head. "Don't know."

Lydia nodded and smiled again at her customers. "Do you think Laura knows her?"

"I haven't had a chance to ask her."

"I've got to go," she said.

When she started to walk away, John grabbed her arm. "We need to talk about my paintings."

"Later. Come by later." She stepped away from him and toward the browsing couple.

His lips narrowed in irritation. She didn't want him to remove his paintings. It didn't take a genius to figure that out. He strode over to the area where the canvases were displayed.

One was gone.

An eagle soared over the open plain before swooping down to earth. When he rose again, he had a small rodent in his claws.

"Yuck," Zora said, trying to keep her eyes on the road and not on the hideous sight.

"It is the way of nature." Joseph sat in the passenger seat of the convertible.

He had persuaded Zora to take him to the hospital in Pierre to see Chet. She resisted at first. How was she going to get him into the car? He'd played on her sympathy by telling her Chet might die and the two would not have said their goodbyes. So she'd loaded the wheelchair in the trunk after Joseph lifted himself into the passenger seat. The old man was a lot stronger than he looked.

The eagle flew over the next ridge of mountains and disappeared. Zora tried to block out the image of the bird feasting on the small animal. "I could never have survived out here a couple of hundred years ago."

"Yes, you would have. You're a survivor, Zora Hughes."

Her laugh was humorless. "I'm not a survivor."

"You are here."

She shook her head. "I was asked to leave my job. I think they thought I was about to crack."

"Like I said, you are a survivor. Too many people let the stress of a high-powered position eat away at them until there is nothing left. You were strong enough to come here and search for answers."

A half-smile tugged at Zora's lips. "You are determined

to make me something I'm not."

He spoke after a moment of silence. "How many generations are between you and your Julia?"

Zora took her eyes off the road and threw him a puzzled glance. His sunglasses shielded his eyes. "I don't know... seven or eight."

"And how many women are there in seven or eight generations of your family?"

Zora didn't know where he was going with this, but she'd play along. "I don't know." She took a wild guess. "Fifty or sixty."

"So if there were sixty women between your time and Julia's, why are you the only one she speaks to?"

A shiver went up Zora's spine. "Julia speaks to me?" She felt Joseph's eyes on her.

"What do you think those dreams are about?"

My screwed-up psyche. She didn't answer, maybe because putting into words the significance of the dreams would be scarier than the actual dreams.

He didn't push her for an answer, and they drove the rest of the way to the hospital in silence.

When they reached St. Mary's an hour and a half later, Chet was sitting up in bed, pushing his lunch around his plate.

"So the mighty spirits threw you back," Joseph announced from the doorway.

Chet's face brightened. "They feared what would happen if I died and you were left in this world alone."

Zora pushed Joseph's wheelchair toward the bed. The two men clasped hands. She touched Chet's shoulder. "How are you feeling?"

His face split into a wide grin, toothless pink gums glistening in his wrinkled face. "Never felt better. I'm alive, ain't I?"

"Heard your aim was a little off," Joseph said.

Chet's face clouded. "I don't care what Iron Hawk said.

There was a coyote in my chicken coup."

"Never heard Oscar described as a coyote before," Joseph quipped.

Chet's eyes narrowed. "Whatever was out there, it walked on four legs."

"John said a young girl was out there when he arrived. Did you see her?" Joseph asked his old friend.

Zora stared at Joseph in stunned silence. *A girl was present during the shooting?*

Chet frowned. "What girl?"

Joseph shrugged. "John didn't recognize her, but she led him to Oscar."

Chet shook his head. "There was no one but me and the coyote."

"Anything else missing from your place, other than a chicken or two?" Joseph asked.

"Like what?"

Joseph shrugged. "Food, blankets…"

Zora glanced at Joseph. He'd picked up on her thoughts. So he also thought she was a runaway or homeless.

"Nope, nothing's missing. If you're thinking it was her stealing my chickens, you can forget it. I found coyote tracks, not human." He folded his arms across his chest.

"Maybe she's not human," Joseph said.

Tentacles of cold apprehension crept up her spine. Surely he was pulling his old buddy's leg. But there was no humor shining from his dark recessed eyes.

"She's definitely human." John stood framed in the door. Dressed in his usual jeans and white shirt, his presence seemed to suck the air right out of the room. He took long strides toward the hospital bed, smoothing his hair back from his face after removing his hat.

Zora's fingers tingled, imagining the feel and texture of his black hair. Reluctantly she pulled her gaze from John and addressed Joseph. "What did you mean, maybe she's not human?"

Joseph glanced at John. "She could be a shape-shifter."

Zora laughed. "There's no such thing as a shape-shifter." She looked to John for confirmation.

The muscles in his jaw clenched with some restrained emotion. After a long pause, he looked her way. "I agree."

Neither of the older men said a word.

"Only a shaman has the power to transform," Chet said. "And there's only one shaman around." He looked pointedly at Joseph.

Joseph was a shaman? She could see the truth in his eyes. So this was why he put so much stock in the visions. She didn't know much about Indian folklore, but she did know shamans were the medicine men of a tribe. They were able to see things others couldn't, communicate with nature and see into the future. "Is this true?"

Joseph bowed his head. "People have used that title to describe me."

"That's why you were so willing—" She caught herself just in time. She didn't want to discuss her dreams with John around. She didn't want to see pity in his eyes.

To Joseph's credit, he didn't say a word. He respected her privacy, and for that, she was grateful.

"So this very human girl must live somewhere." John stared at Chet. "And you never saw her on your property before?"

"I said I didn't know nothing about a girl." His voice rose with his agitation and, as if on cue, a hefty nurse, wearing hospital scrubs, plowed through the door.

"What's going on in here? We can hear you at the nurse's station. Clear out." She made shooing motions at them. "All of you, out of here. You're disturbing my patient."

"I'm not ready for 'em to go," Chet complained.

The nurse placed her hands on her ample hips. "I don't care what you're ready for. I run this ship, and I say it's time for them to go."

Chet shot the nurse a cantankerous glare. She ignored

him and injected something into his IV. He turned his wizened face toward John. "Take care of my animals."

"You don't have to ask," John said.

Zora pushed Joseph's wheelchair out into the hospital corridor, with John following closely on their heels. His attention appeared to be centered on the hustle and bustle at the nurse's station. "I need to find this girl."

"Me too."

Cocking his head, he turned his gaze on her. "You've seen her?"

She realized with all that had gone on she hadn't discussed the sighting of the mysterious teen with John. "She was hanging around Mac's trailer the day you arrested the teens." Had he arrested his daughter? She thought not.

"And you didn't alert me?"

"I tried, but you'd already left." She didn't add she'd been so thunderstruck by the girl's resemblance to Julia that several moments had passed before she could speak. "I spoke with Laura and she says she doesn't know the girl."

"What's your interest in her?"

What did she say to that question? Possible answers tumbled through her mind, all of them sounding more insane than the real reason she was on the reservation.

Joseph saved her from answering by wheeling his chair between her and John. "Maybe the two boys with Laura know the girl."

"They don't know her." Two pairs of eyes fixed on Zora.

"And you know this because…" John asked.

She reasoned she could have lied to him about her talk with Danny and Mac, but time was running out. Maybe if she lit a fire under John, there would be two people working on finding the teen. "She might be a runaway and these kids are protecting her." In for a penny, in for a pound. What did Zora have to lose? "I know you and Laura don't have a good relationship. Maybe she doesn't want you to know anything about the girl."

John pounded his hat on his thigh. "Yeah, that thought occurred to me."

"Have you checked missing persons?" Zora asked.

He'd been studying the traffic in the corridor, but now he turned to face her, moving closer, invading her personal space. Zora fought the urge to step back. He wouldn't intimidate her.

"Ms. Hughes, I've been a police officer for over twelve years. I do know how to find someone. Let me do my job." He jammed his Stetson on his head, turned to leave, and then pivoted to face her. "Don't get involved in this investigation. Do we understand each other?"

She opened her mouth to tell him he wasn't in control of her, but she caught Joseph's eye. He shook his head. She bit down hard on her lip and nodded.

"I'll see you two back at Little River."

Without giving her a second glance, he stalked off down the corridor.

"He's a good man," Joseph said.

"Yeah, yeah, so you keep saying." She turned the wheelchair in the direction of the elevator. "I hope he and your granddaughter will be very happy."

CHAPTER ELEVEN

DUSK FELL AS ZORA DROVE the convertible to the end of the Bearkiller drive and stopped. Emma had left for work a few hours earlier, and Joseph had retired for the night, leaving her with too many hours to think.

A hot desert-like breeze bent the field grass across the road and tugged at the scarf she'd secured around her thick hair. The sun, a fiery red orb, sent the last of its rays over the plain before retiring for the night. A profound sense of melancholy overwhelmed her. It was as though ghosts stood beside her. Generations of people whose restless spirits still prowled the earth, looking for resolution for terrible acts perpetrated against them. She shivered, turned onto the road, and drove quickly away from the Bearkiller house and the land surrounding it.

Cars jammed the casino lot. After parking at the extreme end of the gravel space, Zora walked toward the building, her mood lightening with each step.

When the glass doors slid open, a wall of noise almost sent her staggering backwards. A multitude of voices competed with the gong of bells and the clatter of falling coins. The lights were so bright she needed sunglasses.

She walked to the nearest bar and ordered a chocolate martini. When the drink arrived, she took a sip then sighed with pleasure—excellent. After giving the bartender a generous tip, she wandered around the vast room. Not a gambler, she knew nothing about the different tables but stopped to watch.

The employees were almost exclusively Native American, and the patrons exclusively white. People wore everything from blue jeans to eveningwear with tons of flashy jewelry. Zora thought about the children riding rusty tricycles in their grassless yards and the ancient Singer sewing machine she spotted in the Boys and Girls Club. The amount of money won and lost in one night in this casino could keep the reservation's children in food and toys for a full year.

"Exciting, isn't it?"

Zora jumped. Mike Matisse stood at her side, wearing a smile as big as a used car salesman's and as fake. "Ah…yes, it is." The energy of the place was definitely exciting, but Zora didn't know if it was the type of excitement she liked. Back in New York, she and Terrance attended Broadway plays, ate in exclusive restaurants, and listened to jazz in out-of-the way clubs, but that seemed light years ago.

"Let me show you around," Mike said. Not waiting for her consent, he gripped her elbow in a meaty hand and ushered her toward a table. "Do you play blackjack?"

She shook her head, smiling ruefully. "Afraid not."

He saluted the dealer and smiled at the players who stood around the table. "The first one who gets close to twenty-one without going over wins."

Zora nodded, not really caring, but trying to look interested.

He steered her to another table hosted by a pretty, but very young woman. All the employees wore white tops of some synthetic material that mimicked silk. The male employees wore black pants and the females wore very short black skirts. In fact, as Zora glanced around, she noted that all the front employees, especially the women, were very young, very pretty, and very friendly. Where was Matisse hiding the belligerent Emma Bearkiller?

"This table—"

"Matisse, I want to talk to you."

Zora's stomach flip-flopped at the sound of John's deep baritone. She drank in the wrinkled white shirt, the black hair slipping from its leather tie, the circles under his dark eyes. He in turn didn't spare her a glance but concentrated all his attention on Mike.

Mike turned and pasted on a jovial smile. "Later." He put a hand at Zora's waist to steer her away, but John stepped into his path.

"We can do this in your office or we can have this discussion right here."

Probably aware of the attention they attracted, Mike smiled wider and clapped John on the shoulder as though they were long lost buddies. "In my office," he said through gritted teeth.

Zora stepped back. "I should leave."

"Oh, no, pretty lady," Mike said. "You come on along with me. We can finish the tour once Officer Iron Hawk and I have completed business."

Zora shot John a sideways glance. His eyes were cold black stones that, before he looked away, froze her with their contempt.

Sandwiched between the two men, she found herself in a small elevator that rose to a glassed office overlooking the casino floor.

Once in the office, John closed the door and placed his back against it, barricading them in.

"What's this I hear about you telling folks I'm swindling tribal funds?"

Mike laughed, but the sound was less than jovial. "I just mentioned that some of the casino funds went to the police department, and I didn't know how you'd used the funds. People just misinterpreted my meaning." Rivulets of sweat ran along the side of his moon-shaped face.

That definitely wasn't the tune he'd sung the night of the council meeting.

When John took a step toward Mike, the council president moved behind his desk. "I know what you're doing, Matisse. You're using tribal funds for your own personal expenses, and I'm going to expose you for the thief you are."

Mike's ruddy face turned a darker shade of red. "Don't threaten me, John. I put you in this position. I can fire you just as quickly."

"I work for the Bureau. Any firing will be done by them." John stalked toward the door.

Maybe finding courage now that John was leaving, Mike walked out from behind his desk. "I won't need the services of your department here at the casino. I've hired a private security firm to patrol the premises."

At the threshold John turned, his lips set in a tight line. "As usual, Matisse, you haven't the slightest idea what's going on around you." He slammed the door behind him.

Matisse was silent for a long minute his brow furrowed in thought then he seemed to remember he wasn't alone in the room. Turning to Zora, he laughed. "John's tired. Got a couple of patrolmen out. Working too hard. He'll be okay in the morning. Now, where were we?"

Zora didn't consider herself an expert on John Iron Hawk, but she guessed things between him and Matisse weren't going to improve with a good night's sleep.

———————

John's hair whipped around his face as the Jeep barreled down the dark road toward Chet Tyler's place. He never used the air conditioner, preferring the feel of the wind on his face and the smell of the earth. Tonight, the sharpness in the air signaled rain.

Mike Matisse had to go. He was cheating the people out of money rightfully theirs. The Sioux had been cheated for too many years to be swindled by one of their own. He would put an end to Matisse's thievery. If he couldn't bring Matisse down on his own, he'd ask the Bureau for help. He didn't want to bring the government in on this, but recovering funds meant for the people was too important to let one more day slide by.

And then there'd been Zora. To see her there in the casino with Matisse, and with that son of a bitch's arm around her, made John almost too angry to think straight. Now that Dottie was gone, Matisse was probably shopping for wife number four. If he had his sights on Zora, he'd better look elsewhere. Matisse couldn't afford her. John leaned his head out the window, trying to cool his raging jealousy. Hell, he couldn't afford her, so he should just stop thinking about Zora Hughes. She clouded his judgment and made him ineffective at his job. It had taken Joseph's suggestion at the hospital about questioning Danny and his friend Mac to get John back on track.

Something scurried across the road directly in front on the Jeep. John slammed on the brakes and twisted the wheel to the right to avoid hitting whatever it was. The ditch on the side of the road loomed up. He wrenched the wheel to the left to avoid the deep trench, but the effort was too little, too late. The Jeep skidded into the gully with a bone-jarring thud. John's head whipped back then forward, connecting with the steering wheel. Multicolored lights danced behind his lids to rival his Sun Dance ceremony. The last thing he remembered before darkness claimed him was the face of the girl from Chet's, standing on the opposite side of the road, staring at him with wild dark eyes.

———◆———

Before leaving the casino parking lot, Zora put the top up on the convertible. The idea of driving down the deserted reservation road in the dead of night, exposed on all sides to the elements, raised goose bumps on her flesh. But that wasn't the only thing causing her flesh to crawl. Mike Matisse had the same affect. She shuddered every time she thought of him touching her. After John left, Mike had called for a bottle of champagne. When he'd dimmed the lights in his office, she'd made her excuses and got the hell out of there. Like she'd let him seduce her. She hit the steering wheel, visualizing it as Matisse's head. *Dream on, buster.* She didn't doubt that John's accusations against the tribal leader were true. She didn't need Joseph's endorsements of John to know he had integrity. But she hadn't liked the way she felt when he'd turned those dark eyes on her, as though he painted her with the same black brush as Mike. She didn't care what he thought of her, but she didn't want him thinking she was in cahoots with a sleazeball like Mike Matisse.

She'd flown down this road earlier in the day, but now, when she couldn't see past the headlights' reflection, she literally crept at twenty-five miles an hour. Bright red eyes stared at her from the shoulder. *Don't even think about it. You'll be road kill by tomorrow morning.* She was beginning to know her way around the reservation. She laughed. Okay, maybe she only knew the way to Joseph's house and all the points in between, but that was progress. She knew if you took this road another five miles or so past Joseph's turn-off, you'd come to Chet's—

Rising out of the ditch on the right, a vehicle's front tires rested on the road and the rear ones were in the gulley. The Chrysler's headlights illuminated the police insignia on the vehicle's door.

Her heart nosedived straight to her sling backs.

John!

She slammed on the brakes. The car zigzagged. She jumped out, almost running out of her heels as she closed the distance between the convertible and his vehicle. He had to know every bit of this road. What would cause him to drive his Jeep into a ditch?

His head lolled against the headrest. His long, dark hair partially shielded his face. *Please let him be okay.*

"John!"

He didn't respond. Reaching through the open window, she touched his shoulder. When she felt the unmistakable rise and fall of his chest, she exhaled a trapped breath.

"John, wake up." With a trembling hand, she tucked wayward strands of silky hair behind his ear. She allowed herself the pleasure of running her hand over the contours of his rugged features.

She snatched her hand away. What was she doing? This wasn't Terrance. This was a brutish, uncultured police officer with delusions of living in the Old West.

"John." She slapped him lightly on the face. When the action evoked no response, she hit him harder. "Wake up, you Neanderthal." She raised her hand.

"Hit me again, and I'll shoot you."

One dark eye squinted at her.

She laughed, dizzy with relief.

He rubbed his head, winced then froze. His gaze flew to hers. "Get in your car. Now!"

At the command in his voice, her hackles rose and her eyes narrowed. "Now look—"

"Gasoline."

For the first time, she smelled the fumes. Instead of backing away, she reached for the Jeep's door, her hands clumsy and cold. "Get out. Get out." She pulled frantically on the handle, but her actions were as ineffective as a child's. The door didn't budge.

"Get. To. The. Car." Each word came out in a staccato burst as he shoved against the car's frame. The Jeep groaned and settled deeper into the ditch.

She backed away. Her eyes never left his face. Putting both hands on the window frame, he dove out the window, landing on the road with a bone-jarring thud.

When she reached him, he was already scrambling to his feet. Grabbing her arm, he ran with a lurch that resembled Quasimodo.

The Jeep exploded behind them.

For an instant the night lit up like the Fourth of July. Sparks shot past them as they flung themselves into the convertible. After backing the car up to a safe distance, she turned to him.

"You okay?"

"I'm fine."

"How'd you end up in the ditch?" Trying to add some humor to a situation that had turned critical quickly, she asked, "Didn't brake for a possum, did you?"

"No, I—" He leaned forward, pointing to a spot beyond the burning Jeep. "She was there."

Had he hit someone? Her eyes strained to see into the darkness on the opposite side of the road. "Who?"

The light from the flames made it easy to see the discolored knot on his forehead. Had he suffered a concussion and was now hallucinating?

She didn't know she'd spoken her thoughts aloud until he said, "I'm not hallucinating. She was there...and," he frowned, "she was naked... or nearly naked."

Zora raised an eyebrow. "How's your sex life?" The minute she'd asked the question she wished she could take the words back.

Dark eyes, alive with speculation, studied her. "Worried about my love life?"

She turned away from the heat in his gaze. "I'm not worried, but I'm not the one seeing naked women walking down the highway."

When he didn't respond she glanced over at him. Eyes closed, his head rested against the seat.

"Where's the nearest hospital?"

"Not one."

Of course there was a hospital. He must have hit his head

harder than she thought. "Let's get you to Joseph. He'll know where we should go."

She waited for him to put on his seatbelt. When he didn't she asked, "John, were you wearing a seatbelt?"

"Nope."

She looked at the burning police vehicle then at the bruises on his temple and forehead. "Do you ever wear one?"

"Nope."

Well, that explained why he was unconscious when she found him. "Have you ever heard of lead by example?"

His lips tightened. "I'm not in the mood for a lecture."

She clamped her mouth shut and moved cautiously around the blaze. Five minutes later she slowed to make the turn that would take them to Joseph's house.

"Don't."

She stopped in the middle of the road. "Don't what?"

Face creased with pain, he still didn't open his eyes. "Just take me to Chet's place."

"Why?"

"Animals… his animals need…"

She remembered John's promise to feed Chet's animals. "Those animals can wait a few more hours." She lifted her foot from the brake.

"Haven't been fed in two days."

Zora sighed. "You can't do it."

"Gotta try."

"I don't think so." She placed her foot on the accelerator. From her peripheral vision she saw his hand move toward the door handle. She braked so hard his head jerked forward before falling back against the seat. He let out a groan.

"Gotta feed—"

"Oh, for God's sake. Why do you have to be so stubborn?"

He didn't respond. When she glanced at him, his face

was still strained, and his eyes were closed. She could have turned the car around, gone back to Joseph's, and he wouldn't have been any wiser. She studied his profile.

"He's a good man," Joseph had said.

With a sigh of resignation she asked, "Okay. Where does Chet live?"

John didn't open his eyes. "Mailbox… on the road…red paint…"

After a few minutes she spotted the mailbox. She made the right turn and traveled down a narrow-rutted road that seemed more like a path. Trees scraped the sides of the car. She grimaced, thinking about the scratches on the rental. Just when she thought she'd made a wrong turn, the path opened.

A large Spanish moon hung low in the sky, casting a glow over a corral, small farmhouse and a dilapidated barn.

"John." She shook him gently.

"I'm awake." He lifted his head then fumbled for the door's handle. Once he had the door open, he leaned heavily on its frame.

In that moment she realized she was going to have to feed the animals—she who'd never cared for so much as a goldfish. When she stepped out of the car, the night breeze carried on it the scent of manure, hay and something indefinable. She wrinkled her nose in disgust.

John still clung to the door. She hesitated. This was stupid. He needed to go to the hospital.

Moving to his side, she said, "I'll feed the animals. Afterwards we have to get that head looked at." She took a step away from him and stumbled. Only John's quick reflexes kept her from falling face first into the dirt. Her four-inch heel was securely wedged into the earth.

He snorted. "Those are worthless." His speech and quick reflexes were more like the John she knew.

Leaning heavily on his arm, she pulled the sandals off her feet. "I'll have you know these are Jimmy Choos." She tossed the wispy strapped shoes into the car's back seat.

"Jimmy Whos?"

"Never mind." She pushed him back into the car. "Just tell me what to do."

CHAPTER TWELVE

———

FROM THE PASSENGER SEAT OF the convertible, John watched Zora's tall, slender form tiptoe toward Chet's barn, like she'd die if her whole foot touched the dirt. He'd told her where to find the feedbags for the horses, the rain barrel, and a pair of men's boots. Leaning his head back against the seat, he closed his eyes against the pain. His head throbbed like the day after a two day drinking binge.

The clang of metal hitting metal caused him to jerk awake. He'd been dreaming about a girl in a white dress. He studied the shifting shadows surrounding Chet's barn. Had the girl on the road been Chet's chicken thief?

"Shit," the word floated from the barn on a current of frustration.

John chuckled. His head ached like it was being mistaken for a ceremonial drum, but he could've fed Chet's animals. When Ms. New York offered... well, it was an offer he couldn't resist. He'd needed some humor to this suck-butt day. After scrubbing a hand over his face, he dragged himself out of the car. Time to rescue her. Wouldn't do to have her cut off one of those pretty toes.

He could barely see her when he entered the shed. "What's wrong?"

"How in the h—" She paused, and he could hear a deep exhalation of breath. "How am I supposed to find anything? It's pitch black in here, and I can't find the switch."

"Switch? There's no electricity out here. Chet has a lantern somewhere." He moved his hand along the bare boards until he connected with the lamp. Once he lit the lantern, he held it up and surveyed the barn. Everything looked in place: hay bales lined against one wall, miscellaneous tools, some rusted and in need of repair, hung from hooks. Bertha mooed in her stall.

He let the light play over Zora, from her sea green toenails to her sleek little black dress, a dress that left long, graceful legs exposed.

"You must be feeling better." Her tone was drier than a South Dakota summer without rain.

He raised the light so he could see her expression. With her mouth set in a mulish line and hay sticking out of her fashionable twisted hair, he wanted to kiss away her irritation.

"You shouldn't be on your feet," she said, her tone warming a bit.

"Your caterwauling would have raised the dead."

"My what?" Hands on her hips, she glared at him. Her mouth was doing that kissable thing again. To take his mind off her lips, he moved over to the hay bales, lowered his head slowly and began cutting wire. "Let me show you how to feed the horses."

That took all of ten minutes. Bertha continued to moo.

"What's wrong with her?" Zora asked. "Is she hurt?"

He bit back a laugh. "You could say that. She needs to be milked."

"Milked?" She said the word as though it were foreign. "Where's the milker?" She turned in a circle.

"You're it." At the look of panic in her brown eyes, he said, "Don't worry. I'll show you how."

She glanced from the cow to him. "Can't you do it?"

"Can't bend my head," he lied. "When I do, feels like my brains are rushing toward the front of my skull."

He found a stool in the shadows of the barn and placed

it in Bertha's stall. "Have a seat."

She glanced at her dress. "I can't sit on that."

"Why not?" He had a good idea of what the problem was. The little black number was just that *little*. Her thighs would be exposed up to her—. At the thought of what was hidden beneath that piece of material, his mouth went as dry as scrub brush.

"Don't peek." She hiked her dress up until the tops of her toned thighs were visible.

He swallowed. Every lustful thought he'd ever day-dreamed flew through his throbbing head and down to his throbbing dick. He took a deep breath and cleared his mind.

Once she was comfortable on the stool, he placed a hand on Bertha's haunches. "Talk to her."

"Talk to the cow?" Her face scrunched up as though she smelled something foul, which she probably did. Bertha hadn't been out of her stall in two days. Cow patties were liberally distributed in the straw-covered space.

"She doesn't know you. A soft voice will keep her calm."

Zora mumbled something under her breath that sounded like "Who's going to keep me calm?" She stared at the ani-mal then said, "Here, cow."

He bit the inside of his cheek to keep from laughing. "Give me your hand." She did. Obviously, she'd never done manual labor. Her skin was soft and fragrant like wildflow-ers growing at the base of the mountains. "Stroke her." He moved her hand over the animal's hide. Agitated at first, Bertha's shoulders twitched, but she soon calmed.

He placed a tin bucket under the cow's belly then took Zora's hands and placed them on the cow's teats. "Now pull straight down."

Zora shuddered. "I'll hurt her."

He closed his eyes in exasperation. "Just think of it as giving her relief. You know," he glanced at her breasts, "like a nursing mother."

She caught the direction of his gaze and said sourly, "I've never given birth."

He shrugged. "Trust me, you're helping her."

For the first few minutes John covered Zora's hand with his own so she'd know the exact amount of pressure to apply to the teat. Once she'd got her rhythm, he stepped back. She grimaced with each downward tug, but she got the job done.

"What are we going to do with this milk?"

"Chet sells it to the store just outside the reservation."

Zora pulled on the rubbery warm teat one more time. The bucket was three-quarters full, and Bertha had long stopped mooing. Both of them had gotten comfortable with each other.

———◆———

John sat on the packed dirt floor. His head rested against the stall. His eyes closed.

He had the longest lashes she'd ever seen on a man. They lay black and sooty against his brown skin. Laugh lines shot out from the corners of his eyes like sunrays. He wasn't handsome, but the strength in his hard mouth and broad face made her feel at peace in his presence, made her feel protected, even now as the hairs at the nape of her neck quivered. She glanced out the open door of the barn. Moonlight dappled the hides of the two horses that shifted restlessly in the corral.

She rose from the stool, moving the bucket before Bertha could kick over the contents. Without waking John, she slipped on boots and picked up another bucket. She filled it with feed corn from the bag he'd pointed out. She was getting into the swing of this farming thing.

Stepping out of the barn she headed toward the chicken coup, where she scattered corn. "Here, chicky, chicky." Two chickens scratching around in the dirt strutted over to her.

"Here, chicky, chicky." At least a dozen chickens burst out of the coup, half flying, half speed walking. She threw out more corn, but this time scattered the kernels as far away from her too large boots as she could. When the chickens flew at her and started to peck the area around her feet, she threw them the bucket of corn and fled back into the barn.

John slept. When she touched him lightly on the shoulder, his eyes flew open. They were surprisingly bright for someone just roused from sleep. "Okay, let's get you back to the car." As she tried to lift him to his feet, the feeling of being watched had her looking over her shoulder again. The clouds chose that moment to shift across the moon, creating shadows around the barn. Shadows she could have sworn took shape. Icy fingers slithered up her spine.

"Tired…"

"I know, but you can't sleep here," she tried to suppress the urgency in her voice.

Lifting him was harder than raising a boulder. "Help me, you big lug."

After several attempts he rose clumsily, and the two of them staggered out of the barn. Outside, she shot one more glance toward the barn and chicken coup. Nothing.

"Let's get you into Chet's house so you can rest." The idea of being on a deserted road late at night with a semi-conscious man who'd be no help if they ran into trouble didn't appeal to her. She'd stay awake and watch him for any signs of complications.

"John?"

"Hmmm."

"Is there a spare key?"

"Under the milk jug," he said when they reached the porch.

A steel cylinder with a narrow neck sat close to the front door. Propping John against the house, Zora tilted the jug and retrieved the key.

The upper half of the front door was glass and she could

see into the darkened house. When she opened the door, the odor of garbage and sweat came at her in a rush. *Geez, Chet.* John, obviously beyond caring about the smell, stumbled into the house and collapsed on the sofa.

Once he was comfortable, she took the offending trashcan and placed it outside the back door. She turned her back on the dirty dishes in the sink. There was only so much she was willing to do. Leaving the front door open so she could hear him, she stepped out onto the porch. After being inside, the odor of the farm didn't smell as offensive or the shadows as threatening.

She sat on the railing and studied the stars. They appeared brighter and closer. She could almost imagine how the land must have looked hundreds of years ago when campfires would have provided the only light and teepees dotted the landscape. She and Julia had a lot in common. Both of them were aliens in a foreign land.

Chet's horses neighed at the same time the chickens started a distressed cluck. She leaned over the porch rail. Clearly agitated, the chickens flew around their coop while white feathers dusted the air like down from a busted pillow. Something had disturbed the animals. A coyote? She rose to head back into the house. What if it wasn't an animal but a human causing the disturbance? What if it was the girl?

She hadn't made any progress in solving the mystery of Julia's death. Would she purposely lose the only lead she had by choosing to hide? If she did, she might as well go back to New York. She could hide there.

She turned around and marched down the steps and across the yard toward the barn. For all her boldness, she hesitated. Peering around the corner of the building, she saw chickens hopping around the small space, their feathers ruffled. Almost forgetting to breathe, Zora watched and waited. Just when she decided to make a move, a shadow drifted across the moon.

"Wait." A voice whispered close to her ear.

Zora yelped, the sound lost in the cries of the chickens.

Dressed in the same white shift, the girl from Mac's trailer stood just to the left of Zora. With shaggy dark hair and large luminous eyes, her gaze was focused on something in the yard.

Zora opened her mouth to speak, but the girl placed a finger to her own lips.

"Shhh…He must eat."

"What?" Something shifted in the periphery of Zora's vision. She turned.

Out of the darkness, a dog, no, not a dog, it was too silver to be a dog—a coyote moved in the yard. She didn't know what surprised her more, the voice, or the predator that slunk quietly into the chicken coop.

The chickens took flight, crowing and running into each other. Their cries became frantic and feathers flew like large snowflakes. Holding the limp body of a bird firmly between its jaws, the coyote trotted out of the coop and into the surrounding darkness.

"He is more afraid of you than you are of him," the girl said.

"Right." Zora's pulse slowly dropped down out of the stratosphere.

The girl started to move away.

"Wait." Zora reached for the teen's arm. There was so much she wanted to know. "What's your name? Where do you live?"

"Out there." The girl swept her arm in the direction of the mountains. Then she pointed to her chest. "Sarah." She said the name, hesitantly.

Zora frowned. "Sarah, where do your parents live?"

The girl stared at Zora, her eyes black and bottomless.

"Your mother, your father."

"No mother, no father."

How do you not have parents? Even if you're adopted, you

have a mother or father.

"I go."

"Wait, Sarah."

Following the path the coyote had taken, the teen shot off into the darkness.

———◆———

Someone cried.

John opened one eye. Instead of his bed, he lay on a muddy brown sofa. And it smelled like dirty socks. He opened his other eye. Chet Tyler's living room.

Zora sat on the floor with her head resting against the cushions of the sofa. Her hair, out of its usually restrained bun, lay tousled around her face. Tears seeped from beneath her closed lids. She moaned in her sleep, her lips moved soundlessly.

He slipped to the linoleum then gathered her carefully into his arms.

"Zora." He touched her face. Her skin was soft beneath his fingers. He wiped away her tears.

"Zora?"

She started to thrash.

"Shh." He tightened his arms around her. "It's me... John."

She stopped struggling.

He stroked her face, trailing a finger across the closed lids with their damp lashes and down the side of her cheek. His finger, with a mind of its own, moved back and forth across her full lower lip. When her tongue came out to moisten her lips, he swooped down and captured the delicate pink tip with his mouth. Her body tensed. He started to withdraw, knowing later she'd berate him 'til she stripped the skin off his body.

But her hands caught and held his shirt. Her mouth opened underneath his, allowing him full access.

He took it.

He stroked and sucked until moans issued from her throat. His mouth mated with hers. Feeling her positive response, his hand trailed down her slim body to caress her breast.

She sprang out of his arms. Crouching a few feet away, she asked, "What do you think you're doing?"

"Kissing you."

"Why?"

He couldn't stop the smile that slid across his face. "Because I've wanted to since the night you arrived. Also, you were having a nightmare. I wanted to comfort you."

A look of panic filled her eyes. "What did I say?"

He studied her face. "Nothing. You mostly moaned and cried." He reached out to gather her back into his arms, but she jerked away like a frightened doe.

Flushing, she jumped up. Avoiding his eyes, she glanced around. "We need to get out of here. This place gives me the willies."

She was embarrassed. He didn't know if it was because he'd seen her cry or that he'd kissed her. He wanted to ask about the dream, but he knew this prickly woman wouldn't share anything with him. "Okay." He rose slowly to his feet.

She paused at the door. "Are you feeling better?"

"Yeah, fine," he lied, but it wasn't his head that hurt, more like his pride.

———

The sun crested the horizon. Its rays crept over the land like an invading tide. Zora drove as John stared out the window.

Was he thinking about the kiss? What had possessed him to kiss her? What had possessed *her* to kiss him back? She almost groaned aloud. It had been... it had been everything she thought it would be. Tender, rough, passionate. She almost closed her eyes as the sensation of being in his arms swept over her, leaving a searing heat. The car's tires bumping over the grooves at the road's shoulder brought her back to earth.

She glanced over at John to see if he'd noticed her lapse. His eyes were closed, but she knew he was awake. His body radiated with tension. Had the kiss affected him as much as it had her?

She gave herself a mental shake. She needed to remember why she was here.

"I saw her last night."

His head swiveled toward her. The sudden movement caused him to wince. After a moment his brow cleared. "Who?"

"The girl from the trailer."

She had his full attention. He'd turned squarely in his seat so his back was against the passenger door. "Where?"

"Out by Chet's barn."

"Stealing chickens?"

Zora negotiated the pot-holed asphalt. "No, the coyote took care of that. She was like—its guardian."

A frown marred his rugged features. "Did she hurt or threaten you?"

"No, no, she was protecting me." Pleased with the progress she'd made, Zora smiled at him. "And her name is Sarah."

John grunted. "Watch your speed."

She rolled her eyes. "Are you always in cop mode?"

"Always. Strange, I couldn't get her to say more than two words the other night. Must be because you're a woman."

Zora's mouth twitched. "I doubt that. I've always had a better rapport with men than women." Her face flushed. *Don't go down that road.* Up until this morning, she believed he didn't like her, but the way he'd kissed her....

"Drop me off at headquarters," John said, breaking into

her revelry.

Taking her eyes off the road, Zora stared at him. "I thought I was driving you to the hospital in Pierre."

"Don't have time for that."

She opened her mouth to protest, but his mulish expression stopped her.

"Shouldn't you check on Laura?" Zora wanted to speak with his daughter now that she had Sarah's name. She'd hoped Laura would open up and tell her about the other girl.

"I'll call from the office later. She doesn't get up until late in the morning."

From the tightness around his mouth, Zora could tell his daughter's schedule didn't sit well with him.

They rode in silence the rest of the way to police headquarters. He was out of the car before she'd come to a complete stop.

She stuck her head out of the open window and raised her voice. "You need to see a doctor."

"Later." The word was tossed over his shoulder as he rushed into the building.

She stared at the town hall's closed door. Why had he been in such a hurry to get away? Had she said something in her sleep? Something that made him wary of her company? Or did he regret the kiss?

CHAPTER THIRTEEN

"OSCAR NEEDS A RIDE FROM the hospital," Maggie said as John walked through the door. Reading a copy of *People* magazine, Maggie sat in a chair that threatened to collapse under her weight.

John walked gingerly past her desk and to the coffee pot. The oily dregs that covered the bottom of the pot rolled from side to side just like his stomach. He set the pot down. "Been quiet around here?"

"Yep." She didn't look up from the magazine but extended her hand. One sheet of pink message paper dangled from pudgy fingers. "With Chet in the hospital only had one call on the answering machine this morning."

He took the message. It was from Emma. He balled the slip of paper up and tossed it into the trash. He didn't want to think about Emma right now. Not when he could still taste Zora's lips.

"Have Ted pull my Jeep from the ditch about two miles south of the Bearkiller place and check it out."

Maggie's head popped up. "You ran into a ditch?"

"Yeah." He touched a sore spot on his forehead. He wasn't about to tell her about the girl Zora called Sarah. It would be all over the reservation before noon. He eyed the coffee pot then gave up the idea of making a fresh pot. He'd grab a cup outside the reservation.

He retrieved the keys to Oscar's patrol car from the keyboard. "If Oscar calls back, tell him I'll be there around ten- thirty."With one hand on the door, he stopped. "Maggie, call Parker in the Pierre office. Ask him to send me the latest missing persons list." He didn't wait for a response but headed out the door.

As he drove to Pierre, he cranked up the volume on the one country and western station that reached the reservation. He needed to stay awake. He could have let Zora drive him to the hospital, but he needed to put distance between them. He had a job to do, and so far, he'd fallen shy of his mark since she'd come to his part of South Dakota. He didn't need to get pulled into her troubles, and there were plenty, no doubt about it. He sensed some strange aura encircling her when she woke from her dream. He wasn't empathic like Joseph, but it didn't take an empath to feel the odd vibes that surrounded her.

When he arrived at the hospital, Oscar sat in a wheelchair in his hospital room, his arm in a sling.

"How's it feel?"

Oscar shifted position in the chair. "Hurts like hell." He ran a hand over the limb. "Let's get out of here before they decide to keep me."

With the approval of Oscar's nurse, John pushed the chair to the elevator, which they rode to the first floor. Oscar's patrol car sat at the main entrance. There were some benefits to being a police officer.

Once they were on the road, John turned to his deputy. "So what exactly happened out there?"

Oscar stared out the window. "I don't know."

John frowned. He took his eyes off the road long enough to shoot his officer a disbelieving look. "What do you mean, you don't know?"

Oscar squirmed in his seat. "The chickens started to squawk. I got out of the car and walked toward the barn. I looked around, saw nothing out of the ordinary and started back to my cruiser."

"Where was Chet?"

"Last I seen, he was in the house. Television blaring. The old geezer must be deaf. I could tell you every program he watched."

"Then what happened?"

Oscar threw John an incredulous glare. "Then somebody shot me."

"You didn't see who it was?"

"Nope. As far as I knew, it was just me and the chickens."

"You didn't see the girl?"

"She wasn't there, John. Didn't you check to see if the old man's gun had been fired?"

"Yep. It hadn't."

Oscar's mouth fell open. "Then who the hell shot me?"

Staring at the sun bouncing off the chrome hood ornament, John said quietly, "That's what I'd like to know."

———————

Zora pulled her car off the gravel road and stopped in front of Mac's trailer. Off to the east, dark clouds massed and a slight wind sent miniature cyclones of dust scurrying along the grassless yards. A different mutt from the previous day, one ear twitching to keep the flies off, slept under the trailer. Nothing else stirred.

Reluctantly, she got out of the car. Immediately, beads of sweat filmed the back of her neck. Reaching into her purse, she pulled out a jewel-studded hair band, lifted her thick hair and secured it with the band. Dry, hot air blew across her neck, giving her a little relief. She'd gone back to Joseph's, showered and slipped into a pair of coffee-colored linen pants, a cream halter top, but she could have saved herself the trouble. The heat made the clothes stick to her body as though she'd just stepped out of the shower.

Thunder crackled in the distance. She studied the trailer. Maybe confronting Mac by herself wasn't such a great idea. Danny Matisse and his friends were hoodlums. They could be dangerous, but she didn't know where else to go. Questioning these guys was the only lead she had toward finding Sarah. Before she could talk herself out of it, Zora strode toward the trailer.

After knocking three times, she almost headed back to her car when the door swung open.

Mac, with his thick hair standing up in spikes around his peanut-shaped head, glowered at her. "What the hell do you want?"

"I'm looking for Sarah."

"I don't know no Sarah." He started to slam the door, but she stuck her foot in the opening, preventing it from being shut in her face.

"She's the one I told you I saw hanging around your trailer. Dark hair, short."

Shirtless with jeans riding low on his hip, Mac scratched his belly. "That don't make me know her better."

"She's probably a runaway. Where would she stay if she didn't have any money?"

"How the hell would *I* know?"

She gritted her teeth.

Mac studied her, running his dark eyes up her body and lingering on her breasts. He smacked his lips. "I'll help you for a taste."

Zora had never heard *it* referred to as a taste, but the lewd expression on his face gave her no doubt of his meaning. He reached out as though to touch her, but she stepped back out of reach.

"Don't try that again," she said, "or you'll have nothing to do *it* with."

He grinned and licked his lips. "I like a girl with some spunk."

"I'm not a girl. Now Sarah was hanging around this trailer the day you guys tried to run me off the road."

Mac grinned slyly. "Was that Thursday or Friday?"

Irritation buzzed up Zora's spine like bees released from

a hive. "Do you run people off the road frequently?"

He shrugged. "It passes the time."

She wanted to wrap her hands around his skinny neck and shake him until his eyes popped. *Calm down, girl.* "Look, if you see her or remember anything, call me at Joseph Bearkiller's house." She pulled a sheet of paper from her purse and wrote the Bearkiller number on it. "I'll drop the charges against you guys if you help me find her." She handed him the note.

He took it, unzipped his fly and slipped the note inside his boxers.

He was slime. Zora turned and marched to her car.

"I told Billy Joe when you showed up at the bar the other night that you were a fine piece of—"

Zora slammed her car door, effectively silencing the punk's obscenities.

———◆———

As soon as John pulled into his driveway, he could hear music blaring from inside the house. The tension in his jaw relaxed and he slumped in his seat in relief. He'd tried calling Laura all morning, and finally, after dropping Oscar at his house, he'd driven home. Laura wasn't there and her bed hadn't been slept in. She only made her bed under duress, and he'd forced her to make it yesterday.

Now, after calling all around looking for her, he'd driven by the house again, hoping against hope she'd returned. He just wasn't cut out for this parenting thing. Since Mina was dead, he couldn't very well ship Laura back to his ex-wife. Being a parent was like riding a roller coaster and he didn't like roller coasters. He charged into the house and into her bedroom, relief short-lived and anger quickly resurfacing. "Turn that music off." He didn't wait for her to comply, but stalked across the room and snapped off the radio.

She lay across her bed, studying the ceiling. Resting on

her stomach was a ball of black and white fur.

"What the hell is that?"

She turned her head to stare at him. She had her mother's eyes, dark and capable of hiding secrets in their depths. "A kitten."

"Where did it come from?"

"From its mother."

John bit back a sharp reply. This was what she wanted, to distract him from the main conflict: where she'd spent the previous night. "Laura, I can't deal with this right now. I have a department to run and no police officers. Worrying about you is keeping me from my job."

She didn't look at him but continued to stroke the kitten. When she spoke, her voice was low and soft. "That should be easy for you, not worrying about me."

John frowned. What the hell was she talking about? He spent the last thirteen months doing nothing but worrying about her. "Where were you last night?"

"Out."

John took a step closer to the bed but stopped. He was letting her control the situation. She knew how to push his buttons, make him so angry he'd forget the real issue. "Where? With who?" *Just don't let it be Danny Matisse.*

"With Gilly."

"Doing what?"

She sat upright on the bed. "What do you care?" She resembled the kitten whose claws were embedded in her shirt, both of them young and angry.

He took a deep breath and let it out slowly. "I care. Now quit stalling and tell me where the two of you were last night."

"Or what?" she asked softly.

He drew in a frustrated breath. Or 'what' was right. What could he do? Her grandmother hadn't done such a good job of raising Mina. He definitely didn't want to give Gladys, his ex-mother-in-law, the opportunity to work her black magic on *his* daughter. What were his options? He couldn't restrict her to the house for the rest of the summer because he wouldn't be here to enforce it. "You need a job. You've got too much time on your hands."

Mild interest showed on her face. "A job, where?"

She had him boxed in a corner. He'd just said the first words that had come to mind. There weren't jobs on the reservation for teenagers. He'd be damned if he'd let her work at the casino, and he didn't have the time to drive her to Pierre every day. "The Boys and Girls Club."

She screwed up her face. "That's for babies."

You are a baby. "Well, it's that or work in your Aunt Lydia's shop."

She made a face. "Boooring."

"Then I'll talk to Viola Black Elk."

She scrambled off the bed. "I could waitress at the Iron Horse."

He narrowed his eyes. "Out of the question. Unless you've forgotten, they serve alcohol. And you're underage."

She followed him out of her bedroom. "I don't have to serve the drinks, just the food. Sylvia could serve the alcohol."

"Forget the Iron Horse." John walked to the refrigerator, opened it, peered in and shut it in disgust. It was empty.

"If you give me money, I could go shopping," Laura said.

He filled a glass with tap water. After downing the water, he placed the glass in the sink and turned to his daughter. "How will you get there?" The nearest full-fledged grocery store was on I-92. The Iron Horse had a small convenience store attached to it but didn't sell much beyond beer, soda and chips.

"I could drive."

"You don't have a license."

She turned her hands palm up. "And…"

John glared at her. "If I catch you driving, I'll ship you to your grandmother. Now, where did you spend the night?"

If she thought she could derail him, she was sadly mistaken.

She didn't answer. John marched to the phone and dialed. "Gladys, it's John—"

His daughter grabbed the phone and covered the speaker with her hand. "Gilly and me camped up in the hills."

He stared at her in disbelief. Last fall, he'd found a young woman's mutilated body in one of the caves and he'd never found the killer. He'd forbidden Laura to go into the mountains.

Without taking his eyes off his daughter, he removed her hand and spoke into the receiver. "Gladys, I'll get back with you."

Hanging up the receiver, he turned to his daughter. "Talk."

———◆———

At dusk Zora unlocked Chet's front door but didn't go inside. From her position on the porch the smell of unwashed bodies still hit her in the face, but the underlying scent of garbage had dissipated. None of this mattered, because she planned to spend the night outside. But she left the door open in case she needed the safety of the house.

After removing a flashlight from her Louis Vuitton bag, she plopped down on the steps to wait for Sarah. Zora wouldn't let the girl get away this time until she had some answers.

She leaned her head on one of the porch posts and admired the sunset. When had she had time to sit and contemplate the world around her? Never. Her work had consumed ten to twelve hours of her day, including weekends. Now, that life seemed light years away. Who would believe Zora Hughes, *Haute's* editorial director, would be roughing it among the Sioux, dressing the clueless, and trading quips with a Native American Marlboro man.

She smiled and closed her eyes, forcing her body to let go of the tension it had held on to for several years. John Iron Hawk's face sprang into her mind's eye. He was as in touch with his sensitive side as...

She woke sometime later to darkness and utter silence. Having slipped into sleep as quickly as an eel slid into water, she now fought the tentacles of the dream that threatened to pull her back into its treacherous depths. She shook her head, trying to clear her mind. She listened. Nothing. No sound. No wind whispered through the trees, no animal noises.

How long had she slept? She looked at her watch. Not more than an hour had passed since she'd arrived. As though the forgotten dream still held her in its throes, she rose and walked toward the barn. Her legs felt as useless as overcooked pasta. She rounded the corner of the barn then stopped. More shadow than substance, the coyote watched her. Its silver eyes shone abnormally bright in the darkness. For an insane moment she wondered if the coyote was Sarah. That thought was abandoned when the girl moved into Zora's peripheral vision. Sarah's appearance broke the hypnotic communication between Zora and coyote. The animal loped gracefully off into the darkness. She turned her attention back to the girl just in time to see the white of her dress disappearing into the night.

"Sarah, wait."

Sarah didn't respond but moved quickly toward the foothills.

Zora dashed to the porch. She picked up her flashlight and raced after Sarah. She only knew this one person might provide answers to questions that had haunted her all her life.

Zora stumbled over rocks and tangled in sagebrush as she climbed a steep path up into the hills behind Chet's farm. Like a beacon in the rocky terrain, Sarah's dress became a compass for Zora to navigate by. When she thought she was hopelessly lost, glimpses of white flashed.

A light sheen of sweat covered Zora's body as she climbed higher into the hills. She paused as the wind broke its silence and whispered to her. Turning, she surveyed the path she'd traveled. The flashlight only illuminated a short distance along the path. The rest was lost in darkness. She resumed her upward journey.

She must be insane, following a deranged girl into the hills where coyotes and other wild things made their homes.

Something scurried on the trail in front of her. She bit back a scream, lost her footing and slid down the path. As her body tumbled, a hail of gravel and dirt rained down on her. Dirt filled her nose and mouth. Her knees and the palms of her hands burned as she reached out for anything that would stop her downward plunge. She snagged a protruding tree branch and hung on as her flashlight clunked down the hill.

Coughing and spitting out dirt, she swung her leg over a ledge and hauled herself up and over. Her heart galloped in her chest while her breath bellowed in deep desperate gasps. What had scared her? Another coyote?

A trickle of dust caused her to look up. Something white zigzagged up the path. She wouldn't give up. Not when answers were so close. This time she planted her feet firmly on the trail. Thank God for the moonlight.

When she finally stopped, the twinkle of the constellations filled the inky sky. She guessed she was a mile above Chet's farm. Leaning over with her hands on her knees, she tried to ignore the burning of her palms and the weakness in her legs and struggled to catch her breath. With the exception of her yoga classes twice a week, she'd never been one for exercising. Genetics and her metabolism had kept her in a size six all her adult life, but now she wished she'd spent time on a Stairmaster.

The hill leveled off until she was on a ledge. Taking

advantage of the small space, she lowered herself to the ground and pressed her back against the rocky surface. Dirt and sweat stained her jeans and T-shirt. She grimaced at the eau de toilette of her own sweat. The staff at the magazine would buy tickets to see her in this disheveled and smelly state.

Did Sarah live in these hills? There was no sign of a campfire, so there must be caves. Zora rose and refocused her energies toward looking for a cave. She found the first one further up the hill. Partially obscured by a thorny bush, it wasn't large enough for a small animal, much less an adult. The second cave was larger, but without a flashlight, Zora wasn't venturing past the opening. It could be a bear's den.

A trickle of rubble slid down the hillside from above. She glanced up. Unless the object was white or very light, she wouldn't be able to distinguish it from the shadows. But something had caused the rocks to dislodge. Just because she couldn't see it, didn't mean it wasn't up there.

"Sarah."

No response.

Zora continued climbing until she came to another ledge. After searching unsuccessfully for a cave, she slid exhausted to the ground. Small rocks bit into her legs and butt. This was a wild goose chase. She should retrace her steps back to the farm. If Sarah lived in these hills, she was well hidden. Maybe there was some other way to find the information she needed.

Zora leaned against a rocky surface, grateful for the darkness. Air stirred around her head. She closed her eyes and breathed in the night air. She tasted the dirt in her throat and her eyes felt scratchy. She turned her head to catch the gentle wind and realized the draft was only on her right side. Scrambling to her feet, she started feeling around the mountain face. She wished the sun were up so she could see. Her fingers, raw and bleeding, traveled slowly over the rocky surface as she searched for an opening. The cave was well hidden, and it took her just a few minutes to find the entrance. Smiling in triumph, she stepped into the dark interior. Pausing to allow her eyes to adjust to the murky space, she heard rustling and saw the flash of a white dress up ahead. "Sarah?"

The teen didn't turn around.

"Sarah, wait." With a hand trailing along the cold, dank walls of the cave, Zora took two more steps and free fell into space.

When John walked into headquarters the next morning, a surly Laura trailed behind him. When the Boys and Girls Club opened at ten a.m., he planned to have a talk with Valerie Black Elk about hiring Laura. Hell, Valerie wouldn't even have to pay her, just keep her busy.

He'd quizzed Laura the night before. It seemed she and Gilly had spent the night in the mountains on a dare from Danny Matisse and his buddies. He'd like to stake those guys out in the mountains for scavengers to tear apart.

Maggie gave him a relieved smile, as she cradled a phone under her chin and pointed at the other ringing line.

John grabbed the phone and propped himself on the corner of Oscar's desk. "Police headquarters."

"He's trying to kill me," a female voice whispered.

John tensed, but kept his voice calm, reassuring. "Who are you, ma'am? What's your address?"

"Don't come." Fear and tears made the woman's voice unrecognizable. "He'll kill me if you come."

John pulled a pen from a pencil cup and scribbled "trace this call" on a sheet of paper. He motioned to Laura, whose large eyes were riveted on him. When she reached his side, he crammed the sheet of paper into her hands and pointed toward Maggie.

"Can you lock yourself in a room?" Even though the

woman said she didn't want the police, this was a call for help. Muffled sobs resonated across the phone line. "Ma'am, give me your address."

"I gotta—"

A dial tone buzzed in John's ear.

He looked over at Maggie. "Did that number come up on caller id?"

Maggie scrolled through the phone's LED display window. She shook her head. "I was taking another call. Your call didn't show up."

Anger, red and hot, surged through his body. He wanted to jam his fist down Mike Matisse's throat. He'd asked for money to update the department's phone system, but the request had been denied. Not enough available funds. Although the ruling had come from the council, John could see Mike Matisse's hand in this.

"Daddy."

John blinked. Laura's panicked voice penetrated the haze of anger that fueled his rage. He paused, his hand on the door's handle. He didn't remember the walk to the door.

"What's wrong?" Laura's dark eyes questioned.

He ran a hand over his face. Lost in the urgency of the call, John had forgotten his daughter was in the office. "Domestic dispute."

"What are you going to do?"

He could hear the anguish in her voice. What could he do? With no address and no name, he couldn't very well knock on every door on the reservation. Maggie watched him with understanding in her eyes.

He moved away from the door and plopped down into one of the desk chairs. In his twelve years of being a policeman, he'd gone to the same houses over and over again. Spousal abuse was chronic. If the husband or wife had abused their spouse once, they'd done it before. "Check the logs from the last six months."

Maggie kept a log of all calls received into headquarters.

After a year, the logbooks were placed in storage. She'd have to go through all the calls and weed the domestic dispute from the simple batteries, car accidents, robberies, etc. There was no guarantee the calls received in the past involved the woman who'd phoned a few minutes ago.

"I'll call Oscar," John said.

Oscar might remember being called out to referee such a dispute, but Oscar drew a blank. John replaced the receiver, all the time feeling Laura's eyes on him. Didn't she know there was only so much he could do?

"Oscar able to help?" Maggie asked.

John shook his head. "Nothing came to mind, but he sounded loopy—the drugs probably." John nodded at the log. "Finding anything?"

She rubbed her red-rimmed eyes. "Slow going."

"Maggie, go home. Laura can go through the log."

Laura looked at him in surprise, but she couldn't disguise her excitement.

"You sure?" Maggie stared at him with a hopeful expression.

"It'll be okay. Show Laura how to reach me by phone."

Maggie raised a brow. "Going out on a wild goose chase?"

Without looking at his daughter, he grabbed his keys. "Yeah." Better than staying in the office, knowing somewhere a woman was helpless and scared.

———

John drove down one dusty road after another, looking for anything out of the ordinary. Out of desperation, he drove to Joseph's house.

When he pulled into the Bearkiller drive, he noted Zora's car was missing. He snorted. Probably gone shopping in Pierre. Joseph sat on the front porch. He pushed his chair toward the steps when John got out of the car.

"Did you find her?"

Wondering how the old man had heard about the call so quickly, John answered, "No, sir. But I'm still looking. I just hope I'm not too late. Sometimes these cases don't have a good outcome."

Joseph blanched. "You think someone abducted her?"

John hesitated, suddenly unsure if they were on the same page. "Abducted?"

Joseph leaned forward in his chair. "She didn't spend the night here last night."

John's tensed. "Who's missing?"

"Zora."

The air left his lungs in a rush, and he turned his gaze to where Zora's car should have been. "She probably hopped a plane back to New York." He hoped the disappointment didn't show in his voice. He thought she would have at least said goodbye.

"She's not gone. Her luggage is still in the den."

The look in the old man's eyes, not the tone in his voice, had John feeling uneasy. "How long has she been gone?"

Joseph's hands gripped the arms of his wheelchair until the knuckles stood out in relief. "I don't know. I woke from a nap yesterday evening around seven and she wasn't here. I called Emma at the casino and she said when she left at six, Zora was still at the house. At first, I didn't worry. Sometimes Zora drives to the Iron Horse for food." Joseph looked apologetic. "Emma is not so good a cook."

"But she didn't return last night," John supplied.

The shaman shook his head. "Not this morning, either. I am worried. She is too afraid of things in the night to wander this area by herself."

John stared off across the field. He thought about his last conversation with Zora. He'd been so worried about Laura he hadn't addressed the underlying restlessness he sensed in Zora. He glanced sharply at the old man. "Why is Zora in South Dakota?"

John sensed Joseph knew more than he was telling about

his houseguest. The old man stared at him with impenetrable black eyes. "She is researching her family tree."

"Bullshit. She could do that by computer. Why come all the way from New York to an Indian reservation? She could go to Ancestry.com." John's gaze challenged the old man. "I want the truth."

When Joseph didn't immediately respond, John said, "Come on, old man, she's in trouble, and you hold the key to finding her."

Joseph fingered the amulet around his neck. "The only thing I can tell you is she's seeking information about an ancestor. But I believe this shape-shifter…"

John suppressed a groan of irritation. There was no such thing as a shape-shifter, but he and the old man had been around that corner before. "You mean Sarah?"

Joseph nodded. "Sarah holds the key."

John made a mental note to check on Parker's progress in finding out about missing teens in the area. Zora had seen Sarah out at Chet's place. "Do you think Zora would be crazy enough to go out to Chet's by herself?"

"She is a very determined young woman," Joseph said.

"Mule-headed is more like it." John thought about Zora with the ridiculously high heels, jewelry, and expensive clothes. She wouldn't have gone into the hills. Not the Zora he knew. On the other hand, he remembered the zeal in her eyes when they'd talked about the mysterious teen. There was something going on he didn't understand, and he had a feeling Joseph knew more than he was telling. "I don't think she would have gone into the hills, but I'll drive around to Chet's place and take a look. I need to feed the animals anyway."

John stepped off the porch then turned to face the old man. "If you hear from her, call the office and Laura will relay the message."

Joseph nodded. His eyes held a look of sad resignation. "You will find what your heart seeks, John Iron Hawk."

John stared at the old man, unsure how to interpret his words. Used to Joseph's parables of wisdom coming out of nowhere, John just saluted and moved off to his service vehicle. But the words kept replaying in his head. What exactly did his heart seek? He hadn't given any thought to his heart in years. Life had been about duty and obligation. John turned his vehicle out of the driveway. From his rear-view mirror, he saw the old man return his salute.

Chapter Fourteen

———

SUNLIGHT REFLECTED OFF SILVER AS Julia turned her arm to and fro, admiring the multicolored stones. This was Trades with Horses first gift to her. She smiled shyly at her husband. "It is beautiful."

His mother grunted from her pallet in the corner of the teepee. "It is wrong to give a present meant for another." The old woman spoke in the people's tongue.

Trades with Horses sent his mother a withering glance. "The bracelet was meant for my wife, and I have given it to my wife."

The old woman spat on the ground. "You dishonor us by bringing this woman into our family."

"You dishonor me by not accepting my wife," Trades with Horses said.

Julia glanced nervously in his mother's direction. She had done everything in her power to please the woman, including learning the people's language, but it was not enough. Her husband's mother found fault with every-thing she did. It was not just her husband's mother who shunned her, but most of the women in the village. What had she done wrong? Was it that she had once been a slave?

Julia removed the bracelet from her arm and extended it toward her husband. He frowned. "It displeases you?"

She shook her head and smiled sadly. "I do not want this to cause unhappiness between you and your mother." She lowered her voice. "Was this bracelet intended for another?" She'd often wondered why none of the young women of the tribe had caught his eye and why he was unmarried. He was a handsome man and very wealthy.

A frown darkened his strong face. "No. I found it among the people to the south. I have saved it until I found you, love of my heart."

Julia bowed her head in embarrassment. He had said the words loud enough to be heard by his mother.

"Will you honor me by wearing it?"

His intense black eyes held hers, challenging her, loving her. She took the bracelet and placed it firmly on her arm.

———————

Zora's eyes sprang open. The darkness was so complete she closed and opened her lids again. Panic clawed its way up from her gut. She couldn't see.

Underlying her fear was pain, a throbbing that reverberated through her body.

Tiny pebbles bit into one side of her face and a dank earthy smell filled her nostrils, invading her lungs.

Everything came rushing back, and when it did, her pulse accelerated like a freight train, so rapid and loud she couldn't hear herself think.

She'd followed Sarah into a cave and fallen into a shaft or pit of some sort. She remembered flaying through open air, hitting bottom, the air being knocked out of her lungs, and then nothing.

Lying prone on the earthen floor, she breathed in stale, musty air. She sat up slowly. As she did so, a white-hot pain shot through her right ankle. She reached down to touch the spot then stopped. Exactly how large was the space she lay on? What if she rested on the edge of a crevasse? Even though the air was cool and damp, beads of sweat broke out on her skin. Paralyzed with fear, she didn't dare move. One wrong shift could send her tumbling to her death.

She took one deep breath after another, until the panic subsided. She couldn't stay here forever. She refused to make this her grave. She moved her right arm, inch by inch, trying to determine the boundaries of where she lay. Her fingers encountered nothing but dirt. Encouraged, she moved her left arm. More dirt. Her breath left her lungs in a rush. She wasn't in immediate danger of falling further into the pit. Was her ankle broken? There was no way she could climb out of this hole with a broken ankle.

She wriggled the toes of her injured foot. They moved. She lifted her leg. It hurt like hell, but that pain was not as excruciating as moving the ankle.

Feeling around, she encountered rock. Grimacing, she scooted backwards until her back rested against the stone wall. That small movement caused the pain in her leg to increase from a throb to a searing devil.

She glanced up but could see no difference in the light. She didn't know how long she'd been unconscious. Was it daylight? If so, there should be light coming through the entrance of the cave. Unless…unless she'd fallen so far down into this hole no light reached it. No, she couldn't have fallen very far or she'd be dead or, at the very least, her back would be broken.

Why hadn't she told Joseph what she'd planned to do? Her need for secrecy and fear of ridicule just might result in a slow death in this cave.

As a police officer, John would at least look for her. As she thought of him, Trades with Horses' face materialized in her mind's eye and she remembered the dream. *The bracelet*. Definitely the same one in Lydia's store. How had it found its way to John's sister?

Revitalized by this confirmation she was on the right path, Zora's spirits lifted but soon plummeted as she thought of the predicament she was in. She could only pray Sarah would return.

"Help! Sarah, help me."

Her pleas echoed off the walls of the cave.

If Sarah was in hearing distance, she didn't respond.

John placed his hand on the hood of Zora's car. Cold. The car had been sitting several hours or possibly overnight.

The door to Chet's farmhouse gaped open like the mouth of a rotten pumpkin. John removed his gun from his holster. Keeping it at his side, he took the steps into the house in two strides. "Zora?"

He quickly searched the three-room house. She wasn't there, but he found her purse abandoned on Chet's porch.

John could hear the distressed mooing of Chet's cows. Standing in the shade of the barn, he studied the snow-capped mountains. He hoped she hadn't gone into those hills. All kinds of dangers awaited her up there. Dangers she was unprepared to handle…snakes, mountain cats, not to mention getting lost inside one of the many caves that dotted the mountainous range. He walked to the edge of the property, squatted, and studied the ground.

His father had been a decent tracker. He'd taught his son a few things, but in no way would John consider himself an expert. Two sets of recent footprints crisscrossed each other, one a man's size-ten. This depression was deep, which indicated the wearer was heavy or carried something. The other footprints were a size-seven narrow.

The crushed wheatgrass pointed in the direction of the mountains. John plucked a bent blade. The grass still retained some of its moisture. A full day's sun would have completely dried out the damaged grasses. Someone had passed this way in the last twelve hours.

He strode back to his Jeep and picked up the radio. His daughter answered. "Laura, I'm going up into the hills around Chet Tyler's place. I should be back in the office…"

He glanced at his watch. It was ten-fifteen. "By five p.m."

"Why are you going up there?" she whined.

He pinched the bridge of his nose, biting off a sharp retort. "Zora Hughes may have gotten lost up in the mountains."

He could hear the hitch in her breathing. "Oh."

He strained to hear through the silence.

"Did you find the other lady?" Her anxiety transmitted itself over the phone.

He cleared his throat. "No, but I haven't stopped looking."

"Daddy, be careful."

He longed to have back the early years of her life that he'd missed. She hadn't called him Daddy since she was five or six. Giving himself a moment, he stared over the mountain range and back at the farmhouse. "I will." He replaced the radio and began stuffing a backpack with rope, a water bottle and a first aid kit.

Adjusting his sunglasses against the sun's glare, he secured his hat, picked up a flashlight and moved off toward the hills.

It was easy to follow Zora's trail. Even though she'd traded her high heels for boots, they weren't the best for this type of terrain. There were dislodged rocks and skid marks, probably from new and untested leather soles.

She'd fallen. He could see where she'd grabbed saplings that grew between the rocks to pull up the path, bending the young trees in the process.

Zora Hughes was an irritating, high-maintenance woman who needed to go back to her expensive life of clothes and cars. She had no place on the Great Plain. But the idea of her not being here filled John with desolation so acute, he shut his mind against the feeling. He'd been fine before she'd come. He'd be fine—no better—when she left.

With her ankle throbbing and her throat sore, Zora took a break from shouting for Sarah. The girl either wasn't in the cave or had decided not to come to her rescue. She'd pulled herself up until her back was braced against the cool stone wall. From somewhere close by, she could hear the drip of water. In fact, all her senses, with the exception of sight, were heightened. Small sharp stones bit into her fingers and legs. A wet, pungent odor, probably from the soil, permeated the cave. Rustling and the sound of wings told her—oh God—bats. She flattened herself against the wall. Didn't they carry disease? How long would it take before someone thought to come looking for her? Surely Joseph had contacted John. She knew not to expect help from Emma, but John should come for her. She held that hope close to her heart. In fact, it became her mantra.

John. *John.*

She closed her eyes and conjured up his face, an easy task since his rugged features seemed constantly in her mind's eye.

A frightening thought occurred to her. What if they never found this cave? It had only been by sheer luck she'd found it. In twenty years, some spelunker would find her bones. Tears stung her eyes.

"Stop. Stop it!" Her words echoed off the chamber walls. Now she was talking to herself. She willed the tears to stop and took deep breaths. She needed to judge how far she had to travel to the surface. Maybe if she tossed up a few pebbles...

She scooted around the area, collecting small stones until her fingers encountered something long and hard. Picking the object up, she felt its surface. Her hands followed the smooth contours until she came to the end which was knobby and concaved like the surface of a tooth or a—she dropped it. Recoiling, she backpedaled like a crab. Pressed against the wall of the cavern, she took deep breaths, attempting to conquer the panic and revulsion that robbed her of thought. She'd found a bone. She was sure of it. *Calm down.* It could be an animal bone. Yeah, her mind said, but unless it was an orangutan, that bone was too long to belong to something other than a human.

She couldn't wait for Sarah or John to rescue her. She needed to act now.

Ignoring the pain shooting up her ankle, she slowly pushed to her feet. Once the nausea passed, she hobbled around slowly until she faced the wall. Balanced precariously on her good leg, she searched the dirt wall for protrusions. She'd never been a gymnast and doubted she had the upper body strength to make it out, but she didn't want to die down here. Not like that poor soul whose bone she'd found. Planting her left leg on an indentation in the wall, she started her slow climb toward the top. Every other step was excruciating. She didn't dare stop; if she did, she'd give up. She searched for each protrusion, dug her fingers into it, and searched for another. The pain and pull on her shoulders was beyond anything she'd ever experienced. Her shoulders threatened to separate at the joint and her fingers were numb at the tips from digging into the wall. Reaching up with her right hand, she searched for another perch for her fingers. She found one. Now to find a foothold. She searched until she found an indentation, dug her right foot in and screamed as a red-hot poker of pain shot up her leg. She lost her balance. Her right arm lost its grip on the wall. Zora dangled by her left hand then her perch crumbled, and she fell to the hard earth with a bone-jarring thud.

————◆————

When he reached a ledge, John removed the water bottle from the pack and took a swallow. A jackrabbit bounded from a crevasse and sped across the ground in front of him and dove into a hole in the rocky soil. Removing his bandana from his back pocket, he wiped the sweat from his brow and glanced out over the terrain. The farmhouse appeared small and forlorn. He made a mental note to paint Chet's house and barn. Replacing the bottle, he continued up the path, scanning for evidence of a cave. He'd been pretty familiar with these hills when he was a boy. As an adult, he didn't have the luxury of exploring as he once had. Now, his life consisted of keeping the peace, writing speeding tickets, arresting drunk drivers, and breaking up the occasional lewd and lascivious behavior. He laughed. This was what he'd left the St. Paul police force for? There, he'd seen his share of robberies and murders. He'd longed to get back to the isolation and beauty of the Plains. For a time, he'd been content with this job and painting. But since Zora Hughes had arrived on the reservation, he longed for something more.

Slipping the bandana into his back pocket, he cupped his hands around his mouth.

"Zora." He listened for an answering shout. Not a sound. He continued up the slope, following the prints. About ten minutes later, the male print disappeared. The boot print was smudged and overlapped itself. Zora had turned around, searching for something. Her print didn't continue but stopped. His eyes studied the section of the mountain. Nothing moved.

"Zora," he called again. His hands dropped to his side and he listened over the slight wind that whipped up. Turning, he thought he heard an answering call.

He called her name again. This time, the answer came, tinny, but definitely there.

———

Zora scrambled to her hands and knees. She'd heard a

voice. "Down here," she shouted. "I'm down here." Ignoring the pain in her ankle and now in her head from the fall, she strained to see any light from above. Was she losing her mind? Had she only imagined the voice?

Above, boots crunched on rock. Someone was definitely up there. She remembered the hole a few feet inside the cave entrance. "Watch out."

"Zora, are you all right?"

John. It was John. Even through her pain, she couldn't stop grinning. "John, I'm fine. Be careful."

She blinked, shutting her eyes against the harsh glare from his flashlight. Pinpoints of illumination danced behind her closed lids.

"I'm going to toss down a rope," he said. "When it comes, slip the noose over your head and tighten it around your waist. Use your arms and legs to help you repel."

The rope hit the ground with a thump, causing puffs of dust to rise around her legs. She reached out for the lifeline and secured it firmly around her waist, more than ready to leave this graveyard. For one insane moment, she had visions of hands reaching out of the earth to keep her moored to this cavern. Zora shivered. With teeth gritted in determination, she gripped the rope with both hands. "I'm ready."

Slowly, he hoisted her up. A couple of times, the momentum caused her to hit the dirt wall and reflexively, she put out a hand or foot to prevent her body from crashing into hard rock. On one such occasion, her right foot hit the wall. She swallowed a screech but couldn't prevent the hiss of air that escaped her lips.

"You okay?"

"Fine."

The trip up seemed to take forever. When she reached the top, John grabbed her around the waist and pulled her over the lip of the opening. She threw her arms around him.

"Thank you, thank you," she whispered into his neck. His body smelled of sweat, heat, and man, a potent combination. He returned her hug with one of his own before pushing her away to look at her in the dim light. "Are you okay?" Not waiting for an answer, he ran his hands over her shoulders, torso, and hips then back up to grasp her face.

As much as she wanted to lose herself in this man's arms, she couldn't stop the flood of images of someone dying in that cavern. "John—"

"What the hell were you doing in these hills?"

"John, there's a body down there."

She felt the muscles of his arms and chest tense. "What?"

"A body or at least someone's bones."

He relaxed. "Probably an animal. Now let me get you out of here."

"No, wait." She grasped his hand to keep him from moving away. "The bone is definitely human. It's too long to be an animal."

He stared down into the pit where she'd spent what seemed like a lifetime.

"Did you hear me?"

"Yeah." His jaw tightened. "But I can't do anything about it now. I need to get you out of here. If you're right and there are human bones down there, one more day isn't going to make a bit of difference."

A shiver passed over her body. "I guess you're right. Give me your arm. I hurt my ankle."

Instead of complying, he scooped her up into his arms.

———◆———

After the damp decay of the cave, Chet's place smelled like a field of wildflowers. John deposited her gently on the worn sofa.

"I'll get you a glass of water," he said.

When he returned, Zora drank greedily both of him and the water. His dark eyes ran over her body. She knew she looked a mess and smell worse. She handed him the glass, which he placed on the coffee table.

He stood over her, his face like the sky before a thunderstorm. "What possessed you to go into the hills by yourself?"

She flinched at the anger in his voice. Why had she followed Sarah? It seemed logical at the time, but now… "I had to find her. I knew she lived up there, and I was right. She showed up, and I followed her."

The muscles in John's jaw clenched. "But in the middle of the night? What was so important it couldn't wait 'til morning?"

Her feeling of gratitude was quickly replaced by one of ire. "I needed information. I knew she wouldn't hang around. I had to get it while I could."

"So why didn't you talk at the farm house?"

Zora shrugged. "She didn't want to talk."

John's lips tightened. "Which should have told you something."

She opened her mouth with an angry retort but closed it. His eyes, although dark with anger, telegraphed something else. Fear. Not for himself…but for her. They stared at each other. His shoulders rose and fell with agitation. Deep lines bracketed his lips. Realization dawned slowly. He cared for her. As much as he tried to put on this show of male bravado and displeasure at her presence on his reservation, he cared about her. And she cared about him. She couldn't deny it any longer. When she'd been in that pit not knowing if she'd get out, it was John's face that stayed in her mind—his voice that rang in her head. She didn't just care about him. She loved him. This man who was so different from any other man she'd known.

Her stomach tightened with the knowledge. It scared her but also made her bold.

"Come here," she said.

He moved closer, eyeing her as though she were dangerous. And she was—dangerous with the heady feeling of love and lust that rushed through her. She'd almost died in that cave. But she hadn't. Now she wanted to live—to stop denying her feelings for this man. She wanted him, and he wanted her. She knew it.

Reaching up, she grabbed a handful of his shirt and pulled him down to her. Clasping his beautiful face between her hands, she captured his wide mouth with hers. All the pent-up emotion of not knowing if she would survive went into the kiss.

His lips were both soft and hard. She breathed in the scent of him. She wanted to climb into his skin.

He remained passive under her frantic kiss, so passive she thought she'd made a mistake. Maybe after their first kiss he'd decided he hadn't wanted her after all. Then his rough hands gripped her head, and he returned the kiss with a groan rumbling up from his chest. His tongue parted her lips, bringing the taste of coffee into her mouth. His tongue stroked hers, making her head swim until she gripped his shirt to keep from sliding boneless to the floor.

Abruptly, he broke away. His chest heaved as he struggled to get air into his lungs. "Let's take a look at that ankle."

She blinked. *What?* She waited for the smile that said he joked. Waited for his hands to come back and touch her aching breasts. But instead, he pulled a lethal-looking gun from the waistband of his jeans and set it on the coffee table.

Striving for humor to replace the dawning humiliation, she said, "Planning to shoot me if I misbehave?" Oh, she wanted to misbehave all right. She wanted to run her hand over the bulge in his jeans, wanted to feel his lips devouring her again, wanted to feel the weight of his body on top of hers.

He sat on the edge of the coffee table and placed her

ankle in his lap. "Don't give me ideas." He smiled. Only the slight quiver in his voice betrayed his emotions. The kiss had disturbed him as much as it had her.

She bit down on her lip as he gingerly tried to remove the right boot. When it wouldn't budge past the swollen ankle, he pulled a long-bladed knife from a leather sheath at his waist. She felt a moment's remorse when she realized he meant to cut her Dolce and Gabana boots. Wisely, she kept her thoughts to herself.

The ankle was twice the size of the left one and varied in shades from black to blue.

He gently rotated the foot with long fingers.

She gritted her teeth.

"It isn't broken." He lifted her ankle and placed it on the table. "I'll get some ice." He returned a few moments later with ice wrapped in a dingy dishtowel. Sitting on the table, he nestled her foot in his lap and set the cold compress on the swollen area.

Zora couldn't have said what affected her more, the ice pack and its stinging coldness or the hot flush that traveled over her body at the sight of her foot so close to his crotch. She couldn't take her eyes from the spot, and it appeared to grow as she stared. Her gaze shot to his face. He watched her from behind hooded lids. She couldn't look away. Her whole body hummed.

He held her gaze as his bronzed hand caressed its way up her leg to her cloth-covered mound. Body throbbing with anticipation, she opened her legs wider, wanting his touch, needing his touch. His movements grew rougher with each downward pass over her clit. Finally, he propped her ankle on the coffee table and sat next to her on the sofa.

"Maybe we shouldn't do this now," he said, pointing to her ankle.

In answer, she reached up, grabbed his neck and pulled his face down to hers. The touch of his mouth on hers was electric. She groaned. He captured her tongue, sucking it into the hot cavern of his mouth, while his large hand covered her breast. A bolt of pure pleasure shot to her core.

When his lips broke contact with hers, she cried out in protest and tried to recapture his mouth. He laughed and she realized she'd never heard him laugh before. Though deep and rough, it flowed over her like honey, making her pliant. He reached for the hem of her shirt and pulled the material over her head then stroked the skin that rose above the bra cup. Leaning in, he kissed the area, allowing his tongue to lap the skin. His tongue was warm and wet. When he lifted his head, goose bumps rose on her cool flesh.

He reached behind her for the bra's clasp, released it and tugged the offending garment off, cupping the weight of one breast in his hand. When he ran a callused thumb across the nipple, it beaded. When his warm, wet mouth closed over it, she groaned. She grasped his head to keep him from stopping and plowed her fingers through the thick cap of his black hair. The motion loosened the leather string and thick hair spilled around his broad shoulders.

CHAPTER FIFTEEN

———

JOHN STARED INTO HER MOCHA-COLORED eyes. Damn, she was beautiful and he wanted her. It had been a long time since he'd wanted more than to rut, spill himself, and move on. He didn't want to hurt her, and at this moment, he had enough reasoning left to know he didn't have anything to offer her. "Zora—"

"Oh no, big boy." Her generous mouth widened in a sensuous smile. "You started this. You're going to finish it."

He couldn't stop the smile her words produced. He unbuttoned his shirt.

Her fingers splayed on his chest, touching his nipples before pinching them. His dick answered by pushing against his jeans in a plea to be let out. As though she could read his mind, her hand traveled to his crotch and stroked him. Frissons of pleasure shot up his spine, sizzling his brain. If someone had asked his mother's name at that moment, he wouldn't have remembered.

Her fingers fumbled at the zipper to his jeans, her breath coming in gasps.

Capturing her hands in his own, he said, "Not so fast."

She ignored him. Pulling the zipper down, her hands reached inside his boxers. Greedy fingers closed around him and stroked. All sense of caution threw to the winds. Unsnapping her jeans, he pushed the material down to her ankles. Mindful of hurting her, he carefully removed the pant legs and pulled off her jeans and panties.

Her long-legged length lay before him like an expensive dessert. John closed his eyes and fought for control, but lost it when he felt her hands tugging at his jeans.

"Take them off," she whispered. "I want to see you."

Not taking his eyes off her gorgeous face, he stood and stripped. The widening of her eyes when his dick sprang free made it bob in appreciation.

Zora opened her arms. "Rough and hard."

He tried not to laugh. Even in sex, she was bossy. Well, he was going to comply with the lady's wishes. But first… He reached down and pulled his wallet from his back pocket. Extracting a condom, he tore the packet and sheathed himself, aware of her hot eyes on him.

Settling between her thighs, he positioned himself and pushed.

Molten heat engulfed him. He squeezed his eyes shut and tried to temper the urge to plunge into her, but she took control. Her inner muscles clamped around him, and he couldn't ignore the urge to move.

───◆───

Zora was beyond reasonable thought. She stroked John's back as he plowed into her. Almost inhuman sounds issued from her throat. "More," she groaned. "Give…me…more."

His eyes were half shut and burning with an inner fire. Long black hair lay on shoulders that glistened with sweat. He resembled a warrior determined to win the battle with her as the prize. He never broke eye contact with her as he answered some age-old question that hung like a taunt between them. Zora didn't care who was the victor. She wanted this man at this moment. Ignoring the pain in her ankle, she wrapped her legs around his tight buttocks and pulled him deeper into her body.

She clutched his shoulders and raced toward some beckoning place that wound her tighter and tighter until she broke apart and splintered.

"Did I hurt you?" John asked.

Satiated and floating on a wave of contentment, Zora smiled at him. "Hurt me?"

He pointed to her leg. "Your ankle."

She stared down at her ankle as though it were an alien appendage. On signal, a bolt of pain shot through her leg. She laughed. She was alive. "It hurts like hell, but I'll live."

He nodded in understanding as he pulled his jeans up over muscular buttocks.

His whole body was sculpted, an artist's dream. Her mind flashed to the paintings in his sister's Gallery and the proud chief standing on the Plain. The Gallery...Her mind immediately flooded with images of the bracelet and the last dream of Julia.

"What's wrong?" John asked, hands arrested as he buttoned his shirt.

She gathered her undergarments, suddenly uncomfortable with his scrutiny. She wanted to ask how his sister had come into possession of the bracelet. But if she did, he'd want to know why it was important to her. She couldn't reveal the dreams. Although they just shared the intimacy of their bodies, she wasn't ready to share the affliction of the dreams. She wanted him to continue to think of her as mentally stable. Once he learned of the visions, as Joseph called them, his opinion of her sanity would take a nosedive. "I'm fine. I guess I'm still trying to shake off being in the cave and finding that bone."

"Zora, the bone is probably pretty old."

She eased her panties over her ankle, thankful her hair hid her expression. "I know. That's what I'm afraid of."

"What?" John paused in the act of stuffing items back into his jeans pocket. "What are you afraid of?"

Sometime between finding that bone and being rescued, Zora knew she'd found Julia's earthly remains. And if that bone truly belonged to Julia, someone had dumped her body into that cave. They'd made her disappear.

Zora's fingers tumbled as she fastened the clasp of her bra. "Nothing. Just a figure of speech."

"Listen."

Something in the tone of his voice made her head snap up and her stomach clench.

He ran his hand over his head, an unconscious and telling gesture. "About…" He nodded toward the couch. An array of emotions flitted across his face. "I don't have—"

A year ago, hell, two weeks ago, if someone had told her she'd be doing the nasty with a police officer in the Great Plains, she'd have accused them of snorting coke. That John thought their involvement was a mistake ripped at the soft fabric of her soul. A soul she'd never exposed to anyone, not her parents, not Terrance. John Iron Hawk with his unpretentious manner had touched her like no one else had.

"John, it was just sex." She forced a smile. "Great sex, but just sex."

Something in his eyes darkened and his face went blank. "Yeah," he said, nodding his head, "just sex." He cleared his throat and glanced around the room. "I guess we'd better get going."

For a moment, she couldn't speak around the lump in her throat. "I guess we'd better," she echoed.

———◆———

Bright and early the next morning, John and Pete Montrell hiked up the mountain toward the cave. Pete was one of the few men John trusted. He would've preferred checking out the cave by himself, but he believed in safety in numbers.

Huffing as he trudged alongside John, Pete asked, "Much further?"

"About another half mile."

Face flushed, Pete carried a tire around his middle that hadn't been there three months ago. His wife was seven months pregnant. John figured Pete's expanding waistline must be from sympathy eating.

Pete sighed. "How'd you find the cave?"

"Coyotes were killing Chet Tyler's chickens. Chased one up here a couple of days ago. I spotted this cave and decided to check it out." The lie rolled easily off John's tongue. "It's not much further."

Once in the cave, he drove a heavy stake into the earth. He looped a rope around it, secured the knot, and then tossed the coil over the side. A hollow thud reverberated when the line hit the bottom. After putting on heavy gloves, Pete grasped the end of the rope closest to the stake. Securing the flashlight to his belt, John gripped a portion of the rope and lowered himself into the pit.

The cavern had a surreal silence to it. While in the Marines, he'd been caught in the eye of a hurricane on the Texas coast and the feeling had been the same—a waiting stillness before the fierceness of the storm hit. There was no chance of a storm surge washing through this cavern, but the feeling persisted.

"You okay down there?" Pete called.

John hadn't realized he'd stopped his downward trek. "Yeah, I'm fine." He scanned the space. Rocky walls washed smooth by a millennium of moving water gave off a grayish illumination under the beam of the flashlight. He released the rope and dropped the few remaining feet to the cave floor.

The first sweep of the flashlight revealed an irregular space of not more than eight feet in diameter. Other than the hole above, he saw no other exits. He saw fresh depressions in the floor, probably made by Zora as she moved around. As he swept the cavern again, he spied fragments of bone on the ground in an area that lay just inside the radius of the flashlight's beam. Slowly in grid like patterns, he performed a search of the space. Satisfied the bones appeared to be confined to one spot he replaced his heavy work gloves with latex ones, and squatted to examine the area closely. In addition to the long bone Zora found, a skull lay on its side in the dust.

"You find something down there?" Pete asked. His voice bounced around the walls of the cave like a gunshot echoing through a canyon.

"Found some bones." John had seen a few remains in his twelve years as a police officer. Zora was right. The bones were definitely human. Did he leave them here and call the Feds or disturb the scene by bagging the remains? He extracted a pencil and paper from his shirt pocket and with the limited light available, sketched the area. He worked quickly, including the placement of the bones, and then glanced around for any clothing. Nothing. Which meant the body had been naked when dumped or the fabric had long since disintegrated.

Deciding to leave the bones—they definitely weren't going anywhere—John tugged on the rope. "Coming up."

———◆———

A car pulled into Chet's drive as John finished his call to the medical examiner's office.

Zora hopped out of the convertible and stared at him over the roof. "You could have waited for me."

Wobbling out of the car and oblivious to the undercurrents around him, Chet Tyler looked over his homestead. His wrinkled face broke into a broad grin. "Thought I'd never see the old place again."

"Pete, take Chet inside," John said.

"Sure, sure," Pete said. Moving past John, he took the old

man's arm. The pair ambled toward the farmhouse, Chet leaning heavily on Pete's large frame.

Two horizontal lines of anger on either side of her pinched nostrils marred her beautiful face. She opened her mouth to speak. He raised a hand to stop the coming tirade.

"You were in no shape to go up the mountain again. Look at you. You're in pain."

"I—I still wanted to be here."

"To do what?"

She shrugged and turned her face toward the hills, but not before he saw tears glistening in her brown eyes.

Zora didn't strike him as a woman who cried easily. The fact she looked on the verge of doing so now made him curious. Tired of treating her with kid gloves, he wanted some answers. "You want to tell me why you chased Sarah all the way up that mountain? And don't give me that bull-shit about writing an article. Those must have been some powerful questions to take you into that cave."

"You wouldn't understand." Eyes bright with tears, she pivoted and limped toward the farmhouse.

John caught up with her and grabbed her arm, halting her progress. "Make me understand. Tell me what the hell is going on."

She turned, a sad smile tugging at the edges of her generous mouth. "How can I make you understand when I don't?" She mounted the porch steps and disappeared into the house.

Don't understand what? What was she hiding?

He marched back to the Jeep and honked the horn for Pete. He didn't dare go after Zora. He wouldn't be responsible for what he might do, but he would get to the bottom of whatever she hid.

She stared after the departing Jeep. She'd planned to tell John when they went to the hills this morning that the bones belonged to Julia. But he'd gone without her. Now the moment of sharing her true purpose for being on the reservation was lost.

"Did you say somethin'?" Chet Tyler stood on unsteady legs in the middle of his living room. The very room where she and John had made love not twenty-four hours earlier.

She laughed. The sound was hollow to her ears. "No, just talking to myself. Let's get you comfortable."

Once he was seated on the sofa, she placed his small oxygen tank beside him. "I'm going out to the car for the groceries."

She'd offered to bring Chet home from the hospital. Although he wanted to see his buddy safely home, Joseph realized she couldn't handle two invalids, and stayed home. He did ask her to pick up groceries for Chet, which she now retrieved from the backseat of her convertible.

"What would you like to eat?" she asked, placing the bags on the kitchen table. She plopped into a chair, taking some of the weight off her throbbing ankle. Chet shuffled into the small, square-shaped room.

The kitchen at one time had been white, now it was a grimy gray. Cracked white and black linoleum covered the floor and a small white refrigerator rattled in one corner. Grease stained the wall above a four-burner stove. Not seeing a microwave, Zora knew her options for cooking were limited. Turning on the stove was out of the question since the heat in the room was already stifling.

He lowered himself into a kitchen chair. "A Porterhouse steak, fries, a beer, and a slice of apple pie with vanilla ice cream." He smiled slyly at her.

She narrowed her eyes. "Try again."

He smacked his bony knee. "I'm eighty-five years old. I should be able to eat what I want."

She smiled in sympathy. "You're right." Glancing down

into the grocery bag, she said, "How about a compromise? I'll fix you a grilled cheese sandwich, soup, and some applesauce."

He grimaced.

"That's the best I can do. Tomorrow, I'll bring you an apple pie and ice cream."

He cackled in delight. "You got a deal, little girl."

Later, after she'd prepared his dinner and placed it on the table in front on him, she watched as he said a brief prayer over his food. He looked so fragile. Who was going to take care of him? "You can't stay here by yourself."

He picked up his spoon and scooped up tomato soup. "They've got some woman coming out to check on me a couple of times a week."

What would happen to him between those times? "Do you have any family?"

He put down his soup spoon. "Got a great niece in Minnesota. Haven't seen her in five years. Last I heard she had a house full of kids. She won't have time for an old man."

"Why don't you stay with Joseph?"

He snorted. "I can poison myself with my own cooking. I don't need that granddaughter of his doing it for me. I'll be just fine right here in my house."

Zora sighed. Maybe John could find someone to come and stay with the old man. In the meantime... She glanced around the kitchen. Chet slurped up another spoonful of soup. It wouldn't kill her to spend a night or two here until John could find someone.

"Chet, how long have you lived here?"

He glanced up. "I was born on this land, and my father and his father before him."

Zora's mind started to race. "How far back?"

"At least since the reservation came to be," he said. "Maybe since the 1890s."

Her heart dropped. "Do you know who owned the land before your family?"

He bit into his sandwich. "The land belongs to itself. No one owns land." He chewed thoughtfully. "That's a white man's belief—that the land can be owned and held by one person."

She'd heard that philosophy before and it made her proud that these people whose blood flowed through her veins were so wise.

She must have spoken her thoughts out loud, something she'd been doing a lot lately, because Chet nodded and glanced at her with humor in his faded black eyes. "We're a wise people." He took another bite of sandwich. "So ask me what you really want to know."

"I..." Her eyes met his and she saw the seriousness in his expression—and something else...empathy. She understood why he and Joseph were friends. The men seemed to see beyond the veil people used to shield their feelings. "Joseph told you about my dreams of my ancestor?"

He nodded.

"I think she lived here," Zora paused, wanting to make sure the old man understood, "here on your piece of land."

Chet nodded slowly. "It's possible. This was the original site of the village."

Zora's breath quickened. She sat forward in her seat. Could she trust Chet's memory? Were her words putting suggestions in his mind? But if what he said were true... "There was a river..."

He frowned then his wrinkled face brightened. "There's a dried stream bed across the road, maybe forty or fifty feet further into the bush. My father talked about the days when he and his friends went swimming there."

Zora couldn't contain her excitement. She could venture across the road to the creek bed while Chet rested. She wondered if she would recognize it as the river of her dreams.

The next morning, John stood on the opposite side of the autopsy table from Dr. Steven Foley, St. Mary's hospital's chief pathologist. "What do you think?"

The bones from the cave were spread out on a steel table that had grooves cut into its sides to allow blood and other body fluids to drain during an autopsy.

After the tech from the medical examiner's office had finished with the scene yesterday afternoon, the bones had been brought here to Foley's lab. FBI Special Agent Boyce Tanner had turned the investigation over to John with the admonition to keep him in the loop. Right. One more ball to keep in the air.

A red-haired, ruddy-faced man, Foley ran his hand almost lovingly over the smooth texture of the skull. "Definitely human." He glanced up at John. "Too bad you don't have the pelvic bone. It would make it easier to determine whether these bones are female or male. I'm betting on female."

"Why?" John asked.

Foley picked up the skull. "See these ridges?" He caressed the brow of the skull. "There are distinct differences between male and female, and based on those differences, I'd say this was a woman."

"How long do you think the bones have been in the cave?" John asked.

"Hmm…I'm hazarding a guess of more than fifty years." Foley shrugged. "But that's just a guess. I'd have to do additional testing." He studied the bones longer. "You sure there were no other bones or fragments?"

John shook his head. "Nothing I could see."

"Do you think this person was buried down there?" Foley removed his gloves, dropped them in a waste receptacle and walked over to the sink to wash his hands.

"I doubt it. Fifty years or so ago we didn't bury our dead and definitely not in caves. Plus, it would take a strong man to lug a body up the mountain and then lower the body and him down into that hole. A whole lot easier to just drop it."

"So you're thinking this was a murder," Foley said.

John nodded. "Afraid so."

Foley studied him for a moment. "I'll run some tests and get back to you." He held up his hand to stop the next question. "No, I don't know how soon it will be." He walked into his small office off the autopsy area. "As soon as I know something, I'll call you."

By the time John arrived back at Little River, the sun rode high in the sky and the earth baked with heat and lack of rain. He strode into the office and straight to the water cooler. "Any calls?" He gulped a paper cup of water.

"That Johnny Depp is a character." Maggie glanced up from a magazine and gave John a vacuous smile. "What did you say?" Lank gray hair hung around her plump face.

Trying to keep the irritation out of his voice, John repeated, "Any calls?"

"Yep." She glanced down at the magazine and back at John. "Mike Matisse called and that woman from New York."

John's heart quickened at the mention of Zora. He'd call her later. Best to deal with Matisse first. "What'd he want?"

"Didn't say. Said for you to call him."

John grunted. "Go to lunch, Maggie."

"Sounds good to me." She lost no time getting her purse and magazine and hustling for the door.

"Maggie."

She turned, one hand on the door handle, clearly impatient to be on her way.

"Do you read fashion magazines?"

A shapeless brown dress covered her robust frame. She gave him a withering glare. "A waste of time and money."

That said she stumped out of the office.

John wished he could ignore Matisse's call, but the man was persistent and would keep calling. He secured the gun cabinet before walking toward tribal council headquarters. When he stepped into the small reception area, he could hear Matisse's voice. John started down the corridor toward the man's office.

"What do you mean, there's nothing you can do about it?" Matisse's voice became more strident as John moved closer.

Matisse stood with his back to the door, but he must have sensed John's presence, because he whipped around. Something John could only describe as panic washed over his face and just as quickly disappeared. "Let me call you back," he said into the phone. "Someone's here."

Disconnecting his call, he gave John a tight-lipped smile. "How long have you been out here?"

"Long enough." John wished he'd heard more. In fact, he hadn't heard enough of the conversation to make heads or tails of it, but he wanted to rattle Matisse's chain.

Matisse pocketed his phone. When he raised his head, his face was creased in an unholy smile. "Heard you had a little excitement out at the old Tyler place."

Fuck. How the hell had the news gotten out so quickly? Keeping his face blank, John asked, "What do you mean?"

Matisse studied him. "Come on, John, I'm the tribal council president. My ear's always to the ground and the well being of the people is my primary concern. Do we have a murderer running around on the reservation?"

Matisse didn't give a rat's ass about the people. If he did, he wouldn't be pocketing the casino's profits for his own personal use.

"You don't have to worry about your safety. The bones appear to be pretty old. I say the killer is long dead." John turned and headed for the exit.

Matisse's next words stopped him in his tracks. "Guess

you heard I'm running for state senate."

John forced down his anger and disgust as he retraced his steps back to the council president's office. What was Matisse planning to do, line his pockets with the money from the state coffers? "Don't count on my vote, and I'll make sure everyone in the state knows you're a thief."

Matisse's smile congealed. "That's slander."

"No," John said, giving Matisse his back, "that's fact."

Chapter Sixteen

———

Taking a deep breath, Zora stepped into police headquarters. There was no one in the main room. "John?" She moved toward his office and poked her head in. How could anyone work in such a small space? She had a corner office at the magazine that looked out over beautifully congested New York. She longed for her job, her city, her world. She was like an extraterrestrial in this alien place. Though she had to admit, this land had a strange beauty, especially around sunset.

She stepped into the corridor and right into John Iron Hawk's path.

A slow smile transformed his face, his gaze moved to her mouth. "I got your call."

The hungry look in his eyes had her saying the first thing she could think of. "I need to buy pie and ice cream."

For a heartbeat, he looked confused and then he chuckled. "Let me guess. Chet?"

A foolish grin spread over her face. Like someone dying of thirst, she drank in his face. A feeling of rightness filled her. When she was with him, she felt safe, whole, at home. How could she miss New York in one moment, but instantly feel the rightness of being with this man?

She mentally shook her head. No, no. New York was home, not this place, not this man. Her conflict must have shown on her face because his smile died.

He placed a large hand on her arm. "Are you okay?"

"Yeah, yeah…" She glanced around the corridor. She needed to look anywhere but at his face. "Where's everybody?"

"Maggie's at lunch. Oscar is recuperating, so I guess that's everybody."

"Oh." She'd run out of conversation, but call her crazy, she didn't want to leave.

"How's Chet?"

"Fine," she said absently, still not looking directly at him. She was being stupid. She couldn't let her emotions rule her. Raising her eyes to his, she repeated herself. "He's fine. You need to find someone to come and stay with him for a while, but in the meantime, where do I find pie and ice cream?"

John smiled. "I guess the old guy is feeling better." His forehead wrinkled in thought. "There's a convenience store across from my sister's place that sells ice cream, but the pie…" He shrugged. "I guess you'll have to make that."

She raised an eyebrow. "I don't bake." Or cook, for that matter, but she wasn't going there.

"Then the nearest place would be about twenty miles outside the reservation. Tom Bird has a restaurant in the truck stop there. Annie—that's Tom's wife—might be willing to part with a pie, for a price."

Zora wasn't baking, no matter how much the woman charged. "Sounds good." She cast one last glance at his face before heading for her car.

He detained her with a touch. "Does Chet need me to come out to take care of the animals?"

At that moment, she decided she would be staying with Chet for one more night, especially if it meant seeing John. She turned and gave him her best Zora Hughes glower. "I'm sure not taking care of them." She opened the door and stepped out onto the sidewalk. His chuckle followed her out into the bright South Dakota sun.

———•———

Lydia Whitefeather lovingly picked up the turquoise bracelet and polished it with a soft cloth. Turquoise bracelets were a dime a dozen, but this one was one of a kind. Mined almost one hundred and sixty years ago, the stones were unique. Over the years, she'd had plenty of offers to sell it. One woman had offered a quarter of million dollars. With Lydia's husband, Sam, wasting away and constantly needing medicines to keep him alive, she'd been tempted, but the bracelet wasn't hers to sell.

Twenty years ago, Wanda Matisse, on her deathbed, had given the bracelet to Lydia for safekeeping. To this day, she remembered the words the old woman had whispered, 'Blood stones.' The stones were in shades of pink and Lydia had never understood the words.

A shadow passed over the display case, blocking the sunlight and bringing Lydia back from the past. Zora Hughes stood on the other side of the window, staring in.

The woman had style. Both Laura and Emma had said Zora worked in the fashion industry. Lydia believed it because the woman always looked like she'd stepped off the pages of *Vogue*. She could have been a model except she wasn't toothpick thin.

A moment later, the bell over the entrance chimed.

Lydia stepped out of the recessed alcove. "Good afternoon."

Zora jumped.

Strange, Lydia could have sworn the woman saw her in the display window.

Without acknowledging Lydia's greeting, Zora sat a grocery bag on the counter by the cash register and moved toward the open exhibit case. She reached in and removed the bracelet.

"Don't—" Lydia might have been talking to the wind because Zora seemed oblivious to anyone or anything other than the bracelet.

She held it in the palm of her right hand, using her left hand to turn it from side to side. "It's the same one," she whispered.

Her voice with its eerie calmness caused the hairs on Lydia's arms to quiver. She moved toward Zora, wanting to snatch the bracelet and put it back under lock and key. Zora froze her with a stare. The woman was scary.

"It's the same one." This time, the woman's voice was forceful and solid.

"The same as what?" Lydia asked.

Zora didn't respond but instead held up the bracelet as though she'd never seen it before. "It's beautiful. But how did you get it?"

"I've had it for a long time."

With a lift of the brow, Zora stared first at Lydia then down at the bracelet. "It was stolen."

Lydia glared at Zora. Had she heard her correctly? "Stolen? You're crazy." She moved to take the bracelet, but Zora stepped out of reach.

"Can you prove it? No, you can't," Lydia said, not allowing Zora time to respond. "You can't because it wasn't."

"I—"

The doorbell chimed and Mike Matisse strolled in. Of all the times to visit the shop, why did he show up now? It was like he knew they were discussing the rightful ownership of the bracelet. He smiled brightly at them, but when his eyes fell to the bracelet, his smile faded. Lydia's stomach tightened and she reached protectively for the bracelet. This time, Zora willingly surrendered it.

Lydia locked the bracelet in its case and pocketed the key. When she turned around, Mike Matisse was studying the artwork on the other side of the store. She wasn't fooled. He would be listening closely to everything she and Zora said.

With one eye on Mike, Lydia whispered to Zora, "We'll

continue this discussion another time."

Zora hesitated. For a moment, Lydia thought the woman would start ranting again. Her eyes drifted to Mike Matisse's stout form. Finally she nodded and stalked out.

Breathing a sigh of relief, Lydia hustled over to Mike. She wished she could just ignore him, but like an unwanted houseguest, he'd never leave.

"See something you like?" she asked.

He stood in front of one of John's paintings. Luckily, John used only his initials as a signature. "That's a damn lot of money for something anyone could paint."

Lydia chose to ignore the comment. To defend the painting would draw too much attention to the artist and Lydia knew that was the last thing John wanted.

Touching Mike's arm, she led him toward the hats. Picking one off a mannequin, she replaced his worn hat with a beige Stetson and stood back to admire the man. "It looks good on you." She hoped her dead grandmother wouldn't come back to haunt her for that lie.

Mike removed the hat and attempted to rearrange it on the mannequin's head. His fingers squashed the brim. Lydia grimaced and refrained from batting his hands away. She cautioned herself not to insult him. She'd wait until the toad left.

"I'm running for state senator, and I hope I have your vote."

She gave him a congratulatory smile, all the while knowing she wouldn't vote for him if he ran unopposed.

"Your brother is causing problems." He didn't look at her but instead studied the hat as though he considered buying it.

Lydia's stomach clenched. "Problems?"

His eyes when they held hers were hard and ugly. "Let's just say his nose is somewhere it doesn't belong. I want you to call him off."

Lydia knew better than to pretend she didn't know what

Mike meant. "I don't have any control over my brother."

He glanced slowly around the shop. "When's your lease up?"

Lydia couldn't swallow around the lump in her throat. The tribal council reviewed each lease and had the option of declining renewal for infractions. It wouldn't take much for Mike Matisse to fabricate some offense. Then she'd be without income and couldn't support herself or buy medicine for her husband.

Dark with malice, Mike's gaze bore into hers. "Do we understand each other?"

"Yes," she whispered. Her only option was to leap when he said leap.

"Good." He picked up the Stetson off the mannequin's head and settled it on his own. Glancing in the mirror to the left of the hat display, he smiled. "I think you're right. It does look great on me."

He tipped the Stetson and walked out the door. His old hat lay like a bad-smelling fish on the counter.

Zora breathed a sigh of relief when she pulled into the Bearkiller driveway and didn't see Emma's truck. After the fiasco in Lydia's shop, Zora needed time to regroup. She also needed a phone, something Chet didn't have.

Zora eased open the front door and stepped inside. All was quiet, which meant Joseph was probably taking his afternoon nap. She walked to the kitchen and placed the almost liquid ice cream in the freezer then washed her hands at the kitchen sink.

What had possessed her to confront John's sister in that manner? She had worked out in her mind exactly what she was going to say. She had planned to calmly ask about the history of the bracelet and, based on Lydia's answer, make a decision about her next course of action. But the moment she passed the shop, the bracelet came to mind, and all rational thought fled. And when she'd held it in the palm of her hand, a wealth of emotion, emotion not her own, flooded her. A collage of feelings, love, despair, anger and, above all, regret, flooded her system. All Julia's emotions.

The accusation just flew from Zora's mouth. Now Lydia would have no doubt Zora was certifiable. How long would it take before John knew? How long before everyone knew? Maybe instead of staying around to see John tonight, she'd leave Chet with his pie and ice cream and she'd come back here to Joseph's. Yes, that's what she'd do. She couldn't bear to see the curiosity and questions in John's eyes.

She shut off the running water, dried her hands, then crept past Joseph's closed door toward the den.

A black rotary phone sat on a plant stand. She reached for it and dialed AnaMarie's number. "Are you with a patient?"

AnaMarie's soft, almost languid voice filled Zora's ear. "I'm between patients. Are you okay?"

Zora gave a shaky laugh. "About as okay as a crazy person can be."

"Zora." There was a mild reprimand in her therapist's voice.

Zora told her about the last few days.

"This dream you had in the cave, was it the first time you'd seen the bracelet?" Ana Marie asked.

"No. I saw it in Lydia's shop when I first arrived."

"Any reaction to it at that time?"

Zora thought back to what seemed eons ago but, in reality, had only been a little over one week. "The stones in the bracelet felt warm to the touch and it seemed familiar, but nothing like the reaction I had today."

There was silence on the therapist's side of the phone.

"The bracelet belongs, belonged to Julia. I know it did,"

Zora said. "I didn't imagine my reaction."

"And I wasn't suggesting you did. I just wonder if your unconscious mind placed the bracelet in your dream. If you'd seen the bracelet before you came to the reservation…"

"I know what you're saying. The power of suggestion."

"Exactly."

Zora could hear the smile in the other woman's voice.

A door closed somewhere in the house.

"—tell me, what's happening with that police officer?"

A warm glow spread over Zora's body and she closed her eyes and leaned back on the plaid sofa. "A lot." She suddenly remembered the scene in Lydia's store, and sat up straighter, the glow replaced by apprehension.

"Are you seeing him tonight?"

Zora would rather hide out in Joseph's house than face the questions in John's eyes. But she'd promised him she'd take care of Chet until he found someone to stay with the old man. She couldn't renege on a promise.

"Yes, I guess I will."

———◆———

John stared down at the congealed glob on his plate. Sensing his daughter's eyes on him, he picked up his fork, loaded it with a generous heap of the unidentified mass and popped the fork in his mouth before he could change his mind. His eyes flew open and every bit of saliva evaporated from his mouth. She must have used a box of salt.

"Do you like it?" Laura asked.

He could hear the thinly veiled hope in her voice. "Hmmm." He reached for his water glass and drained it.

"I got the recipe—" The phone rang and she sprang up to answer it. "It's for you," she said, passing the cordless phone across the table. "It's Aunt Lydia."

He closed his eyes in blessed relief and placed the phone

to his ear. "What's up?"

Lydia's voice shook. "I need to talk to you."

"Are you okay?"

"No. Can you come over here? I don't want to leave Sam."

Glancing down at the excuse for dinner, John said, "Sure. I'll be right there."

Pushing back from the table, he replaced the receiver. "I need to see your aunt."

"Do you want me to save your dinner?"

"Uh…no. Better not. I don't know how long I'll be." He paused on the way to the back door. "By the way, where did you say you got that recipe?"

She beamed. "Emma gave it to me."

"Hmmm. Right." Glad for the reprieve, he grabbed his keys off the kitchen counter.

His daughter stood at the kitchen table, staring down at the remains of dinner.

"Laura?"

She glanced up expectedly. "Yes?"

"Thanks for cooking."

Her lips turned up in a slight smile.

As he walked to the Jeep, his step was lighter.

When John pulled into his sister's drive, she sat on her front stoop, puffing nervously on a cigarette.

He walked slowly toward her and stopped short of the smoke. "I thought you'd quit."

She shrugged and took another draw.

He dragged his hand through his hair in frustration. "In case you've forgotten, your husband is dying of lung cancer."

She took one more deep pull before crushing the cigarette under her tennis shoe.

"Want to tell me what's going on?"

She glanced over her shoulder at the lit window. She'd converted her small living room into a bedroom for her husband so he could view the road and the comings and goings of other's lives. Bedridden with lung cancer, he'd first been diagnosed five years ago. He'd gone through a remission, but a year ago the cancer returned. The kicker was Sam never smoked, but Lydia had. His sister lived with the guilt her husband might have contracted the cancer from secondhand smoke.

"Mike Matisse came into the shop this afternoon."

"What did he want?"

"Wanted me to make you keep your nose out of his business. What are you doing that's got him so rattled?"

"I don't know, but I'm going to find out." He wished now he'd heard more of the phone conversation between Mike and the unknown second party.

She placed a rough hand on his arm. "Don't. Let it be." Her voice shook. His older sister had never feared any-thing, not even their drunken father's fists.

"What did he say to you to make you so scared?" John demanded.

She shook her head and stared at her husband's window. Sam's hacking cough sounded like ice formations breaking up in a spring thaw, except in this case, life wouldn't be renewing itself.

"That bastard threatened you. What did he say?"

She turned her face away, probably so he couldn't see the tears in her eyes.

Matisse was a coward. He didn't have the guts to come directly to John with his threat. Well, he would go to Matisse.

"John," her voice broke. "He's going to close the shop."

"How—"

"By not renewing the lease."

About to choke on his own rage, John forced himself to breathe. He took himself away from his anger. Cleared his brain. The setting sun cast splashes of purple and orange over the land, and the rhythmic serenade of cicadas filled the night air. When the red haze had cleared his vision, he placed his hand on top of his sister's. "I'll take care of Mike Matisse."

Dark circles ringed her eyes. "John, tell me you won't do something stupid."

"I won't." He stalked to his Jeep. "I'm going to do something smart." Under his breath, he murmured, "I'm going to bury Mike Matisse."

———◆———

Mike stood in his second-floor office and watched the hustle and flow of customers and workers on the casino floor. Scattered throughout the casino, security kept an eye open for card counters and any other dumb fucks who thought they could beat the house. Some of these employees worked for him outside the casino when he needed private business taken care of. He usually hired his people from the reservation, but three days ago, he'd hired Billy Joe Strickland. Mike watched Billy Joe's blond head as the cocky kid strutted up and down the floor as though he owned it. Mike smiled. He'd hired the kid just to see the expression on John's face.

Mike's smile faded. He needed to do something about Iron Hawk. But it wasn't so easy to make the head of the police department disappear. If something happened to him, the Bureau of Indian Affairs and the Fucking Bureau of Investigation would be crawling all over the reservation. Mike didn't need that, not now, not when he was preparing to run for office.

His gaze settled on Joseph Bearkiller's granddaughter. How many of Iron Hawk's secrets did she know? Mike knew the policeman was tight with the woman's grandfather. Had the old man told his granddaughter anything that might be useful?

Running a hand over his dark blue suit and smoothing

back his hair, Mike started for the private elevator that would take him down to the casino floor.

The noise had picked up as the crowd from Pierre and surrounding areas poured in. Emma stood at the bar, waiting for a drink order. Ed, his floor manager had let him in on a little secret. Hired to serve drinks, Emma had a secret desire to run a blackjack table. Ed had informed him she came to work early to observe the tables.

Matisse walked up behind her and placed a hand on her waist. "Good evening, Emma."

She jumped. Her breasts bobbed under the snug-fitting white blouse. All the employees, male and female, wore white shirts and black pants or skirts. Mike hated the outfits. He'd wanted the women to wear deerskin dresses, but when the employees—especially the women—put up such a stink, he'd conceded. No one could say he didn't take his employees' suggestions into consideration and that he wasn't a reasonable boss. His only demand was the women wear only skirts—short skirts. Men liked pretty legs; the more leg shown, the more money spent.

"Good evening, Mr. Matisse," Emma said.

A slight tremor in her voice made him smile. "Now haven't I asked you to call me Mike?"

Her lids fluttered like a bat caught in a net. "Yes, Mike."

"Learning much about running a table?"

Her eyes widened just a fraction, but otherwise, she kept her face blank. "A little. I'm learning on my own time," she said in a rush.

"Industrious, aren't you?" He smiled down into her face. "We might be able to get Ed to teach you how to run a blackjack table for a few minutes a day."

Her face brightened. "I'd like that."

"How's your grandfather?"

"He's fine."

"Heard you had a houseguest. I think I met her at the last council meeting. What's her name?"

Emma frowned. "Zora."

"That's right, Zora. She seems like a pretty put together lady. Runs a magazine I heard. Must make lots of money. Not like you and me."

Emma's face clouded. "She's got her problems."

Mike raised a bushy eyebrow. "What problems could a rich woman like that have?" He raised a hand to Ed as the other man walked by.

"She's just got her problems." Emma turned away. "How much longer on the drinks, Teddy?"

The bartender held up a hand.

Mike remembered the wild look in Zora's eyes when he'd walked into Lydia's shop earlier that afternoon. She'd been holding his bracelet—no, clutching it.

He felt Emma's intense gaze on his face and realized he'd mentally drifted away. He cleared his throat. "How's old Chet?"

"He's home from the hospital."

"Doing better, huh?"

She shrugged. "I guess." She glanced over her shoulder to the bar.

"Who's helping him out at the farm?" His gaze ran over her compacted form. "You?"

She drew back, a look of disgust etched on her face. "No way. John fed the animals while Chet was in the hospital. I guess he'll continue until the old man gets on his feet."

"Emma!" the bartender yelled at her and pushed her tray toward the end of the counter. She glanced at Mike. "Gotta go." She hesitated. "You won't forget to talk to Ed, will you?"

He'd already forgotten. His thoughts were on the job he had for Billy Joe. "No, of course not."

———◆———

It was dark by the time John pulled into Chet's driveway.

Every light in the house was lit. A smile pulled at John's lips. Zora must be here. Chet normally sat in the darkened living room with only the light from the television as company.

As much as John wanted to see Zora, he detoured to the barn. If he set foot in the house, Chet would jaw for two hours and John would never get the animals fed.

Stepping into the dark barn, he reached mechanically for the lantern inside the door. It wasn't there. It took a moment for him to realize the lantern must be outside in the yard where he'd laid it when he discovered Chet's body. He'd always come during the day to feed the animals.

He walked through the dark barn by rote. The horses snickered in greeting. John made a mental note to let the animals out so they could run around the corral while he mucked out their stalls.

He cursed his stupidity for not bringing a flashlight, but he'd counted on the lantern being where it usually was. He walked toward the area where he judged the old man had lain. Spotting the lantern overturned in the grass, he stooped to pick it up.

The clouds moved across the sky to obscure the crescent moon.

The lamp's glass exploded in his hand. He dove to the ground. Another bullet tore up the ground a foot from his body, stirring up clouds of dirt. He tried to judge the location of the shooter while cursing up a blue streak. He'd left his rifle in the Jeep and his 9mm in the glove compartment. He hadn't figured he'd need them to feed the cows. Blood oozed down his face from a piece of glass biting into his cheek. Who the hell was shooting at him and was it the same person who'd shot Oscar?

CHAPTER SEVENTEEN

"**D**ID YOU HEAR THAT?" CHET half-rose from his seat in front of the television.

"Hear what?" Zora raised her voice to be heard over the sound of the television. She put her finger in the middle of the one-month-old issue of *Haute* magazine to save her place. "I didn't hear anything." How could she? The volume of the TV was turned up to the max.

"I heard gunshots," the old man said and reached for a shotgun propped by the front door.

Never comfortable around guns, Zora scooted back on the sofa and eyed Chet with alarm. Had the old guy gone nuts? "Maybe it's the show you're watching." An old black and white western played out across the screen.

But Chet wasn't listening. His attention was centered on the yard. "Turn off some of these blasted lights." He flipped the television off. When she rose to do his bidding, he shouted, "Sit down, girl, before you get yourself killed."

She plopped down on the sofa, irritated. What did he want, for her to turn off the lights or sit down? Her mouth dropped open when the old guy fell to his belly, crawled to the lamp and pulled the cord from the outlet. They were immediately plunged into darkness. The fool was serious. He really thought someone was outside shooting.

When the back door banged open, Zora's heart jumped into her throat. She let out an involuntary squeal. The lights in the kitchen went out.

"Don't shoot, Chet. It's me, John."

A shadow loomed in the doorway between the living room and the kitchen.

"What's going on out there?" Chet whispered.

"Someone took a couple of shots at me."

John touched her shoulder and Zora jumped, startled. How had he found her in the dark?

"Stay down on the floor," he said. His warm breath fanned the side of her face.

"Where's your gun?" John asked Chet.

Both Chet and Zora spoke almost at the same moment.

"You're no—"

"In my hands," Chet said.

"Well, point it down and hand it over. I left mine in the Jeep—Fuck!"

"What?" Zora asked, lowering herself to the floor.

"I left my car unlocked. Both of you stay down until I get back."

The front door eased open and John was gone.

Who was out there shooting? Zora turned her head in the direction of the kitchen. Could they get into the house? Had John locked the back door? Hell, there probably weren't any locks on any of the doors. If this had been New York… but it wasn't.

From across the room, she could hear Chet wheezing. "Are…are you okay?" Oh, my God. Don't let this old man die on her.

"I'm fine."

He didn't sound fine. In fact, his breathing alarmed her.

Not wanting to scare him, she said, "Chet, I'm coming over." She started to crawl toward him.

"I know that," the old man complained. "Sounds like a herd of buffalo."

Indignant, Zora stopped before her sense of humor kicked in. "Well, this buffalo is worried about you."

When she reached his side, she felt for his pulse. The

irregularity of his heartbeat matched hers. She tried to remain calm. "Who do you think is out there?"

"Some fool shooting coyotes."

And they mistook John for one? Zora didn't think so.

After what seemed like hours, John opened the front door and stepped into the house. His large presence filled Zora with a sense of comfort.

"Did you find him?" Chet asked.

"No."

Zora could hear him fumble around in the dark then the room flooded with defused light. John had pulled an old blanket that covered an even older chair across the lamp's shade. He lifted the old man to his feet and helped him onto the sofa.

"You two okay?" John's eyes skimmed over Zora's body.

Zora glanced pointedly at Chet. "I am."

"What about you, old man," John studied Chet. "You okay?"

Chet grinned, his few teeth flashing in the muted light. "Right as rain. That shot jump-started the old ticker."

Zora eyed him narrowly. His color seemed to be okay and he wasn't wheezing any longer. Still... "I'm going to spend the night out here."

She had John's full attention. "So am I. I want to check out the barnyard at first light. You guys get some rest." He walked out the front door, closing it quietly behind him.

"Who's going to be able to rest? Shots going off all times of night." Mumbling, Chet picked up his oxygen canister from beside his television chair and walked down a small hall toward what Zora presumed was his bedroom.

She studied the front door then followed John outside.

———◆———

John stood in the shadow of the porch's column, staring out over the landscape. Somewhere to the right, an owl screeched. The screen door opened, and Zora stood framed in the muted living room light.

"Get out of the door."

She flinched at the harshness in his voice, but he didn't care. He wanted to keep her safe, not for her to become target practice for some nut.

She quickly closed the door and moved to his side. "Was someone out hunting?"

He snorted. "Yep. Hunting me."

Her head snapped up. "Who would want to shoot you?

"Matisse is my guess."

"But why? What have you done to him?"

John shrugged. "Maybe I'm getting too close."

She touched his shoulder, turning him so she could look in his eyes. "Too close to what?"

He shook his head. "Nothing." He didn't want to bring her into this mess with Matisse. She'd be gone in a few days. It was better to keep her out of it.

"He didn't impress me as the type of man to go around shooting people."

"He isn't. He lets someone else do his dirty work." John scanned the surrounding darkness, looking for anything that moved. He replayed the shooting in his head. He'd heard a motorcycle's engine start up a few moments after the last shot.

Her brown eyes searched his face. "You don't have to protect me, John. I want to know what's going on."

He sighed and stared out over the dark landscape. An owl hooted in a nearby tree, but otherwise, everything was silent, too silent. What the hell. It wasn't as though she could do anything about the problems here on the reservation. "Matisse is taking money from the casino for his own personal use."

She was quiet for a moment. "Can you prove this?"

"Nope."

"How do you know it's happening?"

He bit back a sharp oath. "Because I have eyes. That casino is packed every night, but the Boys and Girls Club doesn't have enough money for instructors or supplies. We don't have enough money to pay for a doctor at the clinic. Hell—" He banged on the porch post. "We don't have enough money to staff the clinic with a nurse three days a week. Families have to drive eighty miles for medical care and most don't have cars." He saw the pity in her eyes and turned away. His people didn't need pity. They needed action.

"What about the Federal government? Don't they supply health care on the reservation?"

"It just barely scratches the surface, and sometimes by midyear, those clinics are out of money. That's why the people voted to have a casino on Indian land. They hoped to have better services, provide essentials for their children they didn't have growing up. Now Matisse is using that money for himself. Probably to fund his campaign."

"Can't you report him?"

"To who?"

"To the Federal government. To the newspapers. There's got to be something you can do."

"Not without proof."

"Oh." She sagged against one of the posts. "Yeah, I guess you'd need proof."

"Yep, You do." All of a sudden, he wished he smoked again. He needed to do something to relieve the tension that coiled through his body. His fingers twitched to hold a paint brush, or if his muse still hadn't returned, he'd go up into the mountains to mediate. Something he hadn't done since he was a teenager.

Thinking about the mountains brought to mind his talk with Steven Foley. "The pathologist said the bones were human and probably female."

She gasped. "Did he say how old they were?"

"Not without running additional tests."

"How long will they take?"

John tried to see Zora's face, but the darkness made it impossible to read her expression. He sensed the tenseness in her body. "Why so much interest in these bones?"

She was silent for much too long. He knew what would come out of her mouth would be a lie or partially the truth.

"It isn't every day a city girl falls down a hole and finds a human bone."

Her flippant tone told him what her words didn't. She was much more interested than she wanted him to know. He swore under his breath. He'd opened up to her, but she wasn't ready or willing to do the same. Why hadn't he believed his gut? This woman was bad medicine. He stepped off the porch. "Keep the doors locked."

"You're leaving?"

He imagined he heard a plea in her voice. Impossible. Zora Hughes only cared about herself. "I'll be in the barn." Why did this woman have to enter his life at this particular time? She had secrets. Secrets she didn't trust him enough to share. Some men were stupid. They always picked women who were bad for them. He'd just joined the ranks of the stupidest.

———◆———

The sun faded fast as John made his way back to the reservation the next evening. He'd spent most of the day at the state crime lab in Pierre. Behind Chet's barn, he'd found two .308 bullet casings. Since both Remington and Winchester rifles fired that size ammo, he decided to switch tactics. Whoever had fired the shots rode a motorcycle. There were few motorcycles on the reservation. It might be easier to start his investigation with those suspects.

He flipped open his cell and speed-dialed Oscar's number. His deputy, his voice eager, answered on the first ring.

"What type of gun does Billy Joe own?"

"Uh… I don't know. What's he done now?"

"Maybe nothing. Someone took a shot at me out at Chet's place." A huge buzzard circled low on the horizon, its dark wings almost blending with the gathering dusk. "Does he own anything other than that beat up F150?" John asked.

"Don't think so. Why?"

"'Cause I thought I heard a motorcycle out on the property immediately after the shots were fired."

"Want me to ask around?"

The buzzard disappeared from sight. "Yep, but don't tip him off." John disconnected, just in time for another call. He glanced at the display and grunted in satisfaction before saying hello.

"Dad, do you want me to cook—"

"No," John said quickly. "How about we grab a hamburger at the Iron Horse?"

———

It was a slow night at the diner. John, Laura, Danny Matisse, and his friend Mac were the café's only customers. The boys played pool.

Laura cast glances in their direction.

"You still seeing Danny?"

Realizing she'd been caught staring, Laura flushed. She shook her head. "He's a jerk."

Like his daddy. Words John didn't utter. He was just grateful she'd come to her senses. "What'd you do today?"

She shrugged. "Hung out at Emma's house. Practiced my cooking."

John kept his face blank. "That's good." He took another bite of his dry bison burger. "How's Joseph?"

"Okay." She glanced at him. "You know something,

Dad? Emma's right. That woman from New York—"

"Zora," John supplied.

"Zora is weird."

"How so?" At the sound of laughter, John glanced toward the back of the café. Danny and Mac racked up balls for another game.

"She has a shrink."

John's head jerked around. Laura had his full attention and she knew it. She took her time spinning the yarn. "She has these dreams—"

"Whoa, what are you talking about?"

"Zora," Laura said impatiently. "Emma overheard her on the phone talking to her shrink."

"And Emma listened to their conversation?"

At least Laura had the decency to blush. "She—"

John held up his hand to stop anything else his daughter might say. As much as he wanted to hear it, he wanted Zora to tell him, not get it as second-hand gossip.

"But Dad, she has these dreams…"

He glared at his daughter. "Finish your dinner." His appetite lost, John pushed his half-eaten burger aside. Laura's appetite must have suffered the same fate because she dragged soggy French fries in and out of a pool of ketchup and shot him black looks.

So Zora was seeing a shrink. Could it have anything to do with why she'd come? He'd always felt her hunting up relatives was a flimsy reason for leaving a job and showing up in South Dakota. People who did impulsive things like that were usually running from something or someone. He pushed Zora from his mind. He had more important things to think about, namely, who tried to kill him last night. "Does Danny have a motorcycle?"

Laura's fingers paused. She eyed him from beneath pencil-thin eyebrows. "Why?"

John shrugged. Billy Joe might not have the money for a motorcycle, but Danny Matisse did. "Just curious."

He could see the wheels turning in her mind. She was angry with him for not letting her gossip about Zora, and she knew he didn't ask idle questions. It would be just like her to retaliate by not answering.

He signaled for Betty to bring the bill. Best to let Laura mull over his motives without seeming to be too interested in her answer. When Betty appeared with the bill, he turned to his daughter. "Sorry, did you want dessert?"

She shook her head.

He glanced at the bill then handed Betty two twenties. "Keep the change."

The waitress gave him a big grin.

"His father bought him a new Kawa... Kawa..." Laura frowned, struggling over the name of the motorcycle.

A Kawasaki. John knew some of the models were loud and could be heard from a long distance. But did Danny's bike have the power? "Some of those toys can barely hold their own on the road." He pushed himself out of the booth.

"He says it's a 750."

John nodded nonchalantly, not looking at the pool players as he followed his daughter out the door. That sounded about right.

———•———

Mike loved a mystery. And Zora Hughes with the secrecy that surrounded her was a mystery. One that he wanted to solve.

She was in the outer office with his secretary, Evelyn, studying a large map of the reservation that hung on the back wall. He could hear bits and pieces of their conversation as he tried to concentrate on the papers in front of him.

Ever since he'd seen the black woman in conversation with Lydia and the two of them cradling that bracelet, his antenna had been twitching. Once John's dispatcher had unwittingly told him about the bone Zora had found in the cave, his interest had shifted from Iron Hawk to Zora Hughes.

Now, he gave up the pretense of work and strolled into the outer office.

The two women's heads almost touched as they bent over the map they'd obviously taken down and placed on Evelyn's desk. Evelyn's family had been on their land for as long as Little River had been a reservation, over a hundred years. Mike had hired her because she knew everyone and was well respected. He knew she also considered herself to be the reservation's unofficial historian.

"So what are you ladies up to?"

He caught a flash of wariness in Zora's eyes when she lifted her head. His antenna, already humming with curiosity, began to quake.

"Just studying the boundaries and layout of the reservation," Zora said.

"There's a more recent map in my office," he said.

She smiled. "Actually for what I need, this one is adequate." She turned to his secretary. "Thank you, Evelyn."

Evelyn nodded. "If you need any more help, just come back."

Zora smiled, nodded at Mike and walked out of the office.

He stared at the frosted pane in the door for moment after it closed. Acid seemed to be burning a hole in his gut. He turned to Evelyn, who'd resumed her place behind her desk. "What did she want?"

Without looking at him, Evelyn started to type. "She needed to locate a lake."

Mike frowned. "A lake? What for?"

His secretary shrugged. "She didn't say."

He scrutinized her face for any indication of a lie. Her features were as guileless as a baby's.

Emma had told him Zora was on the reservation attempting to locate her ancestors. Her interest in a body of water didn't quite mesh with her efforts to fill out her family tree. He studied the map. *Unless she planned to claim a parcel of reservation land as her own.* Mike laughed to himself. Why would someone from a bustling city like New York want a barren piece of land?

His smile died. Maybe she was lying to Evelyn. He needed to find out why Ms. Hughes was really on the reservation.

———◆———

Zora slowed her car as she came around a bend in the road. Puffs of cottony clouds hung low in the noon sky and seemed to touch the road up ahead. A forest of dense hardwoods and pines bordered the road, making it impossible to spot a path. According to the landmarks Evelyn had given her, the turnoff should be within the next few yards, but maybe Zora had miscalculated. Maybe she'd missed it. Just when she decided to turn the car around and go back, she spotted what appeared to be a break in the trees.

Yesterday, she'd stood in the dried gully across from Chet's place and knew it wasn't the one. Even at its fullest it wasn't wide enough to be the river in her dreams. She'd almost given up in despair until she'd talked to Joseph, and he'd directed her to the tribal council offices.

She pulled the vehicle to the shoulder, parked then got out of the car.

As soon as she stepped onto the path, the forest seemed to envelope her in its stillness, no birds sang, no wind whistled through the leaves. Her feet made the only sound as she moved deeper. With each footfall, pine scents rose on the air from the bed of needles beneath her feet. Although the day was sunny, here in the woods, sunlight appeared only in splotches from breaks in the canopy of leaves overhead.

Her nerve endings hummed. At first, it was barely notice-
able, but the deeper she moved into the woods, the louder
the humming became until it vibrated in her ears like the
sound of a thousand buzzing bees. She stopped, afraid to
go forward, but unable to turn around and go back. Some
invisible force propelled her until she reached a glade. This
body of water that spread out before her was wider than
the stream that flowed past Chet's land. Sheltered by the
thick forestry, the water level was quite high, not evaporated into a puddle. Here, the sunlight was profuse, and
Zora sank cross-legged to the ground and turned her face
up to the sun's warm rays. A wave of dizziness washed over
her and she felt herself sinking into a dark void.

The humming suddenly changed, separating into voices,
loud angry voices.

Julia stood well hidden in the trees and watched as Trades with
Horses listened with growing impatience to an elder of the tribe.

"You insult my family," the elder said, "bringing that slave
woman to our village, and into your mother's tent."

"She is my wife. She is not a slave," Trades with Horses said.

Julia could tell from the stiffness of his body and the tone of his
voice he was very angry.

"My daughter was to be your wife. You shared the same blanket
as babies. Do you forget this?"

Trades with Horses bowed his head in acknowledgement. "I do
not forget, but the ways of the heart and the wishes of the family
are not always the same."

"My daughter is shamed," the older man shouted. "Who will
have her now, now that the chief's son has chosen another?"

Trades with Horses didn't answer and his silence seemed to
inflame the old man more. "You will never know happiness with
this woman. And your seed will be cursed, cursed to roam this
land without a spirit." The old man turned and stalked out of
the clearing.

Trades with Horses turned and stared straight at the copse of trees where Julia stood hidden.

———◆———

John spotted Zora's rental car on the side of the road as he made his way to Chet's place. Had something happened to the car? After pulling his Jeep off the road, he stepped out to inspect the vehicle. He walked around the convertible, looking for problems. No flat tires, no radiator leaks. When he poked his head in the car's open window, the keys were in the ignition. He opened the car door and sat in the driver's seat. When he turned the key, the car purred to life. With growing alarm, he stepped out of the convertible, scanning the road then the woods. Where was she? What would make her leave her car on the side of the road? Had someone picked her up? He hadn't passed her on the way, so she was either up ahead or… His gaze traveled to the dense woods to his right.

Securing his Jeep and Zora's car, he treaded carefully along the edge of the road, looking for anything that would indicate Zora had stepped off into the woods. He found it almost immediately—a fresh disturbance of vines and brambles. She'd entered the woods at this point. It wasn't hard to track her. It wasn't like she had tried to elude him. She'd left signs of her passage all along the way, a piece of cloth from a shirt, a broken branch. After about five minutes of getting scratched and stabbed, he stepped into a clearing.

She sat eerily still by the water's edge.

"Zora?" He didn't know why, but he moved toward her as he would a doe he didn't want to startle. "Zora," he called softly. Light glittered off the placid surface of the water, giving the area and the woman seated on the ground a surreal aura. He didn't touch her, but instead, sank to his haunches in front of her. Her eyes were open, but she didn't blink or show any sign of recognition. "Zora?" He touched her, more to reassure himself she was all right than to get her attention.

He saw the change in her eyes when she left the place she was in and became conscious of the here and now. She blinked twice then drew back from him.

"How…" She glanced around the clearing. "Where…"

"Are you okay?"

Abruptly, she turned and stared into the woods behind her. "Did you see…?"

Running his hand up and down her arm, he leaned forward and cupped her chin, turning her face around to his. "Did I see what?"

She shook her head, more, he thought, to clear it than in answer to his question. She made a move to stand and he helped her to her feet.

"What are you doing out here?" he asked.

She opened her mouth then snapped it closed.

"Is this about the dreams?"

Her eyes widened. "How…"

It was his turn to be evasive. He didn't want her to know she'd been the topic of gossip, but God knew how many other people Emma had told. "Does it matter?"

She tried to pull out of his arms, but he didn't let go. He wasn't giving up that easily. He cared about this woman and something serious was going on. Women didn't just ditch their cars and wander into unfamiliar woods.

"You're going to think I'm crazy," she said, more to herself than to him.

His heart sank at the seriousness of her tone. "We're all a little crazy."

Her head jerked up and she frowned.

He tried to give her what he hoped passed for a reassuring smile. "Trust me."

She studied the creek and the trees, shuddering. "Let's get out of here." Before he could agree, she turned, stumbled, and then headed back into the woods. He followed.

When they reached the road, he indicated they should sit in his service vehicle. Once seated, he turned to her. "Now tell me why you were out in those woods."

"I…was looking for answers." She glanced at the dense forestry just beyond the car. "I had to make sure it was all real and not my imagination."

What was all real? A cold tingle shot up John's spine. This conversation was veering out of the normal. She couldn't possibly believe dreams were real, but he had to hear her out. "Did you come to Little River because of the dreams?"

She stared out the windshield. "Yes."

"But there's more, right?"

She moistened her lips. That one gesture bothered him more than seeing her in a trance-like state by the creek. It spoke of uncertainty and fear. This wasn't the stubborn, opinionated Zora he was used to. He wanted back the vibrant woman he'd grown to love. Love? The word slipped so easily into his mind he knew it had been lurking in his unconscious for a while, waiting for him to acknowledge its presence. He leaned toward her and covered her clasped hands with his own. "Trust me, Zora."

It took a long moment before she spoke. "My therapist—" She looked at him quickly, possibly to judge how he'd react to hearing she was under the care of a shrink. "My therapist calls the dreams genetic memories."

John had never been big on therapists. A person worked out his problems by confronting the issue and moving on. For her sake, he tried to rein in his skepticism. "Genetic memories?"

She stared out the window, her body rigid, her hands clasped tightly in her lap. "I've—I have my ancestor's memories," the words coming out in a rush.

Right. What could he say to that bombshell? Nothing sprang to mind.

The silence lengthened. Overhead, a hawk squawked. John wished he were up there, without a care in the world.

"She was murdered."

He frowned. "How do you know this ancestor—"

"Julia."

"—Julia was murdered?"

"I saw it in one of the dreams," she said quietly.

"You saw her murdered in your dreams?" he repeated. Yeah, crazier and crazier.

"Yes." Her voice was soft, distant.

"How long ago did this—did this murder occur?"

"One hundred and fifty years ago."

John rubbed his forehead. "What good is finding out who murdered her?"

"I need to find justice for her so I can finally put her spirit to rest."

John groaned to himself. "You know the murderer is also dead, don't you?"

She gave him a narrow-eyed glare. "Of course I do."

He smiled. This was more like the Zora he knew. "I just meant it's going to be impossible to find the murderer."

"I know."

"So—" John threw his hands up in a gesture of frustration. "What's the point?"

She turned to face him. "I feel compelled to do so. I don't expect you to understand. I don't understand. But it's something Julia wants me to do, and I have to do it."

"Okay. So let me make sure I understand this. She comes to you in your dreams. She was murdered, and you want to identify the murderer?"

Zora nodded. "Yes."

"And let's just say, for simplicity sake, you see the murderer's face in one of those dreams, you won't be able to identify the killer. So you'll be back at square one." A missing piece of the puzzle clicked into place. "Let me guess, Joseph is going to try and contact her."

She must have sensed his skepticism because her eyes held a mute appeal.

Being Sioux, John had grown up with the folklore of spirits, but it didn't mean they really existed. Although, he had to admit since Zora's arrival, the line of distinction between real and spirit had blurred. In the last two short weeks, his deputy had been shot, John had driven his Jeep into a ditch after a waif ran in front of his car—a girl he hadn't been able to find—and Zora had fallen into a pit in a cave and found a human bone.

Bells went off in John's head. The cave, the bone, and Zora's preoccupation with knowing how old the bones were. He studied her. "You think the bone in the cave is…?"

"Julia's."

John studied the road through the car's windshield, noting how the sky met the horizon. He returned his attention to Zora, not letting her see the doubt in his eyes.

"What does Joseph have to do with this whole…" He made a circular motion with one hand. He wanted to say fiasco but refrained.

"I hoped he might have heard through oral history about the murder of a slave woman. Her being here was unusual enough."

"But he hadn't."

She shook her head. "No, neither he nor Chet knew of such a murder." She stared down at her short-nailed fingers.

The sun was now high overhead, and almost in recognition of the passing time, his stomach growled. "Let's get out of here and have some lunch."

She shook her head. "I can't eat." She reached for the door handle. "And I can't leave the car here."

"I have the keys." He opened his palm. "You left them in the car. I'll have someone drive it back to Joseph's."

She snatched them from his hand and stepped out of the Jeep. Leaning down into the open window, she said, "I'm okay. I just need some time to pull this all together."

"I'll follow you back to Joseph's."

She frowned. "Chet…"

"You can't go back out there. Until I find out who the shooter was from last night, it's too dangerous." He stared down the road and made a snap decision. "I'm bringing Chet to stay with Joseph for a few days."

Zora chuckled. "Chet won't like that."

"Tough."

"Go get him. I'll be okay. I'm going to go straight to Joseph's."

She held his gaze for a long moment then turned and moved toward her car. Her stride was long and confident, but John knew underneath that strong exterior was a frightened and confused woman. A woman who'd breached the hard shell he'd built around his emotions and pulled him, John Iron Hawk, a descendant of Crazy Horse, into her Alice in Wonderland world.

CHAPTER EIGHTEEN

———

ZORA HELD HERSELF TOGETHER UNTIL John took the turn off to Chet's place. Then, she jerked the car over to the side of the road. Her teeth chattered and her body shook until she thought she would fly apart and her soul scatter to the four winds.

She'd had a vision. There was no two ways about it. She couldn't call it a dream. She'd been wide-awake, and it had come on her so quickly she hadn't had a chance to prepare. The vision had been so real, she felt she could reach out and touch Trades with Horses. And the emotion she'd felt while watching him wasn't the emotion of an outsider, but the joy of a woman in love. She'd felt Julia's love for this man and it had been in full-blazing Technicolor. For that one moment in time, she, Zora, had become Julia.

Zora tried to remember the vision. It came to her in shattered fragments, first more emotion than substance. Trades with Horses had stood by the creek with an older man. Who was he? He'd argued with Julia's husband— something about the old man's daughter. Banging on the steering wheel in frustration, Zora tried to remember the old man's words. He'd said something about… a curse? That had been it. He'd placed a curse on Trades with Horses' descendants, a curse on her.

Was this what Julia was attempting to communicate to Zora? That she, Zora, was cursed? Well, she didn't need a one-hundred-and-fifty-year-old dead woman telling her what she already knew. Her life was in shambles. If she didn't get rid of the dreams and this obsession with Julia, Zora could kiss her job goodbye. And she missed her job and she missed her city. She felt as out of place here as an Eskimo in Aruba. But until she lay to rest her demons, Julia's demons, she'd be as lost in New York as she was here on Little River Reservation.

But could she help Julia? What did Julia want from her? As John said, all the principal players in this drama were dead. Okay, what if by some freak of nature, Zora identified the killer? What could she do with the information? Nothing. So what did Julia want?

Zora needed to talk with someone who was closer to the spirit world than she was. She headed toward Joseph's house.

As John sped along the main road to Chet's, the sight of Zora sitting in the clearing, so eerily motionless, played over and over in his mind. Was she on the verge of an emotional breakdown? Boy, could he pick 'em. His ex-wife had her own emotional issues. Now he was involved with another fragile soul.

His cell phone rang. "Iron Hawk."

"John, it's Foley."

John could hear the barely suppressed excitement in the pathologist's voice. "What's up?" John made a left turn onto the road that led up to Chet's piece of land.

"You know the bones you brought me the other day?"

"Yeah." Like he could forget.

"Well, I did the carbon dating on it."

Surprised, John slowed the car. "I thought—"

"I know, I know. I love solving puzzles. What can I say? You'll never guess how old this bone is."

Zora sitting eerily still by the creek flashed in John's

mind. "One hundred and fifty years."

The pathologist's breath came out over the airwaves like a hiss from a deflated balloon. "How did you know?"

"I'm a policeman," John said, hedging. "Listen, can you keep this under wraps for a while?"

Silence.

"Steven?"

Foley cleared his throat. "I've already completed a report and sent it to the chief examiner. Sorry, John. I had to justify the expense."

"It's okay. Just ask Dr. Edwards to sit on it as long as possible."

"Sure thing. Ah… John?"

John pulled into Chet's drive and shut off the engine. The house looked forlorn. "What?"

"What's the story behind the bones?

"I don't know. Let me get back to you." He ended the call and stepped out into the day's heat.

———◆———

When Zora pulled into the drive ten minutes later, Joseph waited for her on the front porch.

"What is it?" His worn hands gripped the arms of the wheelchair as she stepped onto the porch.

She studied his aged wrinkled face. Was her anxiety written on her face or was he psychic? "I found the creek."

He frowned.

"The creek in my vision, I found it."

"Around the bend from Chet's?" he asked.

"You know it?"

Wheeling his chair closer to her, he grasped her hand in his callused palm. "Your heart is racing."

She forced herself to take deep breaths.

"I know the place. I haven't been there since my youth, but it was a popular place for the young people to go and be alone." He smiled and a wistful expression filled his eyes.

She sat down on the first step but kept her back to him. She didn't want to see the pity in his eyes when she told him the rest. "I had a vision down by the creek."

He didn't interrupt her so she continued. "It was very..." She searched for a word that would adequately describe her feelings but failed. "...disturbing." Across the road, the sunlight played in the long blades of wheatgrass and a slight wind sent bolls of dust skipping down the road.

Lulled by the normality of the scene, she continued. "Julia, my ancestor, watched her husband and an elder argue by that creek. The elder..." Zora's voice cracked. "The elder placed a curse on Julia's husband and his future descendants."

She turned to gauge his reaction to her revelation. He stared, as Zora had earlier, across the road at the field. For one instant, Zora thought he was asleep with his eyes open, until he turned in her direction. A halo of blue ringed his black pupils, giving him an otherworldly appearance. She frowned. Had that anomaly been there before?

"There's no such thing as curses, right?" Zora searched his creased face for reassurance.

"Curses only work if the cursed believe in them," Joseph said.

Zora frowned. "But Julia must have believed. Why else do her memories keep passing through the generations?"

"Why else?" Joseph muttered. He cleared his throat and his gaze sharpened. "Why did you go to the creek?"

She looked away. His body might be infirm, but his eyes were as discerning as the eagles that soared over the mountains.

"Zora."

The gentle command of his voice brought her eyes back to his. "I had to prove I wasn't losing my mind. I had to know that something about these visions was real and not the hallucinations of a… of someone who's insane."

"And now?" he asked.

"I know the place is real. It looked the same as in my dreams. I've never been there before, so the dreams must be of things that actually happened." She stared out at the long dusty road that seemed to go on forever. To her muddled thinking, it represented time, no beginning and no end. "I know now Trades with Horses was cursed. What I don't understand is what Julia wants of me."

A vehicle emerged out of the dust of the road and turned into Joseph's drive. It was John's Jeep. Zora could see the shrunken form of Chet Tyler in the front passenger seat.

Joseph made a sound between a grunt and a groan. She realized she'd forgotten to inform him he'd have a houseguest.

———◆———

John filled a glass with tap water from the kitchen faucet. His broad shoulders strained against the white shirt until Zora could see the muscle definition underneath. He turned to face her as he gulped the water. Beads of sweat stood out on his face and neck, and she resisted the temptation to push away from the kitchen doorframe, walk over and run her tongue over his neck to taste the salt.

From the den, she could hear the indistinguishable voices of the two old men as they argued over a game of chess. "Do you think this was a good idea?" she asked, nodding toward the den.

John filled another glass and drained it before answering. "No other options. He doesn't have any folks close by. Besides, they'll keep each other company and out of trouble."

Zora nodded absently. "I guess you're right." She leaned against the doorjamb and stared down the hall. Her mind wasn't on the two old men, but rather what had happened this morning by the creek. How was she ever to find out about the curse? Wait for another vision and hope more would be revealed? The appearance of the visions was too irregular, too unpredictable. She couldn't just sit around and wait.

"Steve Foley called me."

She frowned. Had she missed part of his conversation? "Steve Foley?"

"The medical examiner." John rested his hip against the porcelain rim of the sink. "You were right. The bones were old."

Zora straightened. "How old?" She didn't dare hope.

"Over one hundred years old." His gaze was watchful, intent.

She closed her eyes, partly in relief her instincts hadn't been off, partly in sorrow for Julia, who'd been dumped in a cave and her loved ones left grieving.

"The Sioux buried their dead in trees, not in caves."

Her hands knotted. "*That* was not a burial. It was murder."

He nodded almost reluctantly. "I agree. But like I said earlier, what difference does it make now?"

She moved toward him. "That was my relative."

"We don't know that," he said.

"I know it," she said, thumping his chest with a finger. "I know it." He smiled and she drew back, confused. "Why are you smiling?"

He gripped her shoulders and pulled her toward him, kissing her quickly, but soundly. "Because you're once again that stubborn, headstrong woman I love."

She drew back and stared into his black eyes. "You love me?" It came out almost as a squeak.

One corner of his mouth lifted in a smile. "I love you."

"Are we going to get some food, or do we have to cook it ourselves?" Chet stood in the open door, his portable oxygen tank strapped on his shoulder and a cannula in his nose.

Joseph's wheelchair was just inside the entrance to the kitchen. His eyes darted between her and John, a look of pain darkening his eyes.

CHAPTER NINETEEN

Z ORA STEPPED AWAY FROM JOHN. Joseph had wanted John for his granddaughter, not for her, a stranger he'd graciously invited into his home. She felt as though she'd betrayed his trust. She *had* betrayed his trust. She moved to his side and knelt by his chair. "I'm sorry."

He held her gaze with his deep fathomless eyes.

She felt John's presence behind her. "Sorry for what?"

She rose and faced him. He wasn't going to like what she had to tell him. "I—"

"I asked her to help Emma." Joseph's wheelchair moved in front of her.

John's gaze moved from Joseph to her. "Help Emma do what?"

Zora opened her mouth to speak, but again, it was Joseph who spoke. "Help Emma win you as a husband."

Like laser beams of light, John's gaze swung to Zora. His expression shifted from confusion, to disbelief, to finally one of anger. "You agreed to this?"

God, it sounded so bad now. What had been a perfect solution in the beginning now sounded so mercenary. She'd sacrificed him for her own goal. She placed a hand on his arm. "John, I—"

He shook off her hand. "I'm not for sale." He held her gaze. "Not to Emma and especially not to you." He stalked around Joseph's chair, past Chet, who wheezed in confusion, and out the door.

Pain radiated through her chest. She closed her eyes to shut out the looks of accusation and pity from the two old men. The elder by the creek was right. She was cursed. She'd never know happiness because she was doomed to walk this earth making the wrong choices. She'd sacrificed the love of a wonderful man for a goal she couldn't possibly accomplish: bringing Julia's murderer to justice.

"Well, what's got his breeches in a bunch?" Chet maneuvered slowly around Joseph's wheelchair and sat down heavily at the kitchen table.

Zora's first impulse was to rush after John, but on the other hand, she was weighed down by the compulsion to explain to Joseph. He stared up at her with such sorrow in his dark eyes. Sorrow she'd put there.

John would have to wait.

She sat at the kitchen table and turned a chair so she was eye level with Joseph. "I won't lie to you. I'm—I'm attracted to John. It wasn't something I planned. God knows he's not the type of man I'm normally attracted to, but…"

"I told you, you old coot," Chet said, rocking back and forth with glee. "I could see it in their eyes back at my place. Hot enough to set fire to sagebrush."

Joseph silenced his friend with a glance then turned his mournful gaze back on Zora. "Emma would make a better wife for John. She is of the people."

So am I. But she didn't voice that thought. She didn't deserve John. "I know." She stared around the sparse kitchen, unable to meet his eyes, afraid he'd see how much she cared about John. She didn't belong here. What in the world would she do on an Indian reservation?

Maybe it was time to give up. Maybe Julia would be satisfied Zora had made the effort to come and tell a few people her story.

She rose. "I'll pack and head back to Pierre first thing in the morning."

"I will uphold my end of the agreement," Joseph said.

Frowning, Zora turned from the doorway. "I didn't uphold mine, so that lets you off the hook."

Joseph said something Zora missed as she moved down the hall toward the den. It was time to move on, but first, she needed to see a woman about a bracelet.

———————

John removed his sunglasses when he stepped into the Iron Horse. The blast of cold air felt good on his flushed face, a flush not just from the day's heat.

He stepped up to the bar. What he wanted was a double whiskey, but he'd be damned if he'd let any woman, even one as desirable as Zora Hughes, drive him to drink. "Coke."

"How's it going, Chief?"

Turning his head, John stared down into Billy Joe's glassy, unfocused eyes. He appeared to have started his drinking early.

Without speaking, John picked up his Coke and moved toward one of the booths, leaving Billy Joe standing in the middle of the floor. His buddies laughed.

Didn't these kids—men, John amended, have jobs? Or did they just hire themselves out to the highest bidder?

"You think you too good to speak?" Probably spurred on by his friends' laughter, Billy Joe followed John to his booth.

His companions watched from the back of the café. Billy Joe, in John's experience, was one of those people who needed the courage of a group behind him. He'd never have approached John if he were alone.

"What type of rifle do you own?" John asked, intentionally raising his voice to be heard back by the pool table. He didn't look at the young man but continued to drink his Coke. He watched the gang. Billy Joe must have communicated his unease to them because they shifted restlessly, throwing anxious glances at each.

"What concern is it of yours?" Billy Joe's voice lacked its earlier confidence.

John drained his glass and rose. "Just curious." He strolled to the exit. "By the way, give my regards to your boss."

He didn't wait for a response before he stepped out into the sunlight and put on his sunglasses. He felt a little better.

———◆———

Mike smiled into the phone, nodding appropriately, even though William Talbert couldn't see his body language. Mike needed the committee chairperson's support if Mike was to be the next senatorial candidate from South Dakota. "You're so right," he said.

Having picked up some disturbance in the outer office, he swung his feet off the desk, "As I mentioned before, my family history is impeccable."

Billy Joe appeared in the door. Wild-eyed, the boy looked like a cross between a mad dog and a spooked horse.

"Will, let me call you back. Some emergency has come up that needs my immediate attention." He disconnected the call before Peterson could reply. He winced, hoping the abrupt ending of the call hadn't hurt his political chances. He was grateful Billy Joe had the good graces not to start blabbing while Mike was on the phone. "What the hell do you want?" Mike slammed his office door shut once Billy Joe was inside. "Haven't I told——"

"Iron Hawk knows."

Mike stepped out of the range of the man's spittle. "What do you mean, he knows?"

"He knows," Billy Joe repeated. By now, he was pacing around the room, his hands waving up and down in an agitated manner. "He was over at the Iron Horse, and he asked me what kind of rifle I own."

The punk interrupted his call with Patterson for this shit? Mike narrowed his eyes. Billy Joe was one step away from spilling his guts to the wrong person. Mike patted the boy on his shoulder. "You're letting your imagination run away with you."

Billy Joe shrugged off Mike's hand. "I want my money now."

Mike studied the white boy's face. His neck was beet red and the veins stood out on his forehead and throat. Mike again recalled the image of a rabid dog. "You'll have your money."

Billy Joe nodded. "Tonight, and I don't want to be involved in any more of your messes."

Mike smiled. "Tonight."

———◆———

As Zora waited for Lydia to finish with a customer, she bided her time by studying the painting of the Indian Chief. She couldn't explain why the depiction spoke to her on such an elemental level. The artist had eloquently captured the despair of the old man and his longing for a time that would never come again.

"Why don't you buy this one, too?"

Lost in the painting, Zora hadn't heard Lydia's customer leave.

"I could give you ten percent off as a going-away present," Lydia said.

Zora turned to study the older woman. "How did you know I was leaving?"

Lydia shrugged. "You've been here for what—a week? Ten days?"

Had it been that long? It seemed like she'd just arrived. But it felt as though she'd known John Iron Hawk all her life.

"I figured you'd be leaving soon. Little River is not like

New York."

Zora took one last look at the painting before facing Lydia. "I want to buy the bracelet."

Lydia's head jerked in surprise. Her gaze flew to the display case as though she wanted to reassure herself the bracelet was still there. "It's not for sale."

Zora smiled wryly and walked toward the display window. "Everything's for sale. You just have to know the right price."

In their bed of black satin, the stones beckoned to Zora. She placed a hand on the glass, hoping to feel the connection. She wasn't disappointed. A not unpleasant chill snaked up her arm to settle in her chest. "You never mentioned how it came into your possession."

"It was given to me for safekeeping. Not that it's any of your business."

Zora wrenched her gaze away from Julia's bracelet and instead studied Lydia. The woman's chest rose and fell in anger and something else Zora couldn't place.

"Who gave it to you?"

Lydia clamped her jaw shut and folded her arms across her chest.

Trailing her fingers over the belts, Zora moved back to the paintings, ignoring Lydia's stubbornness, feeling she could outwait John's sister. She'd waited a long time for answers. What were a few more minutes? "It first belonged to my ancestor. A wedding gift from her husband Trades with Horses."

The muscles in Lydia's jaw rippled, but she didn't utter a word.

"I found her bones in a cave in the mountains above Chet's farm." Zora studied Lydia intently, wondering how much of the story she already knew. "John said the Sioux don't leave their dead in caves. So that means she was murdered."

"She could have accidently fallen into the cave," Lydia

said.

The vision of Julia being strangled to death in the river flashed in Zora's memory. "No, she was murdered then tossed into the cave." Zora glanced at Lydia. "The question is who murdered her? And why? Did the murderer take the bracelet? That's why I need to know who gave it to you."

"The bracelet could have passed through several hands since your ancestor's death." The bravado in Lydia's voice was in contrast to the paleness of her face. Her eyes darted to the shop's front door. Zora followed the woman's gaze. There was no one out there.

"Let it go," Lydia said. "Go back to New York. Forget about the bracelet. Your ancestor's dead. You can't change that."

She hadn't planned to antagonize Lydia. All she'd wanted was the bracelet, but she couldn't stop the words that poured out of her mouth like a hydrant with a busted main. "Do you think she was murdered for the bracelet? Or…" Zora paused as the vision she'd had by the creek replayed itself in her head. Her body jerked as everything coalesced in her brain. "Julia's husband was someone else's intended. She was murdered because someone wanted her husband. The husband they felt was rightfully their daughter's." Zora glanced toward the display case and the bracelet. "The bracelet they felt was rightfully their daughter's."

Lydia's hand flew to her throat. "Matisse," she whispered.

"Matisse?" Zora repeated. "What does Mike Matisse have to do with this?"

Lydia walked to within five feet of Zora, lowering her voice as though the store were crowded with customers. "Forget about the bracelet. Go back to New York and pretend you've never seen it."

Surprise and unease whispered through Zora's body. "I can't do that."

"If you value your life, you can."

She jerked back as though John's sister had turned into a hissing snake.

Lydia turned on her heels, raced to the store's entrance, and flung open the door. "Now get out before you get both of us killed."

Killed? Zora could only stare at the woman. Who was going to kill them? "Lydia, what does Mike Matisse have to do with the bracelet?"

But Lydia was pushing Zora out the entrance. Before she could take a step to re-enter, Lydia locked the door and flipped the sign to *Closed*.

———

All consuming silence greeted Zora when she stepped inside the Bearkiller residence later that afternoon. Before she could lose her nerve, she knocked on Joseph's bedroom door. She had to apologize. She couldn't leave until she'd spoken to him. In the short time she'd been on the reservation, he'd become like a beloved grandfather.

He didn't answer.

Emma's truck had been missing from the drive. Since Chet wasn't here either, Emma must have taken the two old guys out.

Zora leaned her forehead on the door, sighed, and then headed for the den to pack.

Joseph must hate her. She'd betrayed his trust. John was in love with her not Emma.

Zora paused as she folded a blouse. The rugged lines of John's face had softened when he said he loved her. She hugged the fabric to her chest, an answering smile tugging at her lips. *He loved her.* The smile faded as she remembered the harsh lines and cold blackness of John's eyes when he'd found out about her bargain with Joseph.

She started shoving her clothes into the suitcase. She

needed to leave quickly before Joseph returned. She'd have to go back to the motel. Somewhere close. She wouldn't leave the area without Julia's remains and without the bracelet.

Had she misjudged Lydia? Was the woman loco? What did Mike Matisse have to do with any of this? Zora had hoped Joseph would help her figure it out, but she couldn't ask another thing of him.

She leaned on the suitcase, tugging at the zipper to force it to close. The beige sleeve of one of her favorite dresses peeked out of the case. With a sigh, she unzipped the bag to stuff the offending garment inside.

"It's about time you left."

Zora jumped. The suitcase tumbled to the floor and her clothes scattered over the gray indoor-outdoor carpet.

Dressed in a pair of faded jeans and a plaid shirt, Emma stood just inside the door, leaning on the jamb. What happened to her beautiful clothes? Zora's gaze flew to the other woman's face. Had Joseph told Emma John was in love with her?

Rather than witness the hostility in Emma's eyes, Zora began picking up clothes from the floor. Maybe if she ignored the woman, she'd go away.

Emma stepped into the room until she faced Zora. "Where's Granddad and Chet?"

Zora froze, a pink Donna Karan blouse in hand. "I thought they were with you."

Emma shook her head.

Where could two handicapped old men have gone? And what were they doing? Zora's heartbeat kicked into overdrive.

———◆———

The sound of whispered voices made John grit his teeth. He'd been back from the Iron Horse Café for two hours.

In that time, the door to the department had opened and closed a gazillion times, the phone had rung twice that many, and Maggie had had an on-going conversation with someone for the whole time. He swiped his hand over his face.

How could Joseph have thought Emma meant anything to him? How could Zora have gone along with Joseph's matchmaking scheme? Zora knew John loved her. Okay, so maybe he hadn't said so before now, but she had to have known.

The door to the outer office opened and closed again.

"No!" Maggie's voice.

Someone muttered something too low for John to hear.

"What do you think…" Maggie's voice again.

More muttering by the unknown person.

"Well, you'd better tell John." Maggie's voice, higher now.

John closed his eyes and prayed for patience. He pushed back the desk chair and stalked into the main squad room. "Tell me what?"

Evelyn Singletary, Matisse's secretary, turned to face him, her mouth forming a round O.

"Tell him, Evelyn," Maggie prompted.

"Yes. Please tell me, Evelyn." *So I can go back to my office and pretend to work.*

"Uh…" She smiled apologetically. "It's probably nothing."

John narrowed his eyes.

"Well, Billy Joe Strickland came in this afternoon to see Mr. Matisse. He—he was upset about something. He wouldn't let me announce him. He just marched down the hall to Mr. Matisse's office."

John almost smiled.

"Mr. Matisse closed the door, but I could hear Billy Joe threatening him. When I questioned Mike about it, he told me not to worry, he had the problem under control."

"I figured, with as much trouble as we've had with Billy

Joe in the last few weeks, you ought to know about this," Maggie said. She folded her arms across her massive chest and nodded importantly.

"You did right telling me," John said. "I'll keep an eye on Billy Joe." He took Evelyn by the arm and ushered her to the door. "Let me know if he calls or comes by again."

"Thanks, Captain Iron Hawk."

"John's fine."

She smiled shyly. "John."

"Do you think we should give Mike round-the-clock protection?" Maggie asked after Evelyn left.

"Who do you suggest we get for the job?"

John could see when their manpower situation registered with her.

"Oh…"

"Mike Matisse can take care of himself," John said, walking back to his office. *If we're lucky, the two will kill each other and save the taxpayers some money.*

He closed his office door against any future interruptions. Around six o'clock, Maggie knocked and stuck her head in, her face clouded with sadness. "Something's happened at Joseph's house."

John sighed, picturing Chet clobbering Joseph with a chessboard.

"Joseph Bearkiller is dead," she said.

CHAPTER TWENTY

J OHN DROVE THE TWENTY MILES from police headquarters to the Bearkiller home in thirteen minutes. He'd told Maggie to call for an ambulance and try to locate Dr. Coben, the general practitioner who visited the reservation once a week. He cursed Matisse loudly and profanely as he sped along the highway. If the casino money had been used as it should have been, there'd be a clinic staffed with a physician on reservation land.

John barreled into the drive, stopping inches from Emma's truck. She ran from the side of the house as he jumped out of the Jeep.

"Around back," she shouted. "He isn't breathing."

John sprinted past her. How had Joseph gotten around to the rear of his property in a wheelchair?

The sweat lodge, an igloo-shaped structure draped with animal skins, had been constructed many years ago before Joseph's health had deteriorated. John stepped into the small dark interior. Sweat immediately popped out on his skin. Steam rose from a smoldering fire built in a fire ring in the middle of the lodge. He made out two figures, one hunched in a corner and the other bent over a lump on the dirt floor. The lump was Joseph's prone form.

"One one-thousand, two one-thousand," Zora croaked, her breathing harsh and her shoulders slumped, as she worked over Joseph.

He dropped to his knees on the opposite side of Joseph's

body. "Stop for a minute."

She sat back on her heels and her head sank in weariness.

John tipped the old man's head up to open an air passage. He placed his face near the old man's mouth.

"He started breathing twice on his own," Zora said.

He wasn't breathing now. John blew twice into Joseph's mouth. His chest rose and fell with each breath.

Placing one palm over another, John compressed the old man's chest. "One one-thousand, two one-thousand." He did thirty compressions then checked for breathing. None. *Where in the hell was the damn ambulance?*

———◆———

As it sped down the highway, the ambulance's flashing strobe sent red iridescent light skittering across the Jeep's windshield.

Emma rode in the ambulance with her grandfather. Zora and Chet had piled into John's vehicle.

Zora shifted in the passenger seat, periodically glancing at John's profile as they kept pace with the emergency vehicle. Two lines of concentration marred his forehead and the lines around his mouth were so deep you could hide a penny in them.

He glanced over his shoulder at Chet, who sat huddled in the back of the Jeep. "What were you two doing?"

"Uh…"

Zora could feel the old man's eyes on a spot between her shoulder blades. John turned his attention on her.

"What do you know about this?" His voice had that 'don't bullshit me' tone to it.

While she'd worked on Joseph, Chet, in his hysterical ramblings, had told her about the ill-fated attempt to call forth a vision. She couldn't believe Joseph had gone through with it. She'd told him repeatedly it was too dangerous.

She cleared her throat. "Not much, but I think Joseph was paying back what he thought was a debt. Though I didn't think he owed me anything…"

At the cold, hard glare John gave her, she shut up.

"What happened, old man?" John asked.

Zora could hear Chet shifting position behind her.

"Umm, Joseph was seeking a vision."

John frowned. "What kind of vision?"

"He was calling forth the spirits that walked the land a hundred years ago."

"Cut to the chase, old man."

"He was calling forth the slave woman who lived among the people many generations ago."

"Zora's ancestor?"

"Yeah," Chet muttered.

John grunted. "I told—"

"I think she spoke to him," Chet whispered.

Zora turned to face him. "He spoke to her?" The pulse in her throat was louder than the words she forced out of her mouth.

"I'm not sure—"

"Of course he's not sure," John interjected. "Because it didn't happen. The old man had a heart attack brought on by—"

John jerked around and glared at Chet. The Jeep weaved across the yellow line. Luckily, no other cars were coming. "Did he take something to induce the visions?"

"Ah… he took a little of the peyote mushroom."

"Goddammit." John pounded the steering wheel, making Zora jump.

"Listen, I know this is probably my fault," Zora said.

"You're damn right this is your fault." John's dark eyes shot sparks. "If you hadn't come here with your crazy ideas about seeing your ancestor in dreams—"

"Genetic memories," Zora said. "They're called genetic memories."

John made a rude sound in his throat but kept his mouth shut and his eyes on the road.

The anxiety in the car was as thick as the humidity outside. Zora huddled in her corner feeling guilty, miserable, and heartsick. How dare he make her feel responsible. She'd begged Joseph not to do it. He'd felt honor-bound even after learning of her attraction for John. She would never forgive herself if something happened to this very special man.

Mike Matisse stood at the large glass window overlooking the casino. Ed, the floor manager, escorted a couple toward a detention room. He'd found some suspicious magnetic device in the woman's purse, a device they might have used on the roulette wheel. Normally, Mike would have had the bouncer scare the shit out of them and toss them out of the casino after an ass-whipping, but what if word of what happened got out to the papers? He didn't need that type of attention right now.

The phone on his desk buzzed. "What?"

"Sorry to bother you, Mr. Matisse, but Emma Bearkiller is on line one. She says it's important."

"Take a message." He didn't have time for mealymouthed Emma.

"Joseph Bearkiller's had a heart attack, sir."

Mike heaved a sigh of impatience. If he ignored the call, the employees would make a big hoopla of it. Joseph Bearkiller might be old as dirt, but he still carried a lot of weight on the reservation. And if he recovered, Mike might need the old man's clout to help him get elected. He punched line one. "Emma?"

"Mr. Matisse…" Emma started to cry and babble.

Mike barely suppressed an irritated oath. "How's your grandfather?"

"I don't know if he's going to make it."

Mike picked up the letter opener on his desk and started cleaning under his nails. "Sorry to hear that."

"I was just calling, sir, to tell you I wouldn't be in to work for a couple of days. Just until…"

The old man lives or dies, Mike mentally supplied. "Take as much time as you need." He wasn't going to say her job would be here waiting on her. He wouldn't go that far. "So what happened?"

"He—he was in the sweat lodge…"

Mike almost laughed. "What was the old guy doing in the sweat lodge?"

"He was having a vision. You remember he's a shaman," she rushed on. "It was for that bitch—excuse me—for Zora, that woman from New York who's staying with us. Something about her ancestor."

Mike walked to the casino window. Ed was in an argument with the couple caught cheating and they were attracting a crowd.

"That's good, Emma. Talk to you later." He disconnected the call. What was that fool doing? If word got out about this disturbance Pierre would send a news crew. Mike threw the letter opener on the desk and marched to the elevator.

———◆———

Zora woke the next morning, feeling stiff and with a monstrous headache. She wrinkled her nose. Something ripe and pungent filled the house. Had someone forgotten to take out the garbage? She closed her eyes and willed her body back into the oblivion of sleep.

The night before had been a long one. She, Emma, Chet and John had left the hospital around two a.m. and only after they knew Joseph would live. John hadn't said two words to her in the hospital or on the ride home.

"You up, girl?"

Zora's eyes flew open. Chet stood by her bed. She groaned. "What is it?"

"It's nine o'clock," he said. "Time to get to the hospital."

She sighed. "Can I get some coffee first?"

"Already made it."

Was that what she smelled? Hopefully not. "Give me a minute to get dressed." When he stayed rooted in the door, she cocked her head and asked, "A little privacy, please?"

He looked sheepish. "Sorry." He shuffled off down the hall.

Twenty minutes later, they were on the road. "Why'd he do it?" she asked as the car sped down the highway toward Pierre and the hospital. When Chet shifted in the passenger seat, the sour smell of unwashed clothes and body wafted toward her. She breathed shallowly through her nose.

"He cares about you, girl."

Zora's hands tightened on the steering wheel. She didn't need to hear this. It only made her feel even more guilty and sad. She'd come to love Joseph. She even loved the smelly old goat opposite her. "I care about him, too."

"Well, he wanted to try and help you. Hell, he knew John wouldn't marry Emma."

Zora's gaze jerked from the road to Chet's wizened form. "Then why…?"

Chet shrugged. "He loves John like a son. He would have gone to the spirit world happy, knowing John was taking care of his little girl."

"Well, he might still end up taking care of Joseph's little girl," she mumbled under her breath. John sure didn't want to take care of her, not that she wanted him to. But she'd be a liar if she didn't admit she'd entertained fantasies of curling up next to that warm, hard body at night. She gave herself a mental shake. *Forget it. You'll be back in New York in a couple of days and you'll forget all about John Iron Hawk.*

She let Chet off at the front entrance to the hospital

while she parked the car. As she walked toward the hospital, she spotted John's self-assured and cocky swagger. Her heart leapt into her throat.

"What are you doing here?" he asked when she drew level with him. His black eyes were hard as coal.

"I brought Chet to see Joseph." She pointed to Chet's bent form waiting for her just inside the entrance.

"The hospital staff won't let anyone in but family," John said.

Narrowing her eyes, she studied him. "So, why are you here?" Was he counting himself as family? If so, then poor Chet should be allowed to visit his friend. For all they knew, Joseph might not make it, God forbid.

"I'm just checking on him."

He walked away. She caught up with him just inside the entrance. "Well, so are we."

As he strode toward the elevators, she motioned to Chet. She knew John wasn't going to hold the elevator for them when it came.

They followed him up to the third floor ICU but hung back as he talked with a nurse at the station. The woman, a petite blonde, smiled coyly up at John and hung on his every word. Zora snorted in disgust.

The individual rooms in the intensive care unit were built in a circle around a central nursing station, affording the nursing staff maximum observation of all the patients. Which one was Joseph's?

"This place gives me the willies," Chet said.

Zora glanced at him in sympathy. He'd been in this same unit two weeks earlier. When she turned around, Blondie was advancing on them and John was nowhere to be seen.

"There's a waiting room around the corner," the nurse informed them. Her nametag identified her as Molly Christian.

"Which room is Joseph Bearkiller's?" Zora asked.

"Are you family?" Molly asked, a we-are-here-to-serve

smile on her face.

"Yes!" Both Zora and Chet said at the same time. Zora gave him a wink and a smile.

The nurse's own professional smile dimmed. "Mr. Bearkiller is in unit six, but he's not receiving visitors at this time."

"How's he doing?" Chet asked.

Molly turned her gaze on Chet and her nostrils flared. Zora suspected the nurse had gotten a whiff of Chet's body odor. "He's holding his own."

Somehow that pronouncement didn't make Zora feel very confident.

"The waiting room is around the corner," Molly repeated.

Matching her steps to Chet's shuffle, Zora found seats for them in the crowded room.

"Do you think we're goin' to get to see him?" Chet asked.

"Yes," Zora said with more confidence than she felt. She flipped through several issues of outdated magazines before she couldn't stand it any longer. "I'm going to get some coffee. Want some?"

He shook his head and leaned back in the chair and closed his eyes. She wished she could be that relaxed. There was a vending machine outside the waiting room, but Zora shuddered, thinking about the coffee it produced. There had to be a Starbucks in the hospital. Her search took her past the ICU. She peeped in and didn't see Molly Christian at the station. That meant one of two things, Molly was with a patient, possibly Joseph, or Molly was out of the unit. As Zora walked boldly into the ICU, she was hoping for the latter.

The numbering of the units started at the door to the ICU. Unit six was almost directly across from the apex of the station, so if all nurses were present, their eyes would be trained on unit six. As luck would have it, only two nurses manned the station and they faced away from Joseph's unit.

She slipped into the cubicle and pulled the curtain partially closed behind her. Fully closing the curtain would look too suspicious and bring the staff quickly to investigate.

All the beeps from the electrical equipment, tubes, bags and assorted medical paraphernalia made Zora hesitate at the entrance. She swallowed and eased toward Joseph's bed.

He looked all his eighty-six years. Shriveled, he appeared small and washed out against the white bed linen. Round circular disks were taped to his withered chest. She followed the lines to the EKG machines where the blips of his life were penciled against moving paper.

"Joseph," she whispered.

His eyes flew open so quickly Zora took a step backwards. Only in horror movies was there such a dramatic awakening. Was he dead and his body in the grip of rigor mortis? But his tongue snaked out and moistened his cracked lips. She walked closer to the bed and placed a hand on his arm.

"Joseph? It's Zora."

His head turned slowly in the direction of her voice. His drug-dulled eyes focused then sharpened. He opened his mouth, emitting raspy croaks.

"Shh…" Zora said. "Don't speak. I just wanted to thank you for what you tried to do for me yesterday."

He attempted to say something else. She could see the strain reflected in his face, ropy veins in his neck stood out in relief. She leaned closer, patting his hand in reassurance. This didn't help, but in fact made him more agitated. The beeps for the machine measuring blood pressure and pulse quickened. Zora glanced toward the curtain. If she didn't do something to calm him, a legion of nurses would descend and drag her out of the unit.

"I'll come back later when you're feeling better." She turned to go, but his hand gripped her arm with almost an inhuman strength. He didn't want her to go. She glanced at the heart monitor—his pulse was still climbing.

"I'll stay, but you've got to remain calm." She removed his talon-like hand and placed it on his chest. "Take slow deep breaths."

He closed his eyes and complied. After a moment, his pulse dropped.

"What are you trying to tell me?" She placed her ear to his mouth.

"Mur…" he gasped.

Zora glanced up at him, frowning. "What?"

This time when he spoke, his voice was stronger. "Murder-r-r…"

Zora straightened. She'd never spoken to Joseph of Julia being murdered. Since finding the bone in the cave was at this point a police matter, she was sure John hadn't mentioned it either. But she was not going to fall into the trap of thinking Joseph referred to Julia's murder.

"Someone was murdered in the vision?"

He didn't speak but stared at her in mute appeal.

"Blink once for yes and two for no. Okay?" she said.

He blinked once.

She repeated her question. "Was someone murdered in the vision?"

He blinked once.

"Was the vision of a long ago time?"

He blinked once again.

At this rate it would take forever to get the information out of him. Zora suppressed her impatience. She was acutely aware of the traffic and voices outside the cubicle. Please don't let someone come in before she and Joseph finished.

"Did the woman in your vision look like me?" She pointed to her skin.

He blinked once.

Okay, so now they'd established it was a long time ago and the woman in the vision was a black woman. Where do they go now? In her vision, Julia was alone at the creek bathing. "Was the vision at the same creek we talked about?"

He blinked once again.

"Was her husband there?"

Joseph frowned.

The blood pressure machine beeped and Zora noted his pressure had increased. How long before his nurse came in to investigate? "Take deep breaths. Relax."

When his pulse dropped, Zora continued. "Was Julia alone?"

He blinked twice. No.

"Was the killer with her?"

The machine beeped. Zora glanced up at the machine. The blinking pulse beat at a furious rate. She glanced at Joseph; his eyes had lost focus. Oh, crap. At almost the same moment, the curtain across the cubicle swung open with a loud clink and Molly Christian stood in the opening.

"What are you doing in here?" she snapped. Not waiting for an answer, she removed her stethoscope from around her neck, placed both ends in her ears and moved quickly toward Joseph's prone form. "Take it easy, Mr. Bearkiller. Just calm down." After opening Joseph's gown, she pressed the round disc of the stethoscope to his chest. Finished, she removed the instrument from her ears and rewrapped it around her neck. "You'll have to leave."

"I'm sorry, I didn't mean…"

Joseph turned his head toward her. His lips lifted in an attempt at a smile. Zora touched his arm gently.

"Rest. We'll talk later." She raised an eyebrow at the nurse. A silent question.

"When Mr. Bearkiller has recovered and is moved out of ICU, it's possible you can speak with him at that time." She turned her back on Zora, indicating their conversation had ended.

———

Mike took another sip of his morning coffee and perused the *Capital Journal*. A stack of newspapers from all over the country were piled on the kitchen table. He'd made it a point since he'd decided to run for office to keep up on the country's news.

The scrape of metal against marble set Mike's teeth on edge, and he lowered the paper. Danny, his eyes red-rimmed from lack of sleep and too much drink, sat down at the table. Mike raised the paper, determined to ignore his son, but the stench of stale beer rose off the boy like stink from a landfill. One thing Mike couldn't abide was overindulgence in alcohol. There'd been one too many drunks in the family, and he was determined Danny wasn't going to be another one.

"What are you doing today?" Mike asked.

"Nuthin.'"

Mike gritted his teeth and felt a stab of pain in the region of his left jaw. He forced his jaws to unclench. The boy was worthless, and it was his mother's fault, spoiling him and giving the kid anything he wanted. Thank God she was dead and couldn't influence the boy anymore. Maybe he'd send Danny to Texas to stay with his distant cousin and get him away from the reservation.

The phone rang. Mike ignored it. Anybody of importance called him on his cell. Mike cussed under his breath as the kitchen chair scraped again when Danny rose to answer the phone.

"Yeah…" Danny said into the receiver. A pause. "I ain't seen him since yesterday afternoon."

Mike continued to read the paper.

After another few sentences, Danny hung up the receiver and sat back down at the table.

Mike lowered the paper. "What was that about?"

Danny shrugged. "Mac can't find Billy Joe. Seems he

didn't come home last night."

Mike folded the paper in quarters and began to skim the page. "Probably shacked up with someone he picked up."

"Yeah, that's what I told him."

"What's Mac, Billy Joe's keeper?"

Danny chuckled then rose and walked to the refrigerator. "Mac thought Billy Joe might've had another run-in…"

Mike snatched up the paper and brought it closer to his face. On page three, the caption, *Who is Jane Doe?* caught his attention. He read on. One-hundred-and-fifty-year-old bones had been found in a cave on Little River Reservation.

How had the papers gotten a hold of the story?

"What's wrong, Dad?" Danny's voice came from a long way off.

Pain shot through Mike's jaw. His blood hammered in his head.

He stood. The kitchen chair clattered to the floor.

"Dad?"

Mike grabbed his car keys and charged out of the house.

CHAPTER TWENTY-ONE

JOHN WALKED GINGERLY TOWARD HIS service vehicle with a hat full of eggs. He'd forgotten to check the laying hens the last time he was at Chet's place and now had over a dozen eggs nestled in his Stetson. He sniffed. The early morning air smelled like rain, about time. They hadn't had rain in weeks.

The radio came to life as he placed the eggs carefully on the passenger seat. He pulled a rag from the back seat of the Jeep, wiped his hands and discarded it before picking up the crackling radio.

"Sheriff, where you been?" Maggie's irritated voice came over the airwaves loud and clear.

"I'm feeding Chet's stock. What's up?"

"A couple of kids claim they saw a body at the old quarry."

John closed his eyes. He didn't have time for this. He'd gotten exactly two hours sleep the night before. He'd gone out on three domestic dispute calls and two car accidents. He had paperwork piled up on his desk that hadn't been looked at since Oscar was shot. Being a one-man operation was getting old. "I'm about ten minutes away."

He drove about a mile before he spotted Wilma Dull Knife hanging out her laundry. Her three-year-old boy dug in the dirt with a stick and her newest, now about a year old, clung to her skirts. Leaving the Jeep idling, John jumped out of the car, picked up the eggs and placed them

on Wilma's porch. At her quizzical look, he said, "Compli-
ments of old Chet." The look of disbelief on her face gave
him his first chuckle of the day. Chet had a reputation for
being a cantankerous old miser.

John's humor faded as he pulled into the abandoned
quarry. There'd been big plans for this site ten years ago,
but the Federal monies had dried up and the rest was history.

Three teenage boys, who should have been working
summer jobs, hung out by the entrance. They didn't rush
toward the Jeep as he pulled up, but instead hung back,
waiting for him to approach. A bad sign. It meant they
were guilty of something. But why hang around and wait
for him to show up? Why not call it in and disappear?

"Gentlemen," John said, as he drew level with them. He
only recognized one of the boys, Henry Picotte's son. He
couldn't recall the boy's name. "What we got?"

"A body." The speaker was a tall teen with a large Adam's
apple.

"Actually, all we saw was a hand," Henry's son said.

John studied them. They shifted uneasily under his scrutiny. "How far is this grave?"

"About two hundred yards in." This from the kid with
the prominent Adam's apple.

John reached into the breast pocket of his shirt and
pulled out a notepad and pencil. He turned to Henry's
son. "Your name?"

"Frank Picotte." Frank was short and stocky like his
father. Unlike the other two, this one met John's gaze head
on.

"And yours?" John asked the kid with the large Adam's
apple.

"Lee Black Eagle."

John turned to the boy who'd yet to speak. His eyes
shifted rapidly and his body twitched.

"Name?"

"Matt," he mumbled.

John stared at the young man. "Do you have a last name, Matt?"

"Bradley."

John wrote "check for priors" next to Matt's name. "What time did you discover this... this hand?"

The teens looked at each other, but not one would meet John's gaze. He turned his attention on Frank. "What time?"

"Ahem..." Frank glanced at Black Eagle. "About five a.m."

What the hell had they been doing out here at five? "When did you arrive?"

John held Black Eagle's eyes, so the teen was forced to look at him instead of Frank or Matt. "Around three."

John jotted that down. "What were you guys doing out here at that time of the morning?" This time, he focused on the weakest link. Matt's eyes shifted from John to his friends and back to John. His body twitched. *Coming down off a high.* "You know I can arrest you on suspicion. Do a drug screen on you." It wasn't legal, but they didn't know that.

No one spoke. "Okay, if that's the way you want to play it. I'll deal with that later." He flipped the pad closed and stuffed it back into his pocket. "Did you disturb the site?"

"Aw... no, sir."

This came from Frank, which John interpreted to mean that the site had been compromised. He cussed under his breath. "Wait here."

He found the grave. A human hand stuck out of the ground. No rings on the hand and no identifying marks other than bite marks from some animal. The same animals, rooting around, had uncovered the shallow grave, which probably accounted for the hand being visible. The animals hadn't had a chance to do more than nibble at the fingers, so John was able to determine there was little decay. With this heat, it probably meant the grave had been dug in the last twenty-four hours.

John sketched the gravesite and the surrounding area. He glanced at his watch—eight a.m.— then glanced at the sky. Dark, ominous clouds hung low on the horizon. He needed to get the crime lab team and the medical examiner over here from Pierre before the rain. Any evidence would be washed away. He also needed a tarp to throw over the hand to keep scavengers from feasting off it. He jogged back to the Jeep. He hadn't wanted to bring his vehicle close for fear of obliterating any tire tracks or footprints that might have been present. His cursory inspection of the scene told him no car had been driven up to the gravesite. The victim had been carried here, or he'd come on his own, and probably even killed here.

It was no surprise when he arrived back at the Jeep that the boys were gone. He knew where to find them. He called the crime lab and the ME's office.

Next, he called Oscar. "I need you." He outlined what he wanted his deputy to do. Closing his phone, he pulled a tarp from the Jeep and walked back to the grave.

———◆———

The miles between the hospital and Little River Reservation flew by, and Zora was no closer to figuring out how she would get back into the hospital to talk to Joseph. Chet snored in the passenger seat, giving her time to think. She believed Joseph truly had a vision, but she needed details. Had he seen the killer's face? John's voice popped into her mind. She could hear him asking, "What difference does it make if the killer can be identified? He's dead." Even though Zora knew the logic of this, she felt Julia wanted something more from her.

Zora pulled into the driveway behind Emma's truck. She shook Chet awake. "We're home."

He stared blankly at the little house, confusion then disappointment flashed across his face. He missed his home. Would she miss this place when she was back in New York?

The stench still lingered in the air when they entered the house. Chet shuffled to the den and Zora went straight to the kitchen to dump the pot of coffee and make a fresh one. How could anyone mess up coffee? She took a seat at the kitchen table and opened the morning paper while she waited for the coffee to brew. An article jumped out at her. Folding the paper in half, she started to read. Five minutes later, she had the answer to her question about what Julia wanted from her.

She picked up the house phone and dialed the *Capital Journal*.

Using the back of his hand, John wiped sweat from his face. He heaved another shovelful of dirt onto the tarp.

"That should do," Pete, the crime lab tech said, as he put down his shovel.

Pete dropped to his knees and used his gloved hands to scoop out the remaining dirt that surrounded the head. Within a couple of minutes, the face began to emerge.

John studied the outline as first the nose then the forehead cleared. Pete moved as deftly as a surgeon and cleared the dirt from around the mouth then the eyes. At last the full face emerged from the dirt. John grunted.

Pete glanced at John. "Someone you know?"

John nodded. "Billy Joe Strickland."

"You don't sound surprised," Pete said.

John shrugged. "This is pretty much how I'd expected him to end up. Dead or in prison."

Pete smirked. "Well, I'm sure he's glad he didn't disappoint."

Both men stared at the jagged third eye Billy Joe sported.

"A twenty-two?" Pete asked, raising his eyes to meet John's.

"Looks about right."

John scanned the grave and Billy Joe's body, looking for any evidence he could use to find the killer. Other than the bullet hole in the young man's forehead, nothing jumped out at him.

Pete rose and motioned for the techs from the ME's office. They'd stood off to the side while John and Pete had unearthed the body.

Brushing dirt from his jeans, Pete asked, "Any suspects in mind?"

"A few."

From the intensity of Pete's stare, John knew the crime scene tech expected him to name names. Something he wasn't ready to do.

The rumble of thunder caused both men to glance at the dark clouds.

"We'd better wrap this up quick," Pete said to the techs.

They nodded then rolled the body onto a rubber sheet. Billy Joe lay face down on the tarp, and John took the opportunity to study the back of the body. From the looks of the wound, someone had stood behind the man and shot him at point blank range. Not many people would let someone walk up behind them. They'd have to trust that person. "Who did you trust, Billy Joe?"

———◆———

Zora paced the floor of the police department. "Can't you reach him by phone?"

The dispatcher glared up from the magazine she'd been reading since Zora arrived twenty minutes ago. "John's at a crime scene. He'll be in when he gets here."

Zora bit back a retort. For some reason, the woman

didn't like her. Why? She'd never exchanged two words with the woman. She shrugged. She had bigger concerns than one rude individual. She rapped the wadded newspaper against her palm. How had the reporter learned about the bones? The only person other than John who knew about them was the pathologist. Had he leaked the story? For what purpose? She stared at the ink stains on her hands and willed herself to release the death grip she had on the paper.

The outer door opened and John stalked in. He was so absorbed in his thoughts he almost walked past her.

"John," Zora called.

He turned and a slow sexy smile lit his face. Her heart warmed. Then a cloud crossed his face and the smile died. "What are you doing here?"

Aware they had the dispatcher's complete attention, Zora asked, "Can we speak in private?"

When he frowned, she held her breath. Would he refuse her? Without another word, he turned and strode toward his office. She followed. Windowless, the space was about the size of a storage closet, but the room was tidy. Folders were neatly arranged on top of a cheap but sturdy-looking desk. Zora shut the door, thanking God she wasn't claustrophobic. John took refuge behind his desk.

"Do you know anything about this?" She plopped the newspaper on his desk.

He picked it up, stared at the headlines, frowned up at her and started to read. When he finished, he raised his head, shaking it in confusion. "I wouldn't think Steve—"

"The pathologist?" she asked. "You think he leaked this?"

"Steve's an upright guy. He'd have called me and asked permission before he gave out the story." John reached for the phone.

She placed her hand over his. "It doesn't matter now. It's like my great-aunt said, 'The cow's out of the barn, no need to close the door'. I want to make this work in our favor."

He raised an eyebrow and withdrew his hand. "You mean you want to make this work for *you*."

He stared at her with flat, cold eyes. God, if she could only turn back the clock. *And do what?* Not make the trip? How long could she have lived with the dreams? How long before she'd have found herself in a straitjacket, taking up residency in a padded cell? No, this was the way it was supposed to be. She just hated he'd gotten hurt in the process. "I'm truly sorry. At first, I didn't see any harm in helping Emma."

John rose from his desk. "But I don't care about her." He ran a hand through his black hair, pulling strands of it from its leather tie. "At least, not in that way. Not the way I care—cared about you."

Oh, God. She couldn't meet his gaze. The pain was too much. She studied his bookcase instead. It was crammed full of books. But she couldn't read the titles. The words kept blurring in and out of focus. Had she lost the love of this man before she'd known it?

She blinked several times before she dared glance at his face. When she did, she had to curl her fingers into the fabric of her pants to resist the urge to touch him, to feel the smoothness of his skin against her palm.

Get a grip. This was about Julia, not about her. "I want to have a DNA analysis done. Will you help me?"

He shook his head. "The state won't pay—"

"I'll pay for it. I want the analysis done on me also."

His eyes narrowed. "Why?"

"I can't find her murderer, but if I can prove the bones belong to my ancestor, I can at least give her a proper burial." *Maybe both of us will be at peace.*

"And then you'll go back to New York?"

"Do you want me to?"

Some flicker of emotion passed over his face. She'd like to think it was regret.

"I'm sorry, I can't," John said. "This is still an ongoing case. I can't make such a request. It doesn't aid the investigation."

"So you won't do it?"

They stared at each other over a long heartbeat.

He shook his head. "No. I can't." His voice was as emotionless as his black eyes.

She studied his face. Was this his way of getting back at her for hurting him? Did he hate her now? Could he have stopped loving her so quickly? Stupid tears pricked the back of her eyelids again. Damn. She'd cried more since she'd been in South Dakota than she had in twenty years. She blinked rapidly, turned away, groping blindly for the doorknob. "I won't stop trying." She opened the door, walked through it, and out of the department before he could see the tears trailing down her cheeks.

A dry hot wind blew through Zora's hair as her car sped down the highway toward the reservation. Shades of gray and purple stained the horizon as night approached. Somewhere in the distance, a coyote howled, a lonely and sad song, which resonated with her feelings of desolation.

After she left John's office, she'd gone to the hospital lab in Pierre and had her blood drawn. She'd stood outside the ICU, wanting desperately to go in and see Joseph and tell him about her plans to bury Julia's remains. She wanted to ask if he thought the burial would bring Julia peace. But she knew her presence would do more harm than good, so she'd gotten in her car and headed back to the reservation.

Would she find peace with Julia's burial? Would she be able to go back to New York and reclaim her job? Or would she be splintered with half her mind left behind in the foothills of the Dakotas? Two weeks ago, she'd have gone home to New York and never looked back. But now...

Once on reservation land, she drove slowly down the main road. An ugly yellow dog darted out of a yard and chased her car. The dog's legs churned rapidly to keep pace with the convertible. She glanced in the rearview mirror and saw the mutt give up the pursuit. Soon, he was a small dot on the landscape.

As she crested the hill, the bright lights of the casino drew her eye. Mike Matisse was an influential person. Maybe she could get him to appeal to the state to let her pay for the identification of Julia's remains. As much as she disliked the man, he might be helpful.

After the silence of the long drive home, the cacophony of voices, music and the rattle of slot machines bombarded Zora's senses as she entered the casino.

"Welcome to Little River Casino." A young Native American woman with a wide smile greeted Zora.

"Thank you. Do you have a phone I could use?"

Still smiling, the woman showed Zora to a small cloakroom. Zora dialed Joseph's home number.

"What?" Chet's voice was clipped and abrupt.

Zora smiled. "Have you eaten?"

"Emma made me something to eat before she left for work, but I think I'll save it and feed it to the coyotes out at my place. Save me a bullet."

Zora laughed. "Don't you dare. I'll bring you something once I leave here."

"Where's here?" the old man asked.

"I'm at the casino. See you later." She hung up before he could ask any more questions.

Zora sought out the greeter. "Is Mr. Matisse around?"

"I'll page him," the young woman said.

While Zora waited, she watched the action at one of the roulette wheels. The players stared at the wheel as the ball hopped from one number to another before finally landing on red 19. "House wins." Several players groaned, but it didn't stop them from placing another bet.

Waitresses in short black skirts moved efficiently between tables with trays of drinks. Through a part in the crowd, Zora caught sight of Emma. Why was she working? Zora had thought she'd be at the hospital.

"Ms. Hughes, what a pleasant surprise."

In the noise and flash of lights and coin, she hadn't heard Mike Matisse approach. His smile appeared amicable, but the pleasure wasn't reflected in his eyes. In the *haute couture* world, she'd often been in the company of people she neither liked nor admired, and they never knew how she felt. She turned on that charm now. "Mr. Matisse, may I have a little bit of your time?"

"What can I do for you?"

The whirl and ping of the machines, and the babble of conversations in multiple languages wasn't conducive to a private conversation. "Can we do this in your office?"

"Sure." The hermetic seal of the elevator cancelled out the casino noise but also enclosed her in a box with a man whose cologne failed to camouflage his sweat. When the doors opened, she rushed out.

Once inside the office, she turned to face him. She was aware of his scrutiny. His eyes roamed over her body like a designer looking for those last minute flaws just before the runway strut.

"I need a favor."

He walked to the bar and held up a crystal decanter. "Drink?"

She shook her head.

He poured two fingers of Jack Daniels into a glass. "What kind of favor?"

"You read about the bones discovered in the mountains? The Jane Doe?"

He took a long pull of his drink and placed it on his desk then met her gaze. "I did."

"The bones belong to an ancestor of mine."

Matisse clasped his hands behind his back. "Is that so? I'd heard you were researching your family tree. How do you know this is your relative?"

Her gut warned her not to divulge everything to him. After all, could you trust a man who stole money out of the mouths of babes? "Let's just say I know."

He laughed. "A little psychic connection?"

She didn't share the laugh. "I need you to help me persuade the state to do DNA analysis on her remains."

Mike frowned. "I don't get involved in these kinds of issues. My position—"

Suppressing her irritation, she said, "I came to you, Mr. Matisse, because in order to run this reservation, you have to know how to maneuver around bureaucratic red tape. I'm willing to pay for the analysis. I just want the right to bury my ancestor."

"I don't—"

She was tired of his bullshit. She had no doubt he could just pick up the phone and get it done. But no, he wanted to make her beg. "She was murdered and her body dumped in that cave."

He turned his back to her and poured another drink. He took a healthy swallow. Sweat rolled down his face. The temperature in the room couldn't be more than sixty-five degrees.

"How do you know she was murdered?"

There was no way she'd share the dreams with him. "I know. Will you help me?"

His desk phone rang. After a short conversation with someone on the other end, he turned to Zora. "I'm sorry, duty calls."

She straightened her shoulders and couldn't keep a sigh from slipping from her lips. "Of course, I've taken up too much of your time. Will you think about it and let me know?"

"I'll see what I can do."

She shivered. Simple words but underneath them she sensed a threat.

———◆———

"Bitch," Mike said as soon as he'd closed the door behind Zora Hughes.

He walked back to his glass of whiskey and took another healthy hit then massaged his jaw. It hurt from holding a smile.

The telephone call was a ruse. He had a prearranged agreement with his administrative staff. If anyone showed unexpectedly, one of them would ring his phone after fifteen minutes if his guest hadn't left. This would give him an out if he needed it. Today, he'd needed it.

He hustled to the window overlooking the casino and watched Zora weave through the crowd. Emma Bearkiller stepped into her path. Frowning, Mike moved closer to the window. Agitated as a little beaver, Emma was in Zora's face. He chuckled, for a minute forgetting the seriousness of the situation. What were the two women talking about? The conversation went on for several minutes. Customers stared.

"Shit." He moved to the phone and speed dialed an extension.

"Yes, sir?"

"Send Emma Bearkiller up here."

When he returned to the window, Emma was still yakking at Zora's retreating back.

Flushed, Emma entered his office a couple of minutes later. Her small breasts heaved from the confrontation with Zora. Any other day, he'd have enjoyed the sight, but not after the New York woman's visit.

"What was going on down there?" He pointed to the window. "You caused quite a scene."

She looked down at the carpet. "I'm sorry, sir." She

glanced up, fire in her eyes. "I couldn't help it. That—that woman is trying to kill my grandfather."

Mike cocked his head with interest. "How?"

Emma took a deep breath. "The nurses had to throw her out of my grandfather's room. They said she'd worked him up until his blood pressure was sky high."

Mike walked around to his desk and straightened the edges of a pile of papers. "What was she saying to him?"

"The nurses don't know, but they did say he stayed upset long after she was gone."

"Umm. So what did you say to Ms. Hughes?"

"I told her to stay away from my grandfather."

Mike glanced up from his task. "And what did she say?"

The nipples of Emma's breasts showed dark against the thin white blouse. "—to see him again."

Mike pulled his eyes away from her chest. "What did you say?"

She frowned. "That she needs to see him again. She's got a lot of nerve."

"Why?"

"Why, what?"

Mike suppressed his irritation. "Why does she need to see him again?"

Emma shrugged. "Something about the vision."

"So he did have a vision?"

"Sir?"

He must have spoken his thought out loud. "Do you know what he saw in his vision?"

She shook her head. "Like I said earlier, no one other than Zora and my grandfather knows what went on in that hospital room, and he isn't talking."

"But he's talking to Zora."

She really shouldn't frown so much. It wasn't very attractive.

"I—I don't know…"

He walked up to her and tipped her chin up with a

finger. "Maybe you should find out what he said." He dropped her chin. "I don't want my future blackjack dealer distracted and upset. That is, if you still want to work the blackjack tables."

She swallowed audibly. "Yes, sir, I do."

"Let her see him again."

She opened and closed her mouth.

He lifted a finger. "With you present, of course, so you can control the situation. Keep your grandfather out of danger."

"Well, they are moving him out of the ICU."

Mike nodded. "Good, good." If the information from the vision was too threatening, and before it became public knowledge, he'd get rid of the old man. Who was to say it wasn't the old man's time to go?

CHAPTER TWENTY-TWO

———

JOHN PULLED HIS JEEP INTO the Matisse driveway and parked behind Danny's bright blue Dodge. Matisse was still at the casino, which suited John's purposes. He wanted to talk to the boy alone.

Danny answered the door in dirty low-riding jeans with a bottle of Bud Lite in his hand. John raised an eyebrow.

"I'm in my own house," the teen said.

This kid was bad news, not just the underage drinking but also the blood that ran through his veins. John knew from personal experience blood didn't always tell, but Danny gave every indication of following in his father's footsteps. "I want to talk to you about your buddy Billy Joe."

Danny blanched under his bronze skin. "What's he done?"

"You tell me."

Danny clamped his mouth shut.

"Let's start with three nights ago out at Chet Tyler's place."

"What're talking about?"

"Someone took a shot at me."

Danny didn't flinch.

"Did you know it's a federal offense to shoot a tribal police officer?" John glanced at the garage. "Mind if I look at your motorcycle?"

"You got a warrant?" The boy's eyes didn't match the

bravado of his words.

"See, all I need to do is match up the tire prints from Chet's place with your bike…"

The boy swallowed audibly, his eyes shifting from John's face to the garage. Finally, he seemed to make up his mind about something. "I didn't know why Billy Joe wanted the bike. I didn't know about the shooting. Honest. Billy Joe told me he was going coyote huntin' on old man Tyler's place."

Was the boy a good actor or just stupid? John would bet on stupid. "Who hired him?"

"I told you, I didn't know. Maybe when I find Billy Joe, I'll ask."

"He won't be doing much talking," John said.

Danny lowered his beer bottle to his side, drink forgotten. "Whatcha mean?"

"Billy Joe's body was found this morning in a shallow grave at the old quarry site."

Color drained from the boy's face. The kid looked like he wanted to puke. "Who—What?"

"That's what I want you to tell me."

———◆———

Zora pulled into the Bearkiller driveway and cut the engine. Chet must have gone to sleep without waiting for his sandwich because the house was dark.

She leaned her head against the car's headrest and let the sage-scented breeze wash over her face. In no hurry to get out, she replayed the conversation she'd had with Mike Matisse. She hadn't been fooled by his insincere promises. He didn't want to help her. Why? What difference did it make to him if Julia's bones were identified? It wasn't as though he had any personal stake in the matter.

She yawned. Maybe she was over-reading her conversation with the council president. She needed sleep. She picked up the greasy brown paper bag with Chet's sandwich from the passenger seat. She really needed to talk to him about eating better. She smiled, almost hearing his response. "At my age, I'll eat what I damn well please."

As she stepped out of her car, the rumble of a truck's engine interrupted the night's silence. Zora groaned as Emma's Ford F150 tore into the drive, the high beams catching Zora squarely in the face. Joseph's granddaughter reminded Zora of a gnat, and she was in no mood to put up with Emma's irritating whine. Zora slammed her car door and turned for the house.

"Zora."

She closed her eyes in exasperation then turned to the woman. "Emma, I don't—"

"They're moving Grandpa out of the ICU tomorrow. He's asking to see you."

Something heavy lifted from Zora's chest, and a smile spread over her face. "He's talking?"

Emma cleared her throat. "Yep. Do you want to see him? You can go with me tomorrow when I drive up."

Zora's smile faded. "Okay."

"Fine." Emma bounced past her. "I'll see you in the morning."

Zora stared at the closing front door. What was up with that? One minute Emma was cursing her, the next acting like they were sisters. Call her cynical, but Zora felt suspicious about the change.

———◆———

Though still attached to a multitude of tubes and wires, Joseph looked alert when Zora and Emma arrived the next morning. His grip was strong, even though, his hands felt paper-thin when Zora grasped them in hers.

A nurse adjusted his IV then gave Emma and Zora a stern look. "Don't tire him out," she said before departing.

"I'm glad you're okay." Zora patted his hand. What she really wanted to say was how much she'd worried about him and whether he'd survive. She felt an immense amount of guilt. If she hadn't come to Little River, he'd be sitting on his front porch, watching the grass billowing in the field across the road.

She also felt guilty because she ached to ask more about his vision but was afraid to excite him. She bit her tongue until tears stung her eyes.

"Water." His voice creaked like a rusty wheel.

Emma brought the straw nestled in a Styrofoam cup to his lips. He took a few sips then rested his head on the pillow and closed his eyes. Zora glanced at Emma on the other side of the bed, who shrugged. Maybe this wasn't a good idea.

Joseph's eyes opened slowly. They burned fever bright. "She was murdered."

"You told me." Zora stroked his arm. Didn't he remember their conversation two days ago? "I figured as much when I found her bones in the cave. I'm going to have the state do a DNA analysis of her bones against my DNA. When they release her remains, I'll give her a proper burial."

He squeezed her hand.

"Do you think she'll finally be at peace?" Zora asked.

"I do not know. There is much anger and sadness surrounding her," he whispered.

Zora noted he spoke of Julia in the present tense. "Do you think she knew her murderer?"

He nodded. "Yes. She knew him."

Him? "How—"

"*I* knew her murderer."

For fifteen seconds or so, no one spoke.

Emma broke the silence. "How could you know the murderer? We're talking about something that happened before you were born." She looked at Zora for confirmation.

Zora nodded.

Voices could be heard outside in the corridor. The nurse had returned. Zora focused on Joseph. "Who was it?"

Joseph shook his head. "I did not see his face."

A man? At first when Joseph said the killer had been a man, Zora thought he was confused. "In my dreams, it was a woman who took Julia's life."

Joseph nodded. "A shape-shifter."

She blinked, unsure she'd heard him correctly. John had said there were no such things as shape-shifters.

He continued, not giving her time to assimilate his remark. "He had a mark on his body."

"A mark? Like a wound?"

"No, no." Joseph lifted a hand toward her face.

She raised her hand toward the small pigmentation on her cheek. "A birthmark?"

"Yes, a birthmark, on his side, the shape of the buffalo."

Disappointed, Zora closed her eyes. She'd hoped for a name or at least a facial description.

Joseph squeezed her hand again. "Those marks are often passed down through generations."

"I can't go up to every male I meet and ask him to take off his shirt." She'd come to the end of the road. She realized she would probably never know the identity of Julia's murderer. An immense sadness filled her. She'd let Julia down.

She leaned forward and kissed the old man's brow. "I'm burying Julia. I hope this will bring both of us peace. Then I'm going home." That should make John happy. At least one of them deserved to be happy.

Joseph stared up at her and shook his head. "She will not be at peace, and neither will you, until justice is done."

Zora lifted her hands in supplication. "How can I bring her murderer to justice if he's already dead?"

"You will find a way," the old man said.

———

Rather than rely on Mike Matisse or John Iron Hawk to persuade the medical examiner to do DNA analysis on Julia's remains, Zora decided to plead her case. She left Emma at the hospital and drove downtown. Taking the elevator to the basement, she followed the astringent odor and the directions printed on the green walls, until she found the morgue.

On the ride over, she'd rehearsed what she'd say to him. Now standing outside the doctor's door, her carefully thought out words flew away like prairie dust.

What if he refused to test the bone? Would the state allow her to bury the remains as a humanitarian? If not, she and her ancestor would be forever haunted by that day at the creek.

Taking a deep breath, she pushed open the door and stepped into a small, empty room with floor-to-ceiling bookshelves. A set of double doors sat opposite the entry and led to what she assumed was the autopsy room. Zora sneezed. Dusty three-ringed notebooks filled the book-cases, and an open spiral notebook sat on the surface of a battered brown desk. Housekeeping wasn't dying to get in here to clean. She grimaced at the unintentional pun.

She'd come to see Dr. Foley without an appointment. Would he even see her? Taking a deep breath, she pushed open the double doors.

The chemical order was stronger in this cavern of a room and probably came from the assortment of jars and plastic containers that lined the walls. Repulsion kept her from investigating the brown globs of human tissue float-ing in a sea of fluid. But the main focus of the room was a steel table that tilted down into a large stainless steel sink. She shuddered, imagining blood and other bodily fluids trickling down the channels cut into the sides of the table before draining into the sink. She turned away.

In the far left corner of the autopsy room, Dr. Steven Foley's office door stood open. Even before she reached the door, she knew he wasn't there. His office space was the opposite of John's spartan closet. Books, files and loose papers covered the desk. The legs were the only clue to the color of the desk.

"A live one for once." The male voice boomed in the silent, still room.

Zora spun around. A pair of bright blue eyes in a pale face assessed her. Hand to her chest, she said, "Oh, my God, you scared the crap out of me."

"Wouldn't want to do that." He extended a hand. "Steven Foley, what can I do for you?"

She shook his hand. "Zora Hughes. I came to talk to you about the bones found in the cave out on Little River Reservation."

His face lost its friendly appearance and the blue eyes became guarded. "Are you a reporter?"

She shook her head. "No. I found the bones."

An auburn eyebrow lifted and his stance relaxed. "Did you now?" He studied her. "You don't look like a spelunker."

If she told him she'd followed a strange girl up into the mountains because she resembled a long dead ancestor, Zora risked losing her credibility. "I'm not. I…fell into a pit in the mountains and found the bones."

"Why don't we continue this conversation over a cup of coffee?"

Zora glanced at the coffee pot in the corner of his office. An inch of burnt crud lay at the bottom of the glass pot. "Uh…"

Following her gaze, he laughed. "I'll take you upstairs to the canteen."

She grinned at his infectious humor. "That would be fine."

Once in the canteen, he purchased a bottle of water for

her and a cup of coffee for himself. They sat at one of the unoccupied tables.

"So tell me all the details," he said, sipping his coffee.

She decided to tell him as much of the truth as she could before the tale veered off into the spooky. "I'm from New York—"

"I could tell you weren't from around here." He motioned for her to continue.

"I came to this area to do some research on an ancestor who lived in the area."

"Native American?"

She shook her head. "She was a runaway slave who lived among the Lakota Sioux."

"Interesting." He took another sip of coffee. His blue eyes studied her over the rim.

"I believe the bones John Iron Hawk brought you are my ancestor's remains."

"You know John?" He placed the cup down on the table. He didn't look at her, but stared instead down into the black oily liquid.

"We're acquainted."

He smiled. "Acquainted, huh? So what do you want from me?"

"I want to take possession of the remains and give them a proper burial."

"I don't—"

"I'm willing to pay for a DNA analysis to confirm the bones are indeed my ancestor's."

He shook his head. "This is highly unusual."

She leaned across the table. "What are your plans for the bones after you've finished examining them? Will you burn them or leave them on display to be gawked at like those specimens in your lab?"

He blushed. "Those are for academic research."

"Julia was my ancestor. She deserves a decent burial." Zora reached for her purse and pulled out her checkbook.

"How much will it cost?"

He studied her intently from behind intelligent, assessing eyes.

Would he refuse?

"I'll bill you," he said.

Blinking back tears, she smiled. "Thank you."

———————

John glanced at his watch. His sister had been talking to the same customers for the past fifteen minutes.

Finally she smiled, gave the couple their receipt and ushered them out the door. She flipped the open sign to *Closed* and turned in his direction, eyes narrowed. "What's your problem?" she asked.

"One of my paintings is missing."

"I sold it." Lydia massaged her neck then rolled her shoulders.

"To whom?"

She frowned. "Why do you care? She paid me the asking price. That's all you should be concerned about. They're here to be sold, aren't they?"

"Yep." Whether he wanted them sold or not was a moot point now. Somewhere out in the world beyond the reservation, his paintings graced someone's walls. It was too late to pull them back into the safety of his studio.

"You didn't come over just to ask about that painting. What's bothering you?"

He rubbed his dry, gritty eyes then ran his hands over his face. "Found Billy Joe Strickland's body out at the old quarry."

Her face was a study in blankness. Then recognition dawned. "You mean that kid you're always arresting?"

John looked out the store window. Evening shadows gathered as the sun sank. Traffic had picked up as gamblers drove into the reservation like cattle to water. He glanced at his sister. "I think Matisse is good for it."

"But you don't have any proof."

His mouth tightened. "He worked for Mike Matisse."

"But that doesn't mean—"

John held up his hand to ward off her words. "Danny says it was Billy Joe who took a shot at me that night out at Chet's place. I think Matisse hired him to kill me."

Her lips quivered. "John, Matisse is an evil man. Be careful."

He acknowledged her warning with a nod. "I will."

"So, you think he got rid of Billy Joe?"

"Or had someone do it for him."

"But again, you have no proof."

"No." He beat his hat against his thigh.

She studied him, concern written in deep lines on her face. "What are you going to do?"

"I don't know. Talk to Billy Joe's friends. But unless they were present when Matisse hired him to kill me, there's nothing I can do."

"I'm sorry." She squeezed his shoulder.

"Yeah, me too." He moved toward the exit. The last rays of the sun bounced off the turquoise stone in the display window. He stopped. "Didn't Matisse's mother give you that piece?"

He could hear his sister's light tread as she came to stand beside him. "I think she was afraid Mike would sell it once she died."

John snorted. "She was probably right. How much do you think it's worth?"

"It's probably priceless."

He glanced at his sister. "And Matisse hasn't asked for it?"

"No, not yet. Isn't that strange," she whispered.

John jammed his hat on his head. "You be careful. I don't want you to get hurt when he decides it's time to reclaim what's rightfully his."

"That won't be a problem." She moved to the display

window and unlocked the case. Nestled in its black velvet cloth, the stones in the bracelet sparkled with pink, green and blue lights. "I'm giving it to Zora."

He froze. "*What?* "

"You heard me. I'm giving it to Zora, because I think it rightfully belongs to her." In a low voice, Lydia said, "It belonged to her ancestor."

He stared at his sister, wondering if she'd lost her mind. "Has she been feeding you that bullshit?"

Lydia cocked her head. "You don't believe her?"

"One minute her story's believable, and the next, I think she's loony."

"She's not."

"And how do you know?"

Lydia shrugged. "Let's just say I feel it's all true."

John shook his head in bewilderment. "I'm going to stick to what I know—finding killers." He yanked open the door. The chimes clattered in protest as he stepped through it and out into the fading day.

———————

Pleased with the outcome of her visit to Dr. Foley, Zora hummed as she drove the convertible onto reservation land. Emma sat in the passenger seat, lost in her thoughts.

"There's John," Emma said when they drove past the council offices. Without waiting for Zora to stop the car, Emma unhooked her seatbelt, braced her hands on the windshield's frame and hauled herself up to a half-standing position. Her black hair whipped in the breeze created by the car's motion.

Zora caught sight of John's long-legged body as he climbed into his Jeep.

"Pull over," Emma ordered.

Zora glared up at Joseph's granddaughter. "Sit down. And for once, why don't you let him come to you?"

Emma's mouth tightened in what Zora could only describe as pain. "Because he never will."

"Well, then you don't need him."

"Speak for yourself."

Zora lost whatever sympathy she felt for the woman. As soon as she pulled into a parking space, Emma hopped out of the car and, with a sway of her narrow hips, strolled over to John's Jeep.

She really couldn't lecture Emma on playing hard to get, because in the last few days, she'd driven down this road several times, hoping to catch a glimpse of him. Of course if he'd spotted her, she would have said she was just passing by.

"Hey, John," Emma cooed.

He nodded at Zora, before turning his attention to Emma. Zora gritted her teeth and turned away. Jealousy like a small ugly rodent clawed in her chest.

Lydia stepped out of her store, locked the door, and stopped when she spotted Zora. As strange as their last encounter had been, Zora fully expected the woman to cross to the other side of the street or, at the very least, ignore her. To her surprise, Lydia didn't turn away but moved toward the convertible.

"I'm glad to see you," Lydia said.

"You are?" Zora's eyebrows shot into her hairline.

"Do you still want the bracelet?"

Her breath caught in her throat. She searched Lydia's face to see if she'd heard correctly. When she finally spoke, her voice came out as a croak. "Of course, I do."

John's sister smiled. "Come by tomorrow morning."

Zora sat in stunned silence as Lydia strolled off. She thought she'd have to steal the bracelet in order to get it out of the other woman's possession, and here Lydia dropped it in her lap.

"What was that about?" Emma asked, climbing back into the convertible.

Zora shook her head. "I'm not sure, but Lydia's going to give me the bracelet."

A small gasp escaped Emma's lips. "Mike Matisse's bracelet?"

Zora whirled on her. "No. My ancestor's bracelet." She jerked the car into reverse and peeled out of the parking spot so fast, Emma's head hit the headrest.

———◆———

Mike uncapped a bottle of Gray Goose, sniffed the neck before pouring a generous portion into a beveled glass. The liquor burned a slow path down his throat. When the vodka hit his stomach, molten heat rolled over his limbs. For a moment, he enjoyed the relaxing effects of the liquor and forgot about the irritations in his life.

Billy Joe's body had been unearthed, but Mike wasn't worried. Only his secretary could connect him with the punk. He swirled the remaining liquid around the bottom of the glass. What should he do about her? He couldn't afford to dispose of her. Too much suspicion would be raised by her disappearance.

He raised his glass to take another swallow then froze. The liquor became a sour ball in his stomach. Grimacing he lowered the glass. He was turning into his father.

A quick knock sounded at the door, it opened, and Emma Bearkiller's face appeared. His high dissipated like snow. His displeasure must have shown on his face, because her smile dimmed.

"I just wanted to tell you about my visit to the hospital. About the vision." Without waiting for his response, she retreated and started to close the door behind her.

Though he wanted to pretend she hadn't knocked, her grandfather was too important to lose as a supporter. He reached the door in two strides and pulled it from her hands. "Come on in." He didn't wait for her to enter but moved back to the window overlooking the casino floor, having no doubt she'd follow him. Sure enough, when he turned, her slump-shouldered form stood in the middle of his office, looking like a whipped puppy. "So what happened?"

She lifted her head but didn't look him in the eye. "In the vision…" She cleared her throat, and when she spoke again, her voice was stronger. "My grandfather saw a woman murdered at the old creek." She glanced at him. "You know—the one between town and Chet Tyler's place. He and Zora believe it was her ancestor."

Mike shrugged as though this was of little interest to him, though, in fact, his brain hummed and strained for more information. "This happened over a hundred years ago, right?"

Emma nodded.

"So who was the murderer?

"He didn't see the killer's face," Emma said.

Mike relaxed. "Good."

"What?" Emma's round face crinkled.

"I mean, I'm glad he could answer some of Zora's questions. This must be a big disappointment for Joseph not to identify the killer."

"He did tell her the killer had a birth mark on his body. A buffalo. But that's useless information since no one can see it."

Heat infused Matisse's face. "You're right. It's useless. To come all this way without finding out about her ancestor must have been quite a letdown," he said as he held open the door for her.

She stepped through the door then turned. "Well, at least she's getting the bracelet."

The tips of Mike's fingers went numb as he gripped the door's frame. "Bracelet?"

"Lydia is giving Zora that turquoise bracelet that's been in her store window for ages. I don't know why. It has to be worth a lot of money."

"When?" Mike whispered.

Emma frowned. "When what?"

Mike wanted to reach out and wrap his hand around the woman's skinny throat. "When is Lydia giving Zora the bracelet?"

Emma tried to back up, but Mike reached out and grabbed her arm. Fear flashed across her face. "Soon. Zora's leaving for New York in the next couple of days."

Mike released his grip on the girl, shoved her through the door, and shut it in her face. He stood rooted to the floor. His great-great-grandmother's bracelet was being given to that black slut.

"Over my dead body," he whispered.

———————

John's stomach growled. He couldn't remember when he'd eaten a decent meal. Last night, he'd endured another one of Laura's disastrous dinners. He'd been up half the night with indigestion and decided to paint. He ended up with balls of paper littering the floor. His muse was still on vacation. Maybe the paintings he'd completed were flukes. Maybe he wasn't as talented as his sister seemed to believe.

"He's on his way." Oscar's voice over the radio broke into John's thoughts.

John was parked outside Mac's trailer and had been for several hours. He glanced at his watch. One a.m. Straightening in his seat, he watched the side view mirror. The headlights of an oncoming vehicle glared blue-white in the total darkness of the street. Bass boomed out of the car's speakers. Mac pulled into the rutted path that passed for a driveway.

John was out of his vehicle and standing next to the punk's car before he could cut the engine. He yanked the boy out.

"What the fuck—"

Mac bucked and kicked as John pinned both the kid's arms behind him and cuffed him.

"Let's talk," John growled into the kid's ear and pushed him toward the trailer. "Is it open?"

"Fuck you, man."

John kicked open the door.

Mac twisted in John's grip. "Shit, man—"

John pushed the punk into the trailer but kept him close as he searched for a light switch. He found it and the trailer flooded with light. John wished he'd kept the lights off. Cockroaches skittered out of discarded takeout bags and off food-crusted dishes in the small kitchen sink. Stale sweat and garbage filled his nostrils.

"Nice," John said. He pushed Mac down on a sagging blue cushioned sofa. "Who hired Billy Joe to shoot me?"

The kid shot him a look of pure malice. "Fuck yourself."

"I guess you've heard by now Billy Joe is dead."

Mac continued to glare at John.

"If you know anything about the shooting or Billy Joe's murder, you'd better tell me. 'Cause the way I figure it, whoever killed Billy Joe isn't above killing off anyone who might know about their association. And that would be you, Mac."

"I don't know nothing."

John smiled grimly. "The killer isn't going to take any chances."

Mac spat.

The spittle just missed John's boots. "Okay, if that's the way you want to play it."

John turned toward the door.

"Hey, ain't you gonna take off these cuffs?"

John paused at the door and cocked his head as though considering the request. "If everything is cool, you don't need to worry."

Mac sat up straighter. "Come on, man, you can't leave

me like this."

Watching the kid's eyes, John said, "Why? Afraid Matisse will pay you a visit?"

Mac was a tough kid, but there was a telltale flicker behind those dark eyes. John pushed open the front door.

"What do you want to know?" Mac asked.

John smiled and stepped back into the trailer.

CHAPTER TWENTY-THREE

———◆———

THE SUN CRESTED THE HORIZON, washing the red brick buildings in a soft warm glow as Zora stepped out of her car the next morning. She'd talked with Lydia the night before and they'd agreed to meet at dawn, so Zora could get an early start back to Pierre. She'd decided to wait for the DNA analysis in Pierre. As soon as she could claim Julia's remains and bury her ancestor, she'd return to New York.

A lone car sat out front. Zora stepped into the consignment shop's main room. She stopped, her feet frozen in place. A hurricane couldn't have left more destruction. Hats, belts, and costume jewelry were scattered helter-skelter on the pine floor. Paintings tilted crazily on their easels and a few littered the floor. What in the world had happened here?

"Lydia?" Glass crunched under Zora's sandals as she stepped in further. A sharp coppery smell assaulted her senses. Her heart started to race. Something bad had happened.

"Lydia, are you here?" Zora stopped. A hard sole black military boot extended from behind the counter. Lydia wore that type of boot. Zora rushed up to the case and leaned over.

"Oh, my God." Her hand flew to her mouth.

Lydia lay crumbled on the floor, the cordless phone gripped in her hand. Blood pooled around her head.

Zora ran behind the counter. She crouched at Lydia's side and pressed two fingers to the older woman's throat. At first, she couldn't feel Lydia's heartbeat for the pounding of her own pulse. But finally, she detected a weak but steady beat.

She gently disengaged Lydia's hand from the receiver. It took Zora two attempts to dial 911. This was not the time to fall apart.

According to the dispatcher, it would take the ambulance thirty or forty minutes to arrive, coming from the nearest town. Even though the woman wanted Zora to remain on the line, she disconnected the call.

She needed to locate John. Was he in the office or at home? Although she'd called John's cell before, now the number escaped her. She rose and glanced wildly around the tossed shop. Lydia didn't strike Zora as a person who kept numbers in a cell phone or electronic organizer, so unless she stored numbers in her head, there had to be a Rolodex or a page plastered to the wall. She found a sheet taped to the side of the cash register with the number of Little River Reservation's police department. Maggie, John's dispatcher, answered. The woman peppered Zora with questions.

"Please, just find John," Zora said before disconnecting. She sank back down on her heels and touched Lydia's blood-speckled cheek. "Just hang on. John's coming. Everything will be okay."

———◆———

Ten minutes after leaving Lydia Whitefeather's shop, Mike pulled his car over to the side of the road and opened the glove compartment. The bracelet's stones sparkled dully in the early morning light.

Finally.

As he stroked the bracelet, he heard again the sound of

Lydia's head cracking on the glass counter, and the slump of her limp body hitting the floor. He'd pressed his fingers to her throat. No pulse. Good. Needing to make this look like a robbery, he resisted the urge to pound her face into a bloody pulp. Imagine her trying to steal from him.

He rose and began knocking over mannequin heads, pretending he was destroying Lydia Whitefeather all over again. No one took what rightfully belonged to Mike Matisse.

A car door closed. He peered out the store's window.

Zora Hughes stood by a black convertible, her face turned up to the morning sun. The urge to kill this snotty bitch bubbled like an orgasm in his balls. He had to focus. He was doing this to preserve his chance for a senatorial seat. He'd take care of Zora later. Pulling the bracelet from Lydia's hands, he'd hurried out the back door.

He smiled now and stroked the bauble again before putting it back in the glove compartment. He reached for his cell phone and dialed Lydia's shop. He could hear the suppressed panic in Zora's voice when she answered. He lowered his voice to disguise it. "I have the bracelet. Come and get it."

"Who is this?"

Mike chuckled. "The person who holds the answers to your dreams. Meet me at the river. You know the one." He disconnected the call.

———

A woman's screams rent the early morning air. Gun at his side, John kicked open the door to the Whitehorse residence.

Earl Whitehorse whirled around, fisted hand still raised to deliver another blow.

"Hit her one more time, and I'll blow you to kingdom come."

Mrs. Whitehorse's cries had died to whimpers by the time John handcuffed her husband to the Jeep's bar rail.

"I've been looking for you for a week, you gutless son of a bitch." John glared at Whitehorse then picked up the radio. "Maggie, I'm on the way in with a guest."

"John, Lydia's been hurt."

At first, he wasn't sure he'd heard her correctly. "Repeat!"

"Lydia's been beaten."

Zora's hands shook as she lowered the phone to its cradle. That voice…

"Are you the next of kin?"

One of the paramedics, a stocky female, stood in front of Zora. "We need to transport her to Pierre. Are you the next of kin?"

Zora shook her head. "No." Her voice shook. "I'm," she cleared her throat, "I'm just a friend."

Lydia had been bundled onto a stretcher, a white bandage wrapped around her head and an IV started. The rails of the stretcher came up with a clank, and the other paramedic nodded at his partner.

Switching her attention back to Zora, the female paramedic asked, "Do you want to follow—" Her attention shifted to something behind Zora.

She turned. John's broad-shouldered form filled the store's doorway.

"Where is she?" Not waiting for an answer, he rushed to his sister's side. He stooped, rested his hand briefly on his sister's arm then glanced back at Zora. "Who did this?"

Zora shook her head but realized, even as she denied knowledge of Lydia's attacker, it had been Mike Matisse's voice she'd heard on the other end of the phone, his laughter. "I think—"

"We have to go," said the male paramedic, pushing the

stretcher toward the door and the waiting ambulance.

"I'll follow you," John said.

"John…" She reached out to touch him. She needed to tell him about Mike Matisse.

He moved toward her. "Ssh…" He stroked her cheek with a rough hand. "We'll talk later."

Then he was gone, jumping into his Jeep and tearing after the ambulance.

Zora stood in the door and watched the vehicles speed away. She touched her cheek. What had that caress meant? Was he telling her he'd forgiven her? She felt tears prick the back of her eyelids. She blinked. She would not cry and she would not let John Iron Hawk derail her decision to leave. She belonged in New York, not here. But she couldn't deny the longing she felt for more of his touch.

Now she needed to respond to that telephone call. Not only had Mike Matisse tried to kill Lydia, he'd taken Julia's bracelet. She didn't know how, but she needed to get that bracelet back.

She locked the shop's front door then raced for her car. It took several attempts to insert the key into the ignition. She took calming breaths and focused on getting the bracelet back for Julia. She successfully started the car.

Pulling out onto the road, she aimed the convertible in the direction of the creek.

Trees, landmarks, homes all flew by in a blur as Zora sped toward the river. What part did Mike Matisse play in all this? Why would he harm Lydia? Why would he take the bracelet? None of this made any sense. Maybe she should have been more forceful in telling John about Mike's call. She reached for her cell phone then stopped. John had Lydia to worry about.

She parked her convertible on the shoulder and entered the woods at the same spot she had a few short days ago.

Nothing stirred as she walked through the pine-needled woods. No birds sang, no small animals scurried across her path, just silence. She shivered. It was as if all the animals were in hiding. Once she thought she heard footsteps behind her. Resting her hand on the rough bark of a hardwood tree, she turned and stared back the way she'd come. Her eyes strained to see through the dappled sunshine, but she saw nothing.

When she walked out of the copse of trees, the placid body of water spread out in front of her. The river was not so large Zora couldn't see the boundaries. There was no sign of Mike Matisse.

"Hello. Mr. Matisse?" Her voice reverberated off the distant mountains as she turned 360 degrees, her eyes searching the surrounding area. Where was he? Not for the first time, she cursed the impulsiveness that had brought her out here without telling a soul.

"Walk out into the lake."

Matisse stood at the end of the woods, a gun leveled at her chest.

"What?" She stared in disbelief. Her heart started to pound hard and heavy in her chest. The day seemed suddenly colder. She couldn't take her eyes off the gun. She couldn't make sense of it.

"You heard me. Out into the water." He motioned with the barrel of the weapon.

Zora glanced behind her. How deep was the lake? She turned back toward him. "I—"

The ground exploded around her feet. Pebbles bit into her bare legs like shards of glass. Blood oozed from several cuts.

"Are you crazy?"

"Out into the water or the next bullet won't miss."

Zora shook her head. "Why are you doing this?"

When he started toward her, she backed up slowly. She stopped when the water lapped over her sandal-clad toes. "Just give me the bracelet and I'll be on my way back to New York. We'll forget all this." She pointed a trembling finger at the gun. "I won't tell anyone."

"The bracelet's mine. Now, get in." He advanced on her, his face twisted into a sneer. "Don't stop until I tell you to."

The water was surprisingly cold for September. Its temperature and the pounding of her heart heightened her fear. "Why have me come all the way out here if you weren't going to give me the bracelet?" Maybe if she could keep him talking, she'd think of some way of saving herself.

He smiled, but it wasn't reassuring. "Because it's the best place to dispose of your body."

"My…" Zora gulped and sent an involuntary glance to the middle of the lake. She turned to Mike Matisse, searching his face. His expression was deadly serious. "Why?"

He shrugged. "You've stirred up things that are better left buried." At her frown, he said, "The bones in the cave."

She shook her head, confused. "What does that have to do with you? Those are my ancestor's bones."

Why hadn't she seen the madness in his eyes before?

"You don't get it, do you?"

She shook her head again. "No… No, I don't."

"My ancestor put her there. He murdered her just like I'm going to murder you."

Zora took an involuntary step backwards into the water. "You're crazy. That was a long time ago."

He raised the barrel of his gun. "Unfortunately, the sins of the father haunt the son. I can't let you destroy my future."

She started to shake. John was halfway to Pierre. There was no one to help her. She was going to be murdered out here, just like Julia, and no one would find her body. No one would know what happened to her. A keen sense of loss and regret filled her mind. Regret she and John would never have a future together. Regret she'd never told him she loved him. Regret she hadn't fulfilled her promise to Julia.

What was wrong with her? She needed to get a grip. She

wasn't going to let someone end her life without a fight. She needed to keep him talking until she could figure out how to get away from him. "Why did your ancestor murder Julia?"

"Was that her name?"

Zora nodded. Her teeth chattered. And not from the cold.

"According to what was told to my great-grandfather, this Julia," Mike gestured off in the distance. "This Julia married the Chief's son, and he was meant for my great-great-great- grandmother. So her father decided to do something about it. She was bathing in the creek. "He pointed his gun toward the water behind Zora. "He, my ancestor, came to her in the form of a woman and strangled her. He and his son took her body up to the cave later that night and dumped her."

Through her fear, Zora felt the anger rise. "Then what?"

"My family circulated the rumor she'd run off with another man."

"And Trades with Horses believed this?"

Matisse snorted. "Women can be replaced. He married my ancestor and they had many children. So I guess he didn't grieve too long."

While he talked, Zora studied the surrounding area. If she got away from him, where would she run? "If you kill me, you'll be the first person John will suspect."

"Who says anyone will find your body? They didn't find your ancestor's. He'll just think you left for New York." Matisse smiled. "You know, I kinda like the idea of burying you up in those caves."

At the prospect of being dumped in the black depths of one of those pits, Zora felt bile rise in her throat. And Matisse was right. John would believe she'd left. "You don't have to do this. I'll go back to New York, and no one will know about this meeting. You can even have the bracelet."

"It's too late for that. I can't leave any loose ends." He

advanced on her, stumbled over the land's uneven surface and fell to one knee.

Zora broke into a run. Her shoes slipped on the water's sandy bottom as she tried to put distance between herself and this madman. Not a strong swimmer, she didn't dare move deeper into the water. For her, that would be a death warrant.

The bullet, when it hit, caught her by surprise and the force of it spun her around. Pain like a poker with a dull edge seared through the flesh of her shoulder. But she didn't have time to think about the agony because Matisse bore down on her like a stampeding elk.

Pivoting, she took off.

"Run, run," she chanted through the pain. Her foot slipped and she landed on a large stone. The pain momentarily paralyzed her. But nothing compared to the agony in her scalp when Matisse grabbed her by her water-sodden hair and yanked her to her feet.

"Where the hell do you think you're going?"

In a last-ditch effort, she brought her uninjured knee up and tried to drive his balls up into his stomach. He blocked her attempt then slapped her. Her vision bloomed with black spots. When he started to drag her further out into the water, she dug in her heels, trying to slow the inevitable.

She would not die, not like this. She would not. The mantra rattled around in her brain as she strained and dug in her heels. Her head throbbed from the strain of her hair being pulled by the roots. Strangely, she was aware of life going on around her. She could hear the distant call of a hawk as she was being pulled to her death. The rawness of her throat didn't stop the scream that bubbled up from the depths of her body, a scream rooted in fear and desperation.

He stopped and struck her head with his fist. "Shut the fuck up."

Her vision tunneled and blackness threatened. Cold,

brackish water filling her nose and throat brought her back to consciousness. When she opened her eyes, she could see nothing but the murky depths of the water. She was submerged with Mike's hands on her shoulders keeping her from resurfacing. Her lungs cried out for air. Her chest felt as though an iron band was wrapped around it. She tried to push his hands away, but her injured shoulder and lack of air made her movements weak and ineffective. He tightened his grip on her shoulders. Pain shot up her neck from the injured shoulder straight to her already pounding head. She had to do something, or in another minute, she would be as dead as Julia.

She forced herself to go limp, and when she did, Mike's grip on her shoulders relaxed. She sank, her hands constantly searching for something she could use as a weapon. Her hand closed around a hard object. Still submerged, she swam toward him. Her lungs burned with the need for air. He turned in circles, searching for her. She swung the stone with all the strength she had left. The rock connected with his knee. He howled in rage. Using the last of her breath, she propelled herself to the surface. Gasping and coughing, she took a deep gulp of air and rose, stumbling toward the shore.

"Come back here, you bitch."

Blocking out the pain from her body, she moved faster. Almost to the shore, she felt his hand close around her leg.

"No," she screamed. She twisted in his grip. He loomed over her, his face frozen in a frenzied grimace. He lifted her by her soggy blouse, until they were nose to nose. She stared into the face of madness. With fury and desperation, she swung the rock still clutched in her hand at his head. Poleaxed, he dropped. She watched his body sink below the water.

She half-crawled to the shore. On the beach, she vomited up water before losing consciousness.

The late afternoon sun bounced off the hood of the Jeep as it barreled onto reservation land. When John left the hospital, Lydia was still comatose. Knowing there was nothing he could do for his sister, he'd decided to come back to Little River and find her attacker, the one thing in his control.

He hoped Zora could provide some answers to his questions, but he'd been unable to reach her. Maggie called the Bearkiller place, but neither Chet nor Emma had seen her.

"Any luck?" John asked Maggie as he strode into headquarters.

She shook her head. "No. But Evelyn called and no one's seen Mike this morning either. He had an eight a.m. appointment with the state chairman. Think Zora and he were involved in the same car accident?" She gave him a pointed look.

John ignored her inference. Matisse might have the hots for Zora, but the feeling wasn't reciprocated. For all her protests, John knew Zora loved him.

"Why was she at Lydia's that early in the morning?" Maggie asked.

John cursed. He'd been so concerned with his sister's injury, he hadn't thought about the possible cause of the break-in. Zora had been at the store to pick up the bracelet. Somehow, Matisse had learned what Lydia planned to do. John had warned his sister that one day Matisse would try to regain possession of the bracelet. He just hadn't figured Matisse would kill to do it. He needed to find the son of a bitch.

"Keep the phone and radio lines open," he said, as he raced out the door for his service vehicle. As he backed the Jeep out of its parking space, his cell phone rang. He flipped it open without looking at the LED display, praying it was Zora. "Where are you?"

Silence, then a male voice said, "I'm in my office."

John closed his eyes in frustration. "Sorry, Foley. I expected someone else."

Steve Foley chuckled. "Obviously." His voice took on a serious tone. "I'm trying to get in touch with Ms. Hughes. Have you seen her?"

A horn blew behind John. In his anxiety, he'd stopped the car in the middle of the road. He signaled impatiently for the driver to go around him. When the car had passed he put the Jeep in drive and slowly drove away from headquarters. He didn't want to sit and talk when Zora was out there, maybe needing him. "I haven't seen her." John didn't want to give voice to his fears for her safety.

"I have some exciting news. I wanted to tell her as soon as possible."

Frustrated and more than a little short-tempered, John snapped, "Steve, this isn't—"

"The remains from the cave are definitely in her family tree."

John frowned and slowed the vehicle. "What?"

"I said the bones from the cave definitely belong to an ancestor of hers."

"How did this come about? I thought your budget—"

"That was the strangest thing," Foley said. "Zora offered to pay for the procedure, said she'd already had her blood drawn. What could I say? And to be honest, I was curious so…"

She'd been right. John knew this would make her very happy. He also knew there'd be nothing keeping her in South Dakota now. She'd found her answers. "Steve, I need to go."

Foley continued as though he hadn't heard John. "This sure has generated a lot of interest. In fact, Mike Matisse called me yesterday."

John took his foot off the accelerator and the Jeep coasted. "What did you say?"

"I said Mike Matisse called me yesterday. Said as reservation president, he wondered how the analysis was going."

"Did you tell him anything?"

"Well, since he does represent the reservation, I saw no harm in telling him—"

Impatient, John asked, "What did you tell him, Foley?"

Foley must have sensed his displeasure because there was a moment's silence. "I told him Zora was related to the remains found in the cave."

John ended the call then grabbed the radio.

"Maggie, put out an APB on Mike Matisse."

"What?"

"Just do it. Call Oscar. Have him go to the Matisse residence and see if Mike is there. Tell him to use extreme caution."

John punched the Jeep's accelerator, and the vehicle leapt forward, gravel and dirt flying out from the rear wheels.

The sting of a slap brought Zora around. Bright sunlight filtered through a canopy of trees and Mike Matisse's face loomed over hers. She stifled a scream. She dreamed she'd killed him.

"Time to die," he said, and wrapped his large hands around her neck.

Her lungs strained for air as she bucked and kicked, trying unsuccessfully to dislodge his heavy body from hers. She knew this time she would die. Visions of her life swam before her eyes—her mother and father together with her before their divorce, her graduation from high school, her first day at *Haute,* seeing John standing outside her stranded car, meeting Sarah. *Sarah?*

The teen stood to the side, watching as Zora feebly pushed and clawed at Mike's hands. Why didn't the girl do something? Even as Zora thought the words, she finally understood. Sunlight filtered through Sarah's body. She wasn't real. But both she and John had seen her. How was that possible?

Spittle formed at the corners of Matisse's mouth as he continued to choke the life from her body. His shirt rose from his pants, exposing a large dark pigment on his side. Suddenly, his hands went slack. Zora took in great gulps of air.

The blood drained from his face. "What…" He stared straight at Sarah. Could he see her? Obviously, he could. His jaw opened and closed as he attempted to speak. No sound came out.

Sarah glanced at the ground by Zora's body. Shards from a broken beer bottle lay just a few feet away. Could she reach it? Zora stretched out her fingers. It was just out of reach. A determination to live renewed itself in her. Sarah was telling her to fight.

"No, you're not real," Matisse shouted at the apparition. His grip tightened on Zora's neck.

Stretching, reaching, she strained with every bit of strength left in her body. Blackness seeped into the edges of her vision. She had to hurry. The glass felt cool to her almost nerveless fingers. With her last bit of strength, she wrapped her fingers around the glass and drove it into the throbbing artery in Mike Matisse's neck.

———————

With a white-knuckle grip, John leaned forward in his seat, willing the Jeep to go faster. Why was Matisse interested in Zora and the bones found in the cave? The bracelet, John understood. Matisse would never willingly allow someone to possess anything that belonged to him. Lydia stood in the way. But why try and kill her? And now he might be trying to do the same to Zora.

The radio crackled. "Captain?"

John snatched up the receiver. "Was he there?"

"No," Oscar said. "No one was home."

"Damn," John muttered.

"What now?"

"I'm on the way to the Tyler place. Meet me there." John replaced the receiver. If there was some connection with the caves, maybe Matisse had lured Zora there with the promise of the bracelet. John hoped she hadn't fallen for it. Maybe he hadn't impressed on her how dangerous Matisse was.

John stomped down on the accelerator and took the turn to Chet's place on two wheels. As he completed the turn, Sarah suddenly appeared in the road. He slammed on the brakes and twisted the wheel to avoid hitting the girl. The Jeep did a one-eighty. When it stopped, Sarah was gone. He hadn't hit her. He hopped out and ran over to the ditch. No Sarah. He glanced around. She'd disappeared into thin air.

As he studied the area, he recognized it as the place where Zora had had her vision. From the forest, sunlight bounced off chrome. When he moved into the wooden area, he made out her convertible. Someone had pushed it into the woods to hide it. Matisse.

John broke into a run, plunging into a tangle of trees and bushes. He didn't have time for subtlety. When he reached the open area surrounding the riverbed, he spotted two prone figures further down the shoreline. The breath caught in his throat as he sprinted toward the bodies, praying to the mighty spirits. Pledging his soul, if they'd let her be alive.

Matisse lay across Zora's still form. John stopped. There was so much blood it covered them both. Pushing Matisse's body off Zora's, John dropped to his knees and gathered her in his arms. He ran his hands over her. Except for a small seeping wound in her shoulder, the blood appeared to be mostly Matisse's. Her pulse pounded strong and steady through her veins. John dropped his head in relief.

John spared a glance for Matisse. His eyes stared sight-lessly at the sky.

Averting his gaze, John concentrated on the woman in his arms. "Zora." He stroked her face. "Come on, baby. Wake up."

CHAPTER TWENTY-FOUR

———◆———

THE BROWN PRAIRIE GRASS UNDULATED in the grip of the high wind. A hawk glided on the current like a black kite, then dove into the long grass, and re-emerged with prey between its claws. The sight no longer made Zora shudder. It was the way of the land, a land that hadn't changed in hundreds of years.

Julia's remains were wrapped in a colorful Indian blanket and placed in the center of a makeshift circle. Dancers in full ceremonial costume pounded the earth in dance and sang to the spirits. They asked the spirits to accept this woman and help her transcend the physical world to the world of her ancestors. Even though Julia wasn't Native American by blood, Zora felt this was how she'd want to be buried.

Joseph, Chet, and Emma chanted in time with the dancers. Zora touched her neck. Even if she had known the words, she couldn't sing because of the swollen tissues in her throat. The doctors said it might take weeks before she would sound like herself. She didn't care. Except for being shot in the shoulder, she was fine. She'd survived. Mike Matisse had bled out on the ground where his ancestor had taken the life of hers. She felt no remorse. Julia, and by extension, Zora were at peace.

She'd never know Sarah's story. Zora had to be content with that.

When the ceremony was over and they'd buried Julia,

Zora hugged Joseph and Chet and touched Emma's arm in thanks. She glanced one last time at the road, looking for John's white Jeep. Between visiting Lydia in the hospital, taking care of her husband, and the police force, John had a full plate. But she'd hoped...

Zora gave them all one last glance, then walked to her car, and started the journey home to New York.

Chapter Twenty-Five

Z ORA INSPECTED THE PAGE LAYOUT. "Too busy." She tilted her head and studied the model's picture. "Have Zach retake this without the necklace." She glanced up at Ellen, *Haute's* assistant design editor. "How about a scarf instead?"

Ellen nodded.

"Something long and blue to pick up the color of her eyes." After several moments, Zora said, "Use the fans to create a breeze. The scarf should billow behind her. It's okay if the hair is tossed." She smiled at Ellen. "Artfully tossed. Make sure he doesn't obscure her face. Remember, our client is selling makeup."

Zora rubbed her neck and rotated her head, trying to ease the tension in her shoulders.

"I have some Tylenol in my purse," Ellen said.

Zora shook her head. "I'm fine." She gathered the pages together and handed them to the other woman. "Let's continue this…" Zora glanced at her watch. "Say around five?"

Ellen grimaced. "I have a dinner date at six."

The appeal in Ellen's eyes was too hard to ignore. "Let's move the meeting up to four, and tell everyone it'll be short," Zora said.

Ellen smiled in gratitude and scurried out.

When Zora returned to New York, Claudia had been at her wit's end. She'd fired the twentysomething she'd hired to replace Zora. No photographer had been hired and no location reserved for the magazine's fall spread due to go to press in two weeks.

Claudia, as executive director, raised funds by schmoozing with the rich and famous at cocktail parties and charity events. She was not good at the day to day tasks that kept a magazine running.

Without asking permission, Zora showed up at the office on her second day back in New York, saw the chaos, and took over. Claudia had not protested.

Zora had been back in New York now for two months and hadn't heard a word from John. Several times she'd reached for the phone, just to hear his guff voice, but hadn't placed the call.

She'd spoken with Joseph a few times over the last several weeks. The reservation had a new tribal council president, Pete Montrell. Zora had met him briefly when she'd brought Chet home from the hospital, the day after she'd fallen into the cave. She knew Pete was a close friend of John's. Joseph said the two men were working closely to come up with solutions for some of the reservation's immediate problems. Zora was glad John had someone he could trust. She knew the two men would be very busy cleaning up the mess Mike Matisse had made.

He was probably too busy to call. But still… Her fingers traced the edges of her cell phone. All she had to do was touch the screen. She had his number on speed dial. She clasped her hands on the desk and squeezed them together.

She'd worked so hard for this job. How could she just throw it all away to live twenty-one hundred miles away? She just needed to give it time. She'd get over him.

Who was she kidding? She missed the hell out of that man. Her gaze was drawn to the picture that hung over the black leather sofa. Just looking at the painting transported her back to the Plains. She could see the long grasses billowing in the wind. She could see John on horseback, moving at a canter across the land. Smiling, she shook her head. She was becoming a romantic. She'd never seen John on horseback, never even asked if he could ride, but she knew he could.

The smile faded as she thought about Matisse and how close she'd come to dying on that creek bed. She shook herself. It was over. She'd come back to the only city she loved, and John had gone on with his life on the reservation, protecting and serving. She could never live there and he could never live in this congested, beautiful city.

There was a light tap on her office door and her secretary stuck her head in, wearing a bemused expression.

"There's a *man* to see you." Sheri arched an eyebrow.

Sheri gave a yelp of surprise as the door was pulled from her grip. John filled the doorway.

Zora half rose from her seat.

"May I come in?"

His voice flowed like cool water over her parched soul. Somehow, he looked bigger, rougher than she remembered. Wearing jeans, white shirt, and boots, he looked wonderful. He'd bought a new leather coat. Zora wondered if it was for her. She fought a smile then frowned at her secretary who stood gawking at him. "That's all, Sheri."

Sheri backed out of the office. Zora would bet before her office door had completely shut, her secretary would be on the phone telling everyone about the gorgeous man in the boss's office.

"You look good." He twisted his hat around in his large hands.

"So do you."

He strolled over to the sofa and stared at one of his paintings. After a moment, he turned. "Lydia finally told me you bought them. This one looks good here."

"The other one's at home. How's—" She cleared her throat. "How's everyone?"

"Everyone's fine. Lydia's making progress. She's going to

go to physical therapy, but the docs believe there'll be no lasting damage. Joseph and Chet send their regards." He held her gaze for a long moment, before strolling to the windows. "Nice view."

Her office on the fortieth floor overlooked Times Square. She stared at his broad leather clad shoulders. She clenched her hands into fists to keep from reaching out and touching him.

Frowning, he turned to her. "There's no grass."

Laughing, she joined him at the window. "We have Central Park. It's not the Plains, but…" As much as she loved New York, she'd come to love the wide-open expanse of the Dakotas. To think she'd driven her rental all the way to the reservation with her windows up afraid of the vastness and the sounds of the land.

He studied the New York skyline while she drank him in. His unique scent of earth and musk filled her with a sense of rightness. Without thought, she leaned toward him then caught herself. "Why are you here?"

"The Bureau found more bones in the caves." He moved away from the window—away from her—and started to pace. "All the bones had been in the cave for a while, except for one." He paused, looking over his shoulder at her.

She plopped into her desk chair and waited, breath caught in her throat.

"Matisse's wife, Dora."

"Huh?" Those were not the words she'd expected.

"We thought she'd left him. Someone said she caught the Greyhound." He shrugged. "I guess that was Matisse's doing. Anyway, it seems, he killed her because she and Danny were…" John's face grew dark as the clouds drifting in from the Atlantic before a thunderstorm.

"*What*?" Zora's jaw dropped. Laura had given her heart to that skinny little bastard.

"Yeah, well, I *strongly* suggested the punk leave the reservation if he valued his life. He took my advice."

John rolled his shoulders. "According to Foley most of the bones were from mature females, except one set. They belonged to a young girl just reaching puberty."

John snagged Zora's gaze.

"Sarah," she whispered.

He nodded. "Maybe… probably."

Part of a dream resurfaced. Something about Julia needing to feed her babies. *Babies*—plural.

"There were two children. Sarah was one," she said with certainty.

"Okay. So maybe the same person who killed Julia, later killed her daughter. But why?" he asked.

Zora's stomach twisted with a grave certainty. Through a veil of tears she held John's gaze. His rugged face gave her the courage to voice what she knew was true. "Because she looked so much like Julia. Because the murderer couldn't stand to have Julia's look-a-like walking in the village proclaiming his guilt—mocking him."

Neither of them spoke. The horror of it made Zora ill. She dropped her face into her hands, rocking with the pain. "Oh, John… I didn't understand."

He was there, touching her hair, pulling her hands from her face. Deep grooves had appeared between his brows. "Didn't understand what?"

"Julia wasn't looking for retribution for herself when she came to me in those dreams, it was for Sarah. And I almost didn't come to the reservation." Her voice trailed off into a whisper, her pain so acute she couldn't stand it. "I'd convinced myself I could work through the dreams without traveling to South Dakota." She pressed her hands to her lips to hold back her cries. "I almost turned around out there on the highway and came back home to New York." Now she couldn't stop the tears. "What if I had?"

John lifted her from the chair and folded her in his arms. "Shh…but you didn't. You solved the mystery. We can

bury Sarah next to her mother. Everything is fine now. "
His arms tightened and he whispered into her hair. "And
I'm glad you came."

He pulled back, staring deep into her eyes. "I love you,
Zora."

She couldn't meet his gaze. As much as she wanted to
tell him she loved him, she couldn't. Her pledge to Joseph
stood in the way. "How's—how's everyone?"

John chuckled. "I think you asked that already. You mean,
'how's Emma'?"

She stepped out of his arms, turning to stare out the window. The skyscrapers almost blocked out the sun. "Yeah."

"She's dating Oscar."

Zora blinked once, twice then the ramifications of that
statement hit home. She spun around. "You mean, you and
Emma…"

He gave her a disgruntled look. "I told you that was
Joseph's idea, not mine." He was beside her in a heartbeat,
his fingers gently stroking her face. "Tell me you don't miss
me as much as I miss you."

She opened her mouth to deny it. *Be brave.*

"I miss you." *I love you.* Why couldn't she open her heart
and say the words.

"Anyway, I said I'd be back this summer." She moved
away from him and sought refuge behind her desk.

His lips turned up in a pained smile. "We both know you
didn't mean it." He held her gaze a long heartbeat.

Be brave. Be brave.

An uncomfortable silence descended over the room, a
silence she wanted desperately to fill with the words *I love
you*, but she couldn't make a sound. Her heart and brain
were in combat.

"Well, I guess I'd better be going." He placed his Stetson
on his head.

Her mother's face flashed in her mind. Had her mother
ever told her father she loved him? Somehow Zora

doubted it. Was she destined to share her mother's fate—having a high-powered job, but going home to an empty apartment, an empty bed?

John strode to the door and was through it before she could gather her thoughts.

Be brave. Be brave.

She didn't remember whether she walked or ran out of her office. When awareness returned, she was staring into the faces of her staff who'd assembled outside her door for the four o'clock meeting. She looked beyond them to the bank of elevators that lined the south wall. John was just stepping in.

Her heart hammered in her throat, making the words she shouted as painful as the fear of losing him.

"I love you," she shouted just as the doors closed.

Too late.

She flew down the corridor, losing her fling backs in the process. Punching the elevator's call button twenty consecutive times didn't make it come any quicker. She didn't look back at her staff. She knew they watched her. They'd never seen her this raw, this…this uncontrolled. "Come on, come on." She was practically dancing in place.

John hadn't told her the name of his hotel or what airline he'd flown in on. How was she to find him?

The ping of an arriving car made her pulse spike. Her muscles tensed like a sprinter ready for the starting gun. She'd go down to the mezzanine level—and do what? Okay, so she didn't have a plan, but she had forty floors to come up with one.

The doors opened and the car disgorged a gazillion passengers.

"Come on, come on." She was on the balls of her feet, ready for the race of her life.

When the last passenger stepped out, she realized the car wasn't empty. In the back corner, the elevator's muted light bounced off the Stetson of a tall, well-built magnificent specimen of a man. With a forefinger, he tipped his hat back. His black eyes held hers in a solemn gaze.

She stepped in and the elevator doors closed behind her. She had forty floors to show him how much she loved him. And forty years to prove to him this city girl could make her mark in South Dakota.

She moved into his open arms. They closed around her, welcoming her home.

D EAR READER,

The inspiration for *Lakota Dreaming* came from the independent film *Unbowed*. The movie told the story of an unlikely romance between a Native American prisoner and an African American woman just after the Civil War. The story captured my imagination and I began to wonder, what if...

Over the past several years, I've read several books on genetic memory and the topic fascinated me. What if I could pair the romance of a Black woman with a Native American and use genetic memories in the story line? From all this imagining, *Lakota Dreaming* was born.

I hope you enjoyed Zora and John's story as much as I enjoyed writing it.

ACKNOWLEDGEMENTS

A SPECIAL THANKS TO MY WRITING partners, Mary Barfield, Pamela Varnado, and Tamara DeStefano, who've been there through the rough and good times.

I've received tremendous encouragement and education from my local writing chapter, Georgia Romance Writers, and from individual members within the group: Debby Giusti, Nancy Knight, Dorie Graham, and Berta Platas.

As a 2008 Romance Writers of America Golden Heart finalist, I've had the privilege of meeting and sharing the friendship of the wonderful Pixie sisterhood. Thank you, ladies, for your encouragement and support.

Editing services were provided by Gilly Wright at *www.facebook.com/GillyWrightsRedPin*. Thank you, Gilly, for such a thorough job and an answer for every one of my questions.

Last but never least, a very special thanks to my husband, Jim.

If you enjoyed Lakota Dreaming, I would appreciate it if you would help others enjoy it too by doing one of the following:

Recommend it: Please help others find this book by recommending it to friends, readers' groups and discussion boards.

Review it: Tell readers what you liked or didn't like by reviewing it at one of the major retailers, review sites, or on your blog. I appreciate all reviews.

To find out when my next book is available, you can sign up for my new release email list at *www.constancegillam.com*

Don't forget to follow me on:

Twitter@conniegillam

Facebook

Like my page to get exclusive excerpts, behind the scenes first looks, and upcoming series/book updates.

Made in the USA
Columbia, SC
30 August 2021

44524177R00181